roomies

friends, lovers, and whatevers

lindy zart

Roomies
Lindy Zart
Published by Lindy Zart
Copyright 2014 Lindy Zart
Cover Design by Sprinkles On Top Studios
Formatting by Inkstain Interior Book Designing
Edited by Wendi Stitzer
Author Photography by Kelley C. Hanson Photography

acknowledgements:

Thank you, Tara Bedward, for giving me some fun facts about Lancaster not widely known.

Thanks to Marce Walter, Alysha Webber, and Jessica Wicks for answering some of my foot questions. Also to MJ Fryer for referring me to Sharon Ender, DPM. I had some crazy thoughts and you all, in one way or another, helped bring them back down to the sane plane. (Any mistakes are mine.)

Special thanks to Brenda Tetreault for the tagline used in Roomies: Friends, Lovers, and Whatevers

As always, from book to book, I heart my beta readers, cover artist, editor, photographer, and formatter.

Beta readers: Tiffany Dodson, Tiffany Alfson, Tawnya Peltonen, Judith Frazee, Megan Stietz, Jacinda Owen, Kendra Gaither, Desiree Wallin.
Cover artist: Sarah Foster.
Formatter: Nadege Richards.
Editor: Wendi Stitzer.
Photographer: Kelley C. Hanson

High fives all around!

This is to anyone who ever dialed 867-5309
and hoped to talk to Jenny.

chapter one

S o here I am, at 8:26 in the AM, all smiles for the first victim—I mean, *patient*, of the day. For the record, I hate mornings. I don't know whose record that information is going on, but it's going on someone's. And consciously awake and functional? Not before 10:00.

She (the patient) is looking less than thrilled to be here, but I don't let that deter me or cause my overly perky smile to falter. The air around us is cloaked in a medicinal smell that is astringent to the point of burning nostril hairs if you breathe too deeply, or making your eyes water if you stand in just the right spot. It's from all the many—healthy and completely harmless, of course—chemicals and cleaning solutions used in the office. I'm used to it, so out of habit I take shallow breaths. I'm all about being shallow. Maybe that's the patient's problem—she isn't breathing properly and the fumes are getting to her. I decide that must be the reason for the nasty scowl upon her weathered face. Who *wouldn't* want to be here?

I walk up to where she is sitting in the waiting room—a small area with white walls, five chairs, two large windows, and a wood floor. It also houses framed medical jargon on almost every inch of wall space. Oh, and a big red blow-up heart (the organ, not the pretty one that symbolizes love) that kids are forever trying to turn into a punching bag, much to the receptionist's frustration. Although, I mean, come on, I've even punched it a time or two while passing by. It just screams to be whacked.

Apparently healthy hearts equal healthy feet and the reverse can be said. Everything inside you, from your eyes to your teeth to your toes, is connected. I know, *crazy*.

I extend my already grotesquely large grin and announce, "We're ready for you, Agnes."

Agnes Magnus (yes, that's really her name), a widow in her late eighties, suddenly has saucers for brown eyes and a twist to her red-lined lips. It appears that she may have even decided to throw caution to the wind and not use lipstick at all, going for the 'lip-liner and nothing else' look. Personally, I wouldn't recommend it. The sudden belligerence in her eyes tells me that she may need some assistance down the hall. Not that I would drag her to the examination room or anything. (Insert chuckle here.) But I might give her a gentle shove in the right direction. *Harmless.*

"Well," she says with a wheezing scoff, "maybe I'm not ready for you."

Eyes narrowed, I have the semi-unpleasant thought, *Trust me, lady, we don't want you here anymore than you want to be here.* But I just continue smiling, though maybe tightly at this point, and wait with raised eyebrows.

With an excessively drawn-out sigh, she struggles to her feet and mutters, "Come on. Let's get this over with." As if she is doing us a favor by gracing us with her presence because the office needs her and her money so much that we begged her to set up an appointment. Like we are glad she hasn't taken care of her toenails to the point that they are now growing into her actual toes, and she has no other alternative but to have them surgically clipped. Yes…we have been waiting, years and years and years, for this monumental day.

Please.

I save my eye rolling for after I have my back to Agnes, because I am able to show restraint like that. The lone receptionist of the joint catches my eye as I pass by and smirks. We, the podiatrist and I, have our battles with patients, but Sally Flood, the receptionist, has hers as well up front. Agnes Magnus is not one of our favorite patients, to say the least. She's not the worst, but definitely nowhere near the top of the list for patients we wouldn't mind seeing more than once a decade.

With only minor grumbling on her part, I get Agnes into the operatory; a small, bright white room with shiny metal equipment and products galore seeping out of every crevice that we refer to as the 'op' because we're verbally lazy, and motion to the single chair with the smile of an executioner. She doesn't return the smile. But she does sit.

In her scratchy voice, she says, "I feel like I'm on death row and about to be lethally injected or electrocuted."

I silently open up her chart on the computer.

"Are you going to strap me down too?" she wonders.

It can be arranged. "Of course not, Agnes."

"Hmmph," is her rebuttal.

"We're going to numb up the skin around your toes before cutting the nails. We'll do the left foot today since that has been bothering you the most," I say, meeting her eyes.

Her face pinches up. "Why are you smiling? Are you happy about this?"

My eyes go wide. "I'm not smiling."

"I distinctly see the outline of a smile upon your face, though I'm sure you're trying very hard to hide it. Do you enjoy other people's discomfort?"

"No, of course not," I say, turning away, and add with a mumble, "Maybe yours."

Before I can worry about whether or not she heard that, my boss enters the room. Grant Olman is large. He has to be about six and a half feet tall and weighs anywhere from two hundred thirty to four hundred pounds. Okay, so he probably weighs more like two hundred sixty. His voice is deep and booming, making him seem closer to eight feet tall, and he's perpetually clean-shaven. I've never even seen a hint of stubble upon his face. He's got shaggy brown hair streaked in silver that always seems to be in need of a trim and gray eyes that are alight with humor most days.

"Agnes Magnus! How's it going on this lovely morning?" he greets, then looks at me. "Great day for pizza, right?"

I hold in a sigh. My boss recently turned fifty and the office celebrated by having a pizza party at the local bowling alley. I showed off my athletic ability by routinely getting gutter balls and then I let my inner pig out by devouring most of a cheese pizza. Ever since then, he mentions pizza at least once a week. The guy needs new material.

"It'd be lovelier if I wasn't here," she replies.

For all of us.

My boss just laughs, complete with a snort at the end, and turns to me. "Ready, Freddy?"

"Who's Freddy?" the sweet, sweet lady demands.

"She's Freddy," he says, pointing at me. "I can't remember her name, so I just call her whatever."

3

"As long as you don't call her late for supper, eh?" Mrs. Magnus cackles.

I narrow my eyes on the back of her fluffy gray head. What was that? Was that a fat joke? I glance down at my average frame and frown. Does she think I'm fat?

Dr. Olman commences to widen his eyes and shake his head at me, motioning with his arms and mouthing, "No. No."

I stick my tongue out at Agnes' unsuspecting head and then smile at the readied needle.

Let the fun begin.

"First I'm going to numb up the area and then let it sit for a few minutes before beginning." The boss man looks at the patient. "Are you ready?"

"I can't wait."

With a smile, he pokes the gnarly flesh around her toes with the needle, pumping lidocaine into the skin. All the while Agnes is carrying on like he is slitting her throat. Although, if that was the case, we wouldn't have to listen to her go on and on with her moaning and groaning, so there is actually a certain appeal to it. Not that I would ever tell anyone that.

Once that feat is accomplished, I hurry from the room as quickly as I can move my tired butt, deciding to bother Sally. "Hey. What's up?"

Sally's office isn't really an office at all, but a partially enclosed cubical that's about two feet by two feet. Okay, so that's a slight exaggeration, but really, it can't be much bigger than that. There's enough room for her desk, chair, computer equipment, and that's about it. Oh, and her.

She looks up from the piles of paper scattered across her desk and gives me a woebegone look.

"That bad, huh?"

"Someone shoot me," she pleads.

I laugh, not really sure if that was a comment you should laugh at or not, but hey, I'm all about improvising. Also, I may or may not be an inappropriate laugher.

She gets up from her chair and kicks at an offending piece of paper that had the audacity to fall to the floor, managing to kick the wall as well—which isn't hard to do, considering the limited space.

"Or him. I'm not picky," she continues, jabbing her thumb in the general direction of Dr. Olman's office.

Sally's a nice lady. She's honest, maybe too honest, and when she's ready to keel over from work-related stress, instead she goes on a verbal rampage until she feels better. It's funny. For me anyway.

"Why do you want to shoot him?" I ask, leaning over the counter to better view her murderous facial expression.

She's closer to our boss's age than mine, but you wouldn't know it to talk to or look at her. With feathery blond hair and bright blue eyes reminiscent of Farrah Fawcett, along with a slim and tan frame, she's attractive in an eighties sort of way. She could pass for early to mid-thirties, although I'm pretty sure she's older than that. Not that I'd ever ask her or anything.

I want to live.

"You see this?" She gestures to the messy desk.

Nothing new there, so I shrug. "Yeah?"

"That, that…your boss," she says with gritted teeth, "dumped all of these invoices, months and months of invoices, invoices I didn't even know he had, on supplies I didn't even know he ordered, on my desk this morning, and told me to have them filed by lunch. How?" she asks some unknown entity.

"How am I supposed to do that? And answer the phone, and get insurance payments into the computer, and schedule patients, and every other stupid thing I do around here? How? And I didn't know about any of these bills, and now all the account books are going to be off, and we probably owe tons of money to these medical supply companies. I can't work like this, I really can't. I'm losing my mind." She shakes her head and slumps back into her chair.

I wait for it.

"That man is an imbecile," she announces firmly and loudly.

I dart a quick look down the hall, but Dr. Olman's office door is shut, so there is a good chance he didn't hear her angry litany. Although, I am pretty sure the patient did.

I'm not supposed to know, but Sally and the boss man have a thing going on. And okay, so as of yet, it's unconfirmed, but I know it's true. One minute they hate each other, the next they're shooting gaga eyes at one another when they think I don't notice. It's gross. I mean, they're old. Not that old people shouldn't have love and romance and sex and all that, but…I don't want to know about it, ya know?

Sally pierces me with her eyes. "What am I doing here? Why do I do this to myself?"

"I don't know," I say slowly. "Um, I have to go now." I scurry away, a mouse intent on escape from a broom.

"Kennedy Somers, get back here!"

I cringe, but keep going. My sanity depends on it. And anyway, it's time to slice and dice the offending toenails of Mrs. Agnes Magnus. I fight the urge to rub my hands together in glee and meet my boss at the door to the op. He raises his eyebrows and looks toward the waiting room area.

"Don't ask," I tell him, and he doesn't.

It is time to proceed.

Scrub top, check.

Facemask, check.

Protective eyewear, check.

Gloves, check.

Dr. Olman with his scrub top on…no check.

He holds up a finger and quickly leaves, returning with his scrub top on backwards.

I don't say anything.

Three minutes into the procedure and I am ready to slap the patient. Every time the podiatrist comes near her, she flinches, even kicking her leg out once. Not a good thing to do with sharp instruments coming at your body. Just saying.

Dr. Olman steps back and looks at her. "Do you feel any of that?"

She pops open eyes she's had squeezed shut for the last minute or so. "No."

"Just try to hold still," I say.

She turns her head to glare at me.

"Okay. Let's try this again," he says in a soothing voice.

Mrs. Magnus straightens her leg out, but keeps the toes of her left foot curled. I didn't even know you could do that under anesthesia. I mean, it's supposed to be numb. How do you move a numb appendage?

We wait; I with my hands ready to assist and Dr. Grant Olman with his surgical instrument.

"Mrs. Magnus?"

"What?" she snaps.

My boss and I exchange looks.

"You'll have to uncurl your toes, Agnes," he tells her.

She crosses her arms and sighs, but obliges.

After a minute of letting Dr. Olman dig at her rock hard nails, Agnes holds up a hand. I resist the urge to slap it.

He leans back. "Yes?"

"Are you done yet?" she asks, blood dripping from her big toe onto the towel beneath it and making my stomach squeamish. I know, what am I doing assisting something like this when the sight of blood makes me want to pass out? We may never know.

"No," he says shortly, visibly impatient to continue.

Again with the sighing.

Once again, Dr. Olman has his hands on her feet; strategically slicing away at a layer of tough, protective protein scientifically known as keratin. In one smooth motion he gets it removed, which, in our line of work, is cause for celebration. I smile at my boss, realize he can't see it through the facemask, and nod instead. The look on the upper part of his face is of pure relief before it shifts to determination, as there are still three more to go.

"Are you done?"

"No," we say simultaneously, and maybe more forcefully than is warranted.

He clears his throat. "I have three left," he says in a softer tone.

"Try to remain calm," I tell her, which she ignores.

"You're doing a good job, Agnes. We're almost done," he states.

That seems to pacify her, as she remains silent.

The last nail, on the pinky toe, no less, doesn't want to be accommodating. As much as Dr. Olman tries to finesse a layer of it away from the toe, it will not budge. I am sweating; I am pretty sure the boss is sweating as well. In fact, I can see where his gloves cling to his hands in certain spots; like mine. It is getting hard to breathe behind the facemask and I want to rip it from my face.

After numerous minutes, whispered curses by my boss, and me perspiring profusely and wishing I am anywhere but here, he finally gets the last nail shaved down, leaving bloody toes in his wake. My stomach turns and I look away, pretending I am way savvier than I obviously am.

I love my job. I love it so much I think I should go home right now and celebrate the profound beauty of it with a bottle of wine. I glance at the clock and see it's not even ten in the morning. I scrunch my nose up and turn away.

Wine waits for no one.

I look up from the book I'm reading and roll my eyes. Seriously? Who screams when they have an orgasm? And crying after "making love"? Who writes these things? I toss the book over my shoulder, knowing my roommate is going to be annoyed when he finds it on the floor. He's disturbingly organized. Everything has its proper spot—my book on the floor does not fall into his realm of orderliness.

"What the hell?"

I frown and lift my head to peer behind the couch. "Oh. Sorry. It fell from my hand," I tell my roommate, who was clearly put on this earth for my visual enjoyment.

"Sure it did."

I sit up and twist around to face him. I relish looking at Graham; it is one of my favorite pastimes—right up there with consuming large quantities of wine. He's over six feet tall with an impressive physique and his skin is a perfect shade of golden brown. With messy blond hair and spectacularly green eyes, he is a ten on a scale of one to ten for hotness. I have yet to see him look bad and we've been roommates for over a year now. I just don't think he has it in him.

"I'm disappointed in you."

He plops down in the matching cream recliner, a curious look on his exasperatingly perfect features. "Why?"

"You're wearing clothes."

He rolls his eyes. "Good one, Ken."

"I thought so, Barbie." I smile sweetly as he scowls. I've told him countless times to quit with the Ken nickname, but he insists, and so, I insist on calling him Barbie.

"Really, what's with the book?" He begins to thumb through it.

"It's stupid."

"Why is it stupid?" Pausing, his eyes become riveted to a page I can only assume is one of many graphic love scenes.

I wait. And as I wait, I admire the way strands of golden hair fall over his forehead, the frown between his brows that's terribly adorable, and how he bites his lower lip in concentration.

I can give him something to bite.

"People really read this stuff?" he asks, sounding offended.

I straighten and ban indecent thoughts from my mind. "I told you." Do I sound smug?

Still looking at the pages of the pornographic romance novel, he says, "I mean, I could see you reading it, but other people?"

"Hey."

He looks up, a smirk on his face. "Just kidding."

"No, you're not," I retort, but I can't keep a smile from my face.

"How was work?"

I roll onto my back. "Ugh."

"That good, huh?"

"You don't want to know," I mumble.

"See, that's where you're wrong. I do want to know, hence my asking."

I grab a pillow and smother my face. The pillow is striped in blue and white and scratches my nose. "I'm a bad person."

"What?"

I yank the pillow down. "I'm a bad person."

"I suppose that could be true, depending on who you ask."

I turn my head to stare at him.

"I don't think you're a bad person," he hastily adds.

"Who does?" I ask suspiciously, temporarily forgetting that I stated exactly this a mere minute ago.

"No one."

"You have to say that; I help pay the bills."

"What happened at work?" he asks, redirecting me. He's good at that. Probably why I keep him around. Never mind that his name is on the lease and not mine.

I blow out a noisy breath and sit up, tossing the pillow aside. "Do you want the long version or the short?"

"Short."

I'm trying not to smile, which just proves how vile I am. "Okay, so this old bag was our first patient of the day." I pause and he motions for me to continue.

I rub my forehead and look at a framed painting on the wall above his head. It's a watercolor of yellow and blue flowers. Decorating the apartment is all on Graham because I have no interior design sense at all. The walls of the apartment are white, as designated by the owners, but my roommate has managed to make our living room inviting with paintings, framed sayings on the wall (My favorite is: When the world says give up, hope whispers, try one more time.), and the pale colors of the ocean visible in the variations of blues and greens throughout the room. My contribution is to admire it all.

"She was awful, Graham, she really was," I say earnestly.

"What'd you do?"

A good thing about being so close to someone is that they know you so well. A bad thing about being so close to someone is that they know you so well.

"That sounds like resignation in your tone."

He just looks at me.

"Okay, well, as soon as she walked through the door she had a bad attitude."

"And?"

"She accused me of smiling when I told her what we were going to do today."

"And?"

"I wasn't smiling."

"Naturally."

"So, uh, later, during the appointment, after she'd been mean countless times, I might have told her I was smiling."

He doesn't speak while he digests this.

I twine my fingers together and whistle.

"Maybe you should be more specific," he says slowly.

I know my face is red because it feels really warm. "All right."

Two tawny eyebrows lift in anticipation.

With a deep breath of courage, I say in a rush, "She was acting like we'd severed all of her limbs, saying her toes were stumps and that she was going to sue us, and really, it was a totally regular appointment. I mean, yeah, there was some bleeding, but that's normal when you shave off a layer of nail." He groans, and I ignore that, continuing with, "So, then, you know, by that time I was getting really pissed. And when the doctor was out of the room, I leaned toward her and said very softly, 'Now I'm smiling.' Her eyes went wide and she almost looked scared and I felt a little guilty, but not completely."

Graham laughs, but it has an incredulous ring to it. "Wow."

My shoulders slump.

"Sorry, but that wasn't nice."

"I know!" I groan. "That's what I'm saying. I'm a bad, bad girl." I grin. "You should spank me."

With a shake of his head, he states, "You're just full of sexual innuendoes today, aren't you?"

I shrug, admiring his biceps. "Must have been that book."

"Must have been and quit looking at me like that."

Our eyes meet. A jolt goes through parts of me, all of which shall remain unnamed. "Like what?" I ask innocently.

"Like you want to eat me for lunch."

I just smile.

He sighs. "Your obsession is getting out of hand. Am I going to have to get a restraining order?"

"Psssh, whatever," I say with a laugh. "How are you going to do that when I'm your roommate?"

He scratches his head, disrupting the shaggy locks even more. "Dunno. I'll have you confined to your bedroom until I leave the premises every morning and night."

"You'd miss my unfailing adoration."

He laughs and looks down at the book in his long-fingered hands. "'*Midnight Rogue*'?"

"The book is stupid. This chick is screaming from an orgasm the first time she has sex, mind you, and then, after they, quote unquote, make love, she cries from the beauty of it all. It's ridiculous. All you need is the man crying as well to make the idiocy of it complete."

With a rueful grin on his full lips, he glances at me before returning his gaze to the paperback. "You're such a snot. Maybe some women do those things."

"Maybe not," I scoff.

He tosses the book toward me and I catch it. "What do you want to do for dinner?"

"Eh," is my well thought-out response.

"All right. Guess I'll pick. I've got some chicken in the fridge. I'll grill that up. Can you make a salad?"

I nod and grudgingly remove myself from the couch. I follow him into the kitchen, where he's pulling marinated chicken breasts out of the fridge. The kitchen is small, just big enough for the table and chairs that are in it, and decked out with simple white appliances. The theme is red and black accents with coffee and wine references—favorite things for each of us. Me, I prefer the wine. Graham prefers the coffee.

I lean over him as he's bent down and sniff. "Mmm. Smells good."

"It's Italian dressing and pineapple chunks. Thought I'd try something different."

"I meant you."

"What is with you today?" he questions, sounding more thoughtful than irritated, as he shuts the refrigerator door with his elbow.

I sigh and place my chin in my hand, bracing my elbow on the counter. "Do you think stuff like that really happens?"

"Stuff like what?"

I gesture with my hand. "You know. Women and men who love each other so much they cry after having sex? Having orgasms the first time they have sex? I mean, I know guys do, but girls? And they actually call it making love? Does that kind of stuff really happen?"

Graham stares at me.

"What?"

"I don't really know," he says carefully and carries the plate of chicken through the patio door opening to the deck.

I follow him. "Haven't you ever been in love?"

"Maybe. I'm not sure."

"If you're not sure, then you haven't." Me—who has only had a few boyfriends and only one even close to a serious relationship—the expert on love and dating. It's safe to say I am a virgin.

I am a virgin. There, I said it.

"I suppose."

I sit in a patio chair, watching Graham as he fires up the grill. He has a thing about grilling out as often as possible during the summer. I don't know why. I guess he likes it. I tip my head back. Summers in Wisconsin can be pretty humid, but today the sun is shining and there's a gentle breeze with no sign of dampness. The smoky scent of the heating grill tantalizes my senses as I inhale.

"So—"

"Kennedy."

"Yes?"

"I really don't want to be having this conversation with you."

"I'm just curious."

"Wrong person to be asking." He pierces the chicken with a fork and slaps it on the grill.

"Why?" I demand.

He checks the temperature on the grill and straightens. "Because I'm not comfortable talking about orgasms with you, that's why."

"But Graham—"

"No buts."

"No butts," I snort.

"Not what I meant." He walks to the patio door, stops, and looks at me accusingly. "And you know it."

"You're such a girl," I call after him.

"And you're such a guy." He slams the door shut, leaving me outside.

I frown. *What's his problem?* I can usually tease Graham all day long, but every once in a while, something I mention makes him clam up, like now. Then he gets all huffy and stiff-lipped and I have to make nice, which I'm not very good at. But with him, I make an effort because I love him and not in that way, but actually, yes, in that way. It's complicated. Or not.

I can be mostly upfront about things with him, because even though I wish it were otherwise, my roommate does not look at me as being potential girlfriend material. From the start, I was designated to the friend zone. On the one hand, this is good, because I don't have to try to impress him or anything, so I can say and do whatever. Or maybe that's because I have no tact. Irrelevant! But sometimes, like now, he turns into a stodgy old man and I feel funny, like maybe I shouldn't be so blunt about certain things, or be so much of a buddy. If any of that makes sense and I don't think it does, but whatever.

I trudge back into the apartment to find him mutilating a salad with his back to me. "What'd it ever do to you?" I ask.

He doesn't respond.

"Ah, come on, Graham, let's kiss and make up."

Without waiting for him to respond—or not respond, as he seems prone to do at the moment, I wrap my arms around his waist. I would be completely okay with just kissing, even if we weren't making up. Luckily for me, Graham can never stay mad at me for long. I guess I'm too likable. I smell faint cologne and something fruity, like he got splashed with pineapple juice while preparing the chicken. It smells wonderful. He smells wonderful, like always.

He goes still beneath my touch and it takes him a moment to answer. "It brought up the subject of orgasms."

I rest my cheek on the hardness of his back and close my eyes. It feels like he relaxes into me, but probably he's just resigned himself to my PG fondling. Either is fine with me as I enjoy the nearness of him—his smell, the feel of him, for just a moment.

"So did you," I counter, pulling away.

"I did not," he says, all haughty.

"You just did."

"Really?" All the exasperation in that one word says paragraphs about his discontent with me.

"I didn't know it was a taboo subject between us. I won't bring it up again." I push him out of the way and rescue the salad.

"There are certain things I can't talk about with you, because, well, aside from how you act, you are a woman."

"Like I need reminding."

"Obviously you do."

I give him a look. "Go check the chicken."

He salutes me. I notice his middle finger is saluting me the most. I pretend I didn't see that and turn my attention back to our vegetables. My phone rings and I wipe my hands on a towel before fetching it from the end table in the living room.

I grimace as I answer. "Hello?"

"Your mom burned peas. How do you burn peas?"

My dad has this thing about calling me. All the time. About random things. Graham says it's his way of reaching out to me, but I sort of doubt that.

"You cook them too long?"

"They're already cooked. All you do is heat them up."

"I guess if you heat them up for too long, they burn," is my awesome reply.

"What are you doing?"

"Getting ready to eat supper."

He grunts.

I wait, about to tell him I have to go, when he says, "Guess I'll go eat some burned peas."

"Have fun."

He grunts again before hanging up.

I shake my head and finish preparing the salad.

Within the hour, all is well once more in world of Grennedy as we sit on the patio, eating poultry and lettuce. I cut my chicken into microscopic pieces so I can taste it but not think too much about what I'm eating.

Don't ask.

"Mmm, this is good." I point my fork at the plate and smile at Graham. It is too; sweet and tangy, like citrus fruit bursting on my tongue with enough sweetness to keep it from being sour.

He grins back. "Thanks. The salad's not too bad either."

I shrug. "What can I say? I'm gifted in the kitchen."

"Yes, you are. Remember the last time you baked?"

"Did anything exciting happen to you at work today?" I hurriedly ask, scowling at him. We don't need to talk about the time I almost burned the whole apartment building down by testing my culinary skills—and let's be honest, I don't have any.

He squints through the sunshine and shakes his head. "Nah. Just the usual."

"Not even one person threw a golf club or beaned someone on the head with a ball?"

"That *is* the usual."

Graham's a golf instructor at the local golf course. A lot of his students are women, and I think they're there more to gawk at him than anything else. He's just way too easy on the eyes. And he's nice. He's like a magnificent work of art you can't look away from. When God put Graham Malone together, He had beauty in mind, I'm sure, but that isn't even the appeal, not really. The appeal is him—the way he laughs, the sound of his voice, and his sweet, sweet nature. Yes, he is beautiful, but what makes him even more beautiful is that he has no idea.

He has his quirks; his little bits of crazy, but even they endear him to others.

I know men think they need to be tough and hide their true selves, and society tells them they need to as well, but the fact that he isn't like that, in no way deflects from his attractiveness. In fact, it enhances it. How can you not admire, respect, and covet a men who is perfectly okay with the way he is, even if the world says it's not the way he should be? He's definitely not a badass, but he doesn't need to be.

He's just...he makes your heart fill with something like joy and all of you turns warm when you're near him. You respond to him with not just your mind and your body, but all of you. At least, that's how it is for me. I sort of wish it was that way only for me, but I've seen how women act around him. I know—it's so not just me.

Yep. He's *that* guy.

"Did Mrs. Strang hit on you again?" I try to sound innocent as I ask this, but I have a hard time unclenching my jaw to get the words out.

"She does not hit on me. She's married. She merely flirts."

"Outrageously."

He gives me a look that clearly states, *And you don't?* But all he says is, "She doesn't have lessons today, remember? Only Fridays."

"Oh, that's right." I perk up. "How about Janice and Melanie? I'm sure they embarrassed themselves somehow in their attempts to woo you."

"Uh-uh."

I purse my lips. "Something exciting had to have happened."

"Nothing at all," he says quite cheerfully.

"How very dull."

"Well," Graham comments, pouring us each a second glass of wine, "we can't all be such badasses like you. Giving the grannies the what for and all that."

I sigh. "I am pretty terrible, aren't I?"

He leans toward me with a grin on his face. "You're not bad, you're not terrible, you're not even evil. You're just you." And he kisses my nose.

chapter two

O kay, so I shouldn't have had the third, or even fourth, glass of wine. I'm staring at my ceiling, but it's dark, so everything's blurry and fuzzy, and of course, *dark*. I feel kind of woozy. Like too much wine kind of woozy. It doesn't take much to get me happy. I distinctly remember Graham telling me to slow down on the alcohol and I may or may not have growled at him and snatched the bottle out of his hand. I can't be sure 'cause the details are hazy.

I sigh. Why's he always gotta be right about everything?

I keep replaying his words in my head. It was only like a whole sentence, but still, it had meaning behind it. *You're not bad, you're not terrible, you're not even evil, you're just you.*

It's funny how just the right words, or maybe it's not the words at all, but the person saying them, can make all the difference between self-loathing and understanding of oneself. Graham has a way of making me realize certain things about myself. He makes me feel like I'm worth knowing, bad traits and all. Possibly redeemable even. If I wanted to be—which I don't.

I think about this as I stare at the darkened ceiling of my bedroom that I can't really see. I also think of Graham kissing my nose. He *kissed* my nose. He kissed my *nose*. Which really shouldn't be all that significant and maybe it isn't even to him, but to me, it is. I absolutely hate my nose, revile it, detest it, wish it wasn't mine, etc. etc. It's much too long and not pretty at all. It's like, on the whole, my face isn't too bad, but once you focus on that particular part of my face (the proboscis), it's not so great. (And I only know what that word means 'cause I looked it up once, for research. Don't ask me why I was researching noses.)

I mean, I've been complimented on the deep brown of my eyes and the way they tilt up at the corners. They have even been referenced to as being almond-shaped. Which...score! Because almonds are awesome. Who doesn't like almonds? Even the slenderness of my neck received praise from one boyfriend. He might have had issues, so I'm thinking I really should disqualify that observation (but I won't because a compliment is a compliment). And my lips. They are small, but full, and yes, an ex said he liked them (not the same one). Even women like the silvery blond shade of my hair and the way it hangs down my back in a semi-straight sheet.

But have I ever received one positive word about my nose? No. Or had my nose kissed? Negative.

So it makes me feel, I don't know, happy or something, that Graham would do that, to a part of me I think is repulsive. And he must not, or he wouldn't have been able to do that. I groan. Why can't he be awful, horribly deformed, cruel, smelly, missing teeth, gay, *something*? Then I wouldn't be so stupidly in love with him. And I know I am, even though I deny it every other thought. It is so very pointless to be.

Graham is older than me, and even if he wasn't, I'm smart enough to realize he's more mature than me, probably more than I'll ever be. He's twenty-seven, so he's been around five whole years longer than me. But like I said, I don't think it's the age gap that's the problem; it's just the *gap*. Something indiscernible that says no to us ever being together. Maybe it's my lack of maturity? Pffft. Yeah right. I can't really be *that* immature. And anyone who says otherwise can kiss my butt. But not really, because that would be weird.

It's ridiculous how fast it happened. I answered an ad for a roommate in the local newspaper, met him, fell in love. He grinned—his eyes crinkling at the corners, the striking green of them slamming right into my heart—and I was done for. I shove the pillow over my head and scream. Thankfully the sound is muffled. At least I think it is until there's a knock at the door. It has to be Graham, because, well, he's the only other person living here.

I fling the pillow across the room and sit up. "Yeah?" I hurriedly try to smooth my hair and adjust my breasts in my tank top 'cause I'm currently bra-less. I arrange the blanket around my hips just as the door opens a crack.

"Ken?"

"Yes, Barbie?"

The door opens wider, revealing half of his body, the other half remaining in shadow, which is just plain disappointing. He's got on dark pajama pants and nothing else. My mouth goes dry. A streak of light spotlights me and I know I don't look nearly as good as he does. I make a face. Oh well—not much I can do about it.

"You okay?"

"Yep. Mmm-hmm. Why?"

His feet softly pad into the room and he sits at the foot of the bed. Like, right by my pinky toe. If I move it less than an inch it'll be touching him through the blanket. Hot dog!

"I thought I heard something." I can feel his eyes on me, but can't really see them. They maybe glow, which could be spooky, but I'm really not sure about anything I'm seeing or not seeing in my possibly inebriated state.

"Nope. Nothing from here."

"Huh." His head turns. "Why is your pillow on top of your dresser?"

"Psssh," is my clever response.

Even in the shadows I can feel the intensity of his eyes on my face and body. Okay, so, on my body, I *wish*. "You feel okay?"

"Wonderful!" I giggle. I'm not sure why. What I said wasn't funny.

"I told you not to have those last two drinks. You're drunk, aren't you?"

"I am no such thing!" I declare—and hiccup. "Hey! Listen to this, I just thought it up." I pause dramatically. "Here today, wine tomorrow. Good, right?"

"Bra off, wine on."

"Risqué, especially for you." I think, or try to think, as my brain is submerged in alcohol. "What the world needs now, is wine, sweet wine."

"Got wine?"

"Lame!" We have this thing with thinking up catchy wine phrases. I don't know why or how it even started—probably during one of our wine drinking nights, and there have been many.

He scoots up by me and gives me a shove. I almost hit the wall with my head, but catch myself in time. "Move over."

"Easy with the outstanding merchandise."

"Learn to handle your booze."

"Oh ho! It's going to be like that now, is it?"

He laughs. "Fo sho."

"Do not start with the gangster talk. My ears can't take it."

"Yo, you know what happens when you get shit-faced. Gangster Graham comes out," he says in a horrible imitation of street talk that has me laughing and groaning at the same time.

About seven months ago, I stumbled home from a party with all kinds of wisdom to impart. Apparently, I hung out with some faux rappers or thugs at the party 'cause by the time I got to the apartment, I was a wannabe of a wannabe and put on quite a show for Graham and his then girlfriend. For my big finale I puked—on his girlfriend.

Needless to say, he's never let the incident go, and every time I become intoxicated, as my penance, I guess, he does this. You'd think one of us would learn by now. Oh yeah, and his girlfriend dumped him. On the plus side, he wasn't too beat up about that. Or maybe the plus side was that she dumped him—plus side for *me*, that is.

With the side of his body against mine and his warmth seeping into me, I have a hard time playing along and keeping it PG. I want to jump on him and attack him and practice all kinds of sordid things I've read about in my smut books.

"Yo yo yo, check this out." He does some weird hand movements that look like he's trying to make shadow puppets—or mime.

"Graham, stop. No more," I plead, holding my aching sides.

He goes still. "If you puke, I'm not holding your hair for you."

"That's so not nice. I would hold your hair for you."

"And if you're hung over tomorrow, I'm going to bang pots around and hide all the pain meds," he threatens.

"You're so mean to me."

He gets up and I instantly miss his warmth. But all he does is grab the pillow off my dresser and comes back to the bed. "Sit up," he commands.

So I sit up.

He plumps the pillow up and places it on the bed. "Lie down."

"Are you going to tie me up too?"

"Not quite."

"Your loss."

Graham is quiet. I look up at him. He stares down at me.

What would you do if he kissed you right now? And on the lips?

Kiss him back.

Kiss me. Kiss me, kiss me, kiss me.

But he doesn't. He does get back in the bed to stretch out beside me. Which is enough, because it has to be enough. We lie beside one another in quiet camaraderie. Although, I am tempted to jump his bones, so it's not exactly peaceful on my part. My head touches his shoulder and I have to fight the urge not to rest it there. And then, I do anyway. Graham doesn't move away or tense up.

"Are you sobering off at all?"

"Yeah. Party pooper."

"You'll thank me in the morning."

I'd thank you in the morning if you didn't leave my bed all night. "We'll see in the morning, I guess, huh?"

"Indeed."

"You sound so pompous when you say that."

"Indeed."

"Stop it," I tell him, a grin curving my lips.

"Indeed."

"Graham, I swear…"

He turns his head and looks down at me, dislodging my head from his shoulder in the process. "You swear what?"

My face feels hot. "I don't know. Something bad."

"In—" He laughs when I groan. "Just kidding."

I slap his chest and then immediately rub the spot in apology.

"Kennedy?"

The seriousness of his tone has me frozen. "Yes?" I ask, not really sure I'm going to want to hear what he has to say.

"There's something I have to talk to you about."

"Do you really?"

He chuckles softly. "I really do."

I grab the blanket from the foot of the bed and clutch it near my waist like it is literally my security blanket. It's a fluffy silver and plum comforter I've had for ages. *Oh no, what's he going to say? He's moving out, he wants me to move out, he's in love, he's getting married, he's dying, what?*

"Hey. You okay? You're all tense."

I release my death grip on the blanket and smooth it over my stomach. "Mmm-hmm. Yep. Wonderful."

"Do you remember me telling you about my brother?"

I frown and search my brain. *Younger brother with mental issues, suicidal tendencies, not close with Graham, hasn't seen him in years. Ca-razy.*

"Yeah. Sort of. What about him?"

He rubs his face. "This is really hard to say."

"Did he die?"

"What? *No.* Nothing like that."

I'm an impatient person, so I urge a little forcefully, "Spit it out already."

"He wants to stay here. For the rest of the summer."

"Okay. Why?"

"Because he's on summer vacation from school and he hasn't seen me in years and I guess he wants to spend some time together. I got him a job. He's going to help out at the country club."

I sit up and face him. "Wait. So this is already all planned out? You didn't even ask me if it was okay for some person, some stranger I don't even know, to temporarily live here?" Well, of course I don't know him if he's a stranger. I frown, hoping he didn't catch that.

Graham sits up too. "I know. I'm sorry. I just didn't know what you would think of it and I did intentionally wait until the last minute to tell you. But really, you'll hardly ever see him. I'll keep him busy so he's not pestering you. We'll try to make ourselves scarce."

My mind wraps around something. "What do you mean, waited until the last minute? When's he showing up?"

I can see him wince. "Tomorrow."

"What?" I shriek. "You're shitting me! Tell me you're just doing this for the ultimate payback to that time I puked on your girlfriend. Or you're sobering me up the rest of the way. *Something.*"

"I'm right here. Please stop yelling."

"I'll yell if I want to yell!" I yell and jump to my feet. Not a good thing to do on a mattress 'cause all I manage to accomplish is the unknown ability to land on the floor with my face. Now that takes talent. The jolt jars another thought into my way too-sober brain. I sit up and give him a woebegone look. Graham can't see my face, but I'm sure he can feel the sorrow in my gaze.

"So you won't be around much the next couple of months?" My voice sounds so pitiful I could slap myself. But I don't want to, because that would hurt.

He sighs. "I don't want him to be a burden, so yeah, I'll keep him out of your hair. I don't even know what he's like anymore. It'll be like having a stranger around."

I roll my eyes. "Duh."

"I'm sorry for springing this on you at the last minute. I really am. But I couldn't say no. He's my brother." He sounds sad and in return I feel bad for him.

"You owe me," I tell him without a shred of guilt.

"I so owe you."

"Where's he going to sleep?"

"With you."

"Ha ha. Very funny," I say and grab his offered hand. He pulls me to my feet and wraps his arms around me and it feels so wonderful I almost sigh. But I don't. I'm way reserved.

"Good night."

"Suck it," I tell him saccharinely.

His laughter follows him out the door.

A pounding has me bolting upright in my bed. I look around the room, sleepily thinking there's an earthquake presently going on, even if we do live in Wisconsin. There's a gray cast to the room so I know it's before six. And I don't like to be awake before six, earthquake or not. I slump against the headboard of the bed and blink at the clock on the nightstand. The evil red numbers glow 6:12. Close enough to before six to be irate.

"Kennedy?" comes through the door.

"What?" I growl, flipping my hair out of my eyes to better glare at the door.

It opens, revealing a freshly cleaned head of messy blond hair and eyes that dazzle green even in the dullness of the morning light. My heart does a dippy thing into my stomach at the sight and smell of him, but I'm supposed to be annoyed, so I do my best to look…annoyed. Graham saunters into the room with a coffee mug in each hand. He's got on a pale pink polo shirt only a man with infinite self-confidence can pull off and khaki cargo shorts. I glance at his feet, unsurprised to find them in worn tennis shoes. His standard country club ensemble, although the color of the shirts and shorts changes daily. He's even got a purple and lime green-striped polo he pulls out of his closet on his really flamboyant days.

"It's 6:12," I announce, my voice gravelly and unhappy.

His eyes flicker to the clock. "6:14."

I don't have to try hard to put the scowl on my face this time.

"I brought you coffee." He carefully places a black mug that reads 'You'll always be my best friend; you know too much' on the stand beside my bed. Graham fits his lanky frame into the lone chair in the room, a flimsy rocker I picked up at a garage sale and am to this day stupefied is still in one piece, and gazes at me.

I shift uncomfortably, knowing I have eye boogers and my hair is a ratted mess. It's hard to look your absolute best at all times when you live with the guy you most want to impress, and it's downright impossible when the guy bombards your bedroom at all hours of the day and night. I want to seethe at the injustice of it all, but the coffee smells heavenly, and honestly, I've puked in front of him, so…who cares?

"Thank you," I tell him grudgingly, lifting the steaming liquid ambrosia to my mouth. I sigh in pleasure as the first drop of bold, black coffee touches my sleep-gunked tongue. I totally forgot to brush my teeth last night. Shame on me and *gross*. I redeem my poor opinion of myself when I remember I *did* floss.

"You're welcome," he murmurs in his deep voice.

We sip our coffee in silence. I start to feel semi-human.

"How do you feel?"

"Wonderful. No hangover."

"Good. I'm glad."

"You're glad I don't have a hangover? You care so much whether I'm miserable or not?" I'm grinning. We both know he really does.

"Well, I just don't want you to be unkind to the elderly folks that go to the foot doctor today."

"Oh, yeah, bring that up." I add, "And I don't need to have a hangover to be mean."

"Sadly, I know this."

I give him a curious look. "Why the coffee and early wake up?"

He then does something so out of character that I'm stunned. Like, mouth hanging open stunned. He fidgets and hesitates and finally stumbles out, "Well, my brother's coming today, remember?" Actually, I had forgotten. Why'd he have to remind me? "I want to make sure you'll be decent to him." What does he think I'm going to do, traumatize the poor kid? I can be nice. Sometimes. "You know, that you won't hold a grudge against him because of me, waiting till the last minute and all to tell you. I'm sorry about that."

"Why would I take my anger at your stupidity out on your innocent brother?"

Graham sighs. "I apologized! I do really feel bad. I should have told you sooner, but I didn't want to give you an extended amount of time to think about it, and dwell on it, and plan all kinds of mischievous ways to get back at me."

"Silly boy." I chuckle. "I only need a couple hours to do that."

The morning light is changing from steel to shades of sherbert and I can see him better now—I can also see the disaster that is my room. He looks nervous. This visit with his brother must mean a lot to him.

"I just wanted to touch base with you before I leave for work. Sorry for waking you up early. I know how much you hate the unsleeping state of life."

I give him a glare for that comment. A girl needs her beauty rest; all ten to twelve to fourteen hours of it. On a good night, that is.

"I thought the coffee would help. Be a salve to the morning monster's grumbly attitude."

He is *so* not getting a Christmas present.

He stands and the light through the window seems to illuminate his good looks all the more, casting a golden glow to his already golden physique. "I'm going to go hit some balls while I wait for my first lesson."

"Who is it today?"

Something like jealousy shoots through me when I think of a few of his younger, perkier, prettier students—the ones that wear skimpy clothes, and bat their eyelashes at him, and sigh as they gaze at his handsomeness. Oh, and make obvious sexual innuendos, which is counterproductive. If you're trying to be inconspicuous, you don't grab at a guy's arm and press your breasts against him, telling him your husband is out of town for the weekend. And that's just one of the times I saw it firsthand; I'm sure it happens all the time in all kinds of interesting ways.

All of my advances are much more subtle. Okay, so they aren't. But that isn't the point!

"It's Friday. Mrs. Strang."

I make a *grrr* sound through clenched teeth. She's the exact married woman I witnessed hitting on Graham in a not-too-subtle way.

He laughs. He always laughs it off. "She promised she'd behave."

My face scrunches up. "I'm sure she did."

"Kennedy."

"What?" I snap.

"Quit acting like my mother."

I sit back. That completely wakes me up and not in a good way. His *mother*? Seriously? "Get out," I hiss and point a finger at the door.

"What? What's the matter?"

"I have to get ready for work and *you* need to go flirt with your *student* and I am *not acting like your mother*!"

He hurries to the door, casting an anxious look over his shoulder. "Remind me never to wake you up early again." He pauses. "And I don't flirt. You know that."

I menacingly scoot off the bed. Yes, it is possible to scoot off a bed in a menacing way. It's all about the expression on your face. Mine is schooled for murder.

He disappears like magic, popping his head back into the room to say, "And remember to behave around my brother."

The look of fury on my face hurries him along, luckily for Graham.

I'm jamming along to Avril Lavigne on my short, five minute commute; give or take a couple seconds, to work. I cut someone off at a four-way stop, apparently going when it wasn't my turn (and that's saying something in a small town like Lancaster. Like, I'm a bad driver) and give them a one finger salute when they honk and wave their fist at me.

Besides, I have stuff on my mind—Graham and Younger Brother stuff. Okay, so I'm slightly irritated that he didn't mention this whole two month visit to me before the day before his brother is supposed to show up. It's not like he's staying for a couple days; it's a couple *months*.

Most likely this kid is going to sleep on the couch and want to stay up all night playing video games and be a nuisance. He's probably like sixteen or seventeen and thinks he's all cool. I'm sure he's not. He also probably won't work like he's supposed to, after Graham got him the job and everything, and he'll just be a slacker. A smelly slacker. 'Cause there's no way two Malones can be so perfect. The younger one definitely has to be the outcast. I realize I already know he is, based on what Graham's told me of his troubled past. Wonderful. I'll probably say the wrong thing and he'll slice his wrists open, which…not cool.

What if he sees me in my undies or opens the bathroom door while I'm in there going pee? And yeah, the door does lock, but still, that's not the point. If he's observant in any kind of way, I'm sure he'll realize in about two seconds that I have the hots for his older brother. What if he tells him? Graham would be mortified to know such a thing. He really would. Everything would be ruined between us.

My shoulders slump. This is going to be a horrible two months, I can tell already.

I hit the brakes at the last possible second and whip into a right turn, tires squealing. Cripes, I almost drove past my workplace. I slam the shifter thing (I don't know the technical term for it so that's what I call it. Lay off.) into park and twist the key in the ignition (I do know the name of this one. That R. Kelly song helped with that. Even though he's a perv, he did have that one good song. Not the flying one—that one was just strange.) to off.

With a loud sigh and a sense of foreboding, I grab my hot pink purse, lock the car doors, and head for the gray building. At the door, I impulsively fumble around in my purse for my cell phone and hit Graham's number.

"Hello?"

"Hey, are you busy?"

"Well, I'm working."

"Yeah, so, are you busy?"

He sighs. "What's up?"

I nibble my lip. "So this brother of yours? He's not going to, like, freak out and kill himself during his visit here, is he?"

"What are you talking about?"

"Well, because, remember, you said he had problems? Or something? Like, he's depressed and suicidal and shit. So is he, like, going to off himself if I say or do the wrong thing?"

There's silence for an extended amount of time and then, "Only if you mention the color red."

I go still. "What?"

"Yeah, something really traumatic happened to him when he was a kid and it involved the color red. So whatever you do, don't say that word."

I pull the phone away from my ear and narrow my eyes at it. "Are you funning with me?"

"Jesus, I thought you said something else," he says faintly.

I grin when it dawns on me what he thought he heard me say. "Don't swear."

My parents may be whacked, but they did teach me some things you never say, and anything in relation to biblical terms spoken in a negative way was one of them.

"I didn't…oh…yeah…sorry."

"So you're telling the truth?"

"Definitely."

I don't know if I really believe him or if I think he's just saying this to get back at me for me being me—like, calling to ask if I have to worry about his brother ending his life in my apartment. Which isn't very fair 'cause I can't help the way I am. Maybe I'm a little callous, a little insensitive, a little self-centered, but hey, that's how I roll.

"Okay. Well. 'Bye."

"Goodbye."

I don't hang up. Neither does Graham.

"The word red, huh?" I just want to make sure I'm getting this straight.

A pause. "Yes."

"What if he sees the color red? Same thing?"

Another pause. "No."

"Oh, good, 'cause we have lots of red in our apartment."

"Uh-huh."

"And that would get tedious if whenever he went somewhere, there was the possibility he'd see the color red and attempt suicide. Like, if I grabbed the bottle of ketchup out of the fridge and he went berserk and hung himself. That would be a bummer."

"Yes, it would," he says evenly.

"What if it's already in a word? Like…" I search my brain. Not easy to do this early in the morning. "Redwing. Or something."

It sounds like snickering from his end of the phone. "That's…fine," he says, his voice sounding strained.

I purse my lips, feeling pretty suspicious. "Really, you're not messing with me?"

"Really."

I hesitate. "Okay then. 'Bye."

"'Bye." His second farewell may have sounded curt, but I'm sure I imagined it.

I unlock the door and scoot inside, willing the day to start fast and end faster. I'm always the first of the crew to show. Me, the doc, Sally, and a part-time massage therapist make up the glamorous team of foot care pros. We're open four days a week, with Tuesdays off. Phoebe Kuntz, the massage therapist, makes bucket loads of money and only works Wednesdays, Thursdays, and Fridays. Must be nice. She makes in an hour what I make in five. Although, she did go to college for two years, and ya know, she has to massage feet.

Cringe.

I was hired right after I graduated from high school and was trained by Dr. Olman. The ad read 'Willing to train the right individual', and of course, that was me. Four years now I've been a foot doctor assistant. Amazingly, I find it fascinating. For the most part. The least part is blood and bad smells and procedures that don't go as planned and running behind in the schedule and people that don't clean between their toes—ever.

I glance at the schedule and can't quite hold in a moan. Of course, the first procedure is multiple bunion removal. Yay. Talk about party in the office.

I'm just putting the final items on the surgical tray when Dr. Olman and Sally show up. Together. I narrow my eyes as I watch them walk through the back door. It's possible they just arrived at the same time, but came in different vehicles from different houses. Then again, I'm thinking not. Call it the blush on Sally's face or the way Dr. Olman isn't meeting my eyes.

I smile—a really big smile.

He clears his throat, and in his thunderous voice, asks, "What are we doing on the first patient?"

Oh, so it's going to be like that, is it? All business. Okay. Fine. I can be business-like. I'm profoundly versatile.

"Multiple bunion removal on both feet. Here's the x-ray." I slap it against his palm.

He holds the x-ray up to the light, grimaces, and nods. "Could be extensive."

"Yes! I love extensive procedures." I punch the air in mock enthusiasm.

"Should be exciting."

"That's exactly what I was thinking."

"Excuse me," Sally says and slithers by. She glances at me as she passes. She blushes even redder when I left an eyebrow at her and hurries to her area.

"Have you seen Phoebe yet?"

I look at my boss. He never asks about Phoebe. Could be he's trying to deflect the attention from him and Sally. And…no. That's not happening. "Uh, no. Her first patient is at 8:30, so she should be here soon."

He brusquely nods his head. "Good. I'm just going to…" he trails off, practically running to get to Sally.

I hold in a laugh and go about my duties.

Two hours later, Dr. Olman bandages up two feet, wishes Richard Hermsen a good day, and exits left.

"You have to come back one more time. We didn't get as far as we'd hoped to today," I tell the patient.

Richard is in his sixties, has two hearing aids, and mumbles a lot. I don't know if it's on purpose or something he has no control over. But how can you not be able to control such a thing? I always want to yell at him, "Enunciate! Enunciate!", but of course I don't.

He runs a hand over his gray head, mutters something, and gets out of the chair.

"What?"

Mr. Hermsen blinks his brown eyes at me. "Huh?"

"What did you say?"

He leans his hands on the chair and slowly straightens to his full height of about five feet three, three inches shorter than me. "What?" He looks confused.

I let out a helpless sigh. I know I have a soft voice, but really, he has his hearing aids in so he should be able to understand me. I almost want to ask him if they're turned on, but I do have enough sense to realize that could be interpreted as rude.

"You have to come back one more time and Dr. Olman will finish working on the last bunion."

He stares at me. I stare back. I don't know if he comprehends a thing I'm saying. I'm about ready to shove him from the room and let someone else deal with him when he nods. I let out a deep breath and follow him from the room. I tell Sally what's going on and quickly escape back to the op, but not before I give her a wink. *Have fun*, that wink says.

I remove the dirty instruments from the room, toss them in the ultrasonic unit (which basically vibrates germs and other gross stuff from the instruments) in the lab, return to wipe down the room, and go back to the lab. I take the dirty instruments out of the ultrasonic unit and put some of them in the heat sterilizer, the rest of the instruments that can't be cleaned with heat in the cold sterile container, and head back to the op to set up the room once more. I finish typing my notes in Richard's computerized chart, and click out of it just as the office door chimes, most likely signaling the arrival of the next victim—*patient*. There I go again.

Phoebe pops her head in the doorway. "Hey, Kennedy. How's your morning going so far?"

My co-worker's lucky, and not just because she's almost too skinny, tan, blond, and blue-eyed; although none of those things hurt, but because her patients actually want to see her. When my boss tells someone they need treatment, it's not exactly something they want to hear. Let's just say, it doesn't make their day; it even infuriates some of them. People seriously look at him sometimes like he's lying about their podiatric health. It would be humorous if, well, if it was.

"Oh, you know. Like butter." I grin at her.

She smiles back, showing off her straight, whitened teeth that appear to glow. I tried whitening my teeth once, but they got so dang sensitive, I had to stop.

She hovers somewhere in the above average height and below average weight category. She's got her fine blond hair pulled back in a ponytail, which just accentuates her facial beauty all the more. Her eyes are large and she has a small chin and dainty ears. Phoebe's just so cute even I can't hate her. And believe me, when I first met her, I tried. She even looks good in her pale blue scrubs, whereas I *feel* like a scrub in my dark purple ones. And yeah, I got my hair pulled back in a ponytail as well, but my hair is thick and probably weighs twice as much as hers, so it just doesn't look nice pulled back. It looks heavy.

"I think your patient's here," she tells me, nodding in the direction of the waiting room.

"The suspense is killing me."

She blinks. "I know you're being sarcastic, but I don't know why. It's *Nathan Mezera*," she whispers, leaning close to me.

Her one flaw: she smokes. Therefore, she smells like a big butt most of the time. Cigarette butt, that is. And don't get me wrong, I've tried smoking a couple times, but I just didn't have the talent to make it a habit. I know—I am such a disappointment. And sometimes, when I drink, I feel the urge to smoke, but otherwise, I'm not a smoker. It's sad, really. I can't even be an overachiever at that.

"So?" I know why she's looking at me the way she is, but I'm going to play dumb. Nathan Mezera is a construction worker, which isn't to say he's naturally buff and hot, but he is.

She closes her eyes and counts. I know this 'cause even though she's not speaking, her lips are moving—in the form of numbers. Phoebe pops her eyes open and states, quite loudly, "He is hot! On fire hot. So hot he sizzles when he moves. Do you not *see* this?" She widens her already slightly too large eyes and makes a sweeping motion with her hand.

"So hot you could catch a fever?"

"Yes!" She nods her head up and down so fast I fear she may get whiplash.

"So hot he's smoking?"

"Yes, yes!"

This is getting to be fun. I try to think of another analogy, but Dr. Olman ruins my good time.

"Hey!" He snaps his fingers in front of our faces. "Stop drooling over the next patient and *get* the next patient. You, Phoebe, Sally has a question for you. Move it, move it," he commands, sounding like a drill sergeant.

Phoebe sprints from the room, but I just stand there and look at my boss. He returns my stare until I raise an eyebrow. He sighs and leaves the room, mumbling something about good help being hard to find. Then I snap to it and hurry for the next patient. I don't want to appear too eager, like Phoebe. I wouldn't want my employer to actually think I *listen* to him.

chapter three

nathan Mezera is twenty-four years old. I know this because I looked at the date of birth on his chart. He's probably about five feet ten inches of all muscle. He's got light brown hair that curls on the nape of his neck and over his ears, and it looks so soft, like silk. Of course, his brown eyes are dreamy and always have a sleepy look to them, like he just got out of bed or had great sex. His skin is tanned dark brown from being outside in the sun most days. He always wears these straight-legged jeans that mold to his thighs and butt, and stretchy t-shirts that show off his awesome physique. Phoebe's right—he is hot. Definitely drool-worthy.

"Nathan, how's your mom and dad?" Dr. Olman asks in a booming voice, shooting a look my way and completely interrupting my daydream.

My face burns and I fiddle around with the mouse pad. I suppose I can at least try to look like I'm working, and straightening the mouse pad counts in my book—which is yet to be written. I would so buy that book. Because, I mean, if the mouse pad isn't straight, then the mouse on top of it won't be, and how will I get anything done in the chart with an imbalanced mouse sitting on a crooked pad? Exactly! Aligned mouse pads are key to a productive workday. That could be the opening line of the book.

"They're doing really good. Their twenty-fifth wedding anniversary is this weekend. You should come. There's an announcement in the paper; everyone's welcome. They'd be thrilled to see you—as long as you don't bring your scary instruments." He and the doc laugh. I somehow refrain. "It's at the country club. Tomorrow night. Seven o'clock. Bring your staff," Nathan adds and wiggles his eyebrows at me when the boss man isn't looking.

My mouth drops open—not because he can wiggle his eyebrows, or even that he did so at me while in the presence of my boss, but because I think maybe he just flirted with me. My boss and I exchange looks. I try to shrug discreetly, but I have a sneaky suspicion I look ridiculous bobbing one shoulder up and down, so I stop.

"Sure, sure. We'll try to make it." Dr. Olman gives me a pointed look. I pretend I don't see him, which is hard to pull off as he is standing directly before me.

"So, uh, Nathan has some callouses on the soles of his feet that he'd like treated," I rush to tell him.

"We'll shave them off for you, how's that sound?"

"Sounds good," he tells him, fairly oozing self-confidence from where he sits in the patient chair.

"We'll numb the areas up first."

"Nah. I'm good. Go at it." He puts his hands behind his head to show just how good he is.

My boss and I look at each other, and then he shrugs. "Kennedy, where is the scalpel?"

"Uh..." I force my gaze from Nathan and try to think. *Scalpel. Where's the scalpel? What* is *a scalpel?*

Dr. Olman gives me a look of disgust. I lift my hands, palms up. I can't help it. He's really good at making my brain mush, to the point where words I should know, I no longer do.

"I'll get the scalpel," he says.

I nod, not really paying attention. Nathan's smiling at me. Why does he keep smiling at me? It makes me want to smile back, especially with him looking all cute and into me. And then I realize, on top of all of this, we're about to shave callouses off his feet. My smile dims. I mean, the whole experience seems odd. Here, flatter me and make me blush while I watch my boss remove hard, dry skin from your feet. Yeah. Weird. I have an epiphany as I am mulling this all over—I so could not date him.

Well, at least I know. It would just—feet, him, me? No. I'd be thinking of his feet while kissing him and that is totally gross.

"I'll get the scalpel," Dr. Olman says again, and his voice sounds ominous.

Then he waves at me to follow. With a sigh, I do. Once in the hallway, he wordlessly points to the lab. I enter and twirl around to face him. He closes the door and leans against it, crosses his arms, and waits. I wait too, wondering what we're waiting for.

"Something you want to tell me?"

"Um…your scrub top's on inside out?"

"What?" He glances down. "Why didn't you tell me sooner?"

I shrug. "It was funny."

He quickly pulls the article of clothing off, rearranges it, and shoves it over his head. "Anything else?"

I look him over, but no, I don't find anything else to point out to him—at the moment. He has two facial masks hanging around his neck, but I'll mention that when he tries to put them both on—as he's done in the past.

"Noooo. Why?"

He jerks his head at the door behind him. "What was that in there with Nathan? Is he hitting on you or something?"

"I really don't know," I say, quite honestly too.

I don't know what that was about. I can count on one hand the number of boyfriends I've had (and the most recent before I moved in with Graham. Sad, I know. He has kind of ruined other guys for me). I'm pretty much clueless about men and have almost no experience. Especially when nothing serious happened and I didn't really like any of them. Except for one, and that was lukewarm.

When the silence gets awkward, I say, "I think we should get back to the patient."

He nods, looking relieved.

Amid lots of blushes and restrained giggling (completely out of character for me), I get through Nathan's appointment. Dr. Olman looks ready to shoot either me or himself by the end of it. My mind has wrapped around, and won't let go of, Nathan's parting words: "See you Saturday?" He said this to *me*, while looking at *me*, and waiting for *me* to answer. So I nodded. Of course. I'll just try to keep the image of his feet out of my head from this moment on.

"I'm glad I don't have kids," my boss says as we await our final patient of the morning.

"Why's that?" I ask, leaning against the counter in the lab.

"I feel like I need to protect you, or give you some advice, or ground you."

I raise my eyebrows.

He gets a helpless look on his face. "Do I?"

I vehemently shake my head. "No. No way. You just don't worry about a thing with me and boys, okay?"

A curious expression forms on his features. "What would your father tell you in a situation like this?"

I think of my dad, a manly man with black hair pretty much everywhere but on his head, brown eyes, and an inclination to call me on a whim. He wanted a boy to hunt, fish, and watch football games—and let's not forget, burp and fart—with, but got me instead. Poor guy. Or rather, poor me.

I laugh. "He wouldn't say a thing. He still thinks I'm a guy."

He looks perplexed.

"Never mind."

"Okay," he says slowly.

The bell chimes from the waiting room, saving me from explaining my dad's curious view on life, and saving Dr. Olman from the confusion of listening to it all. I give him a cheeky grin and head for the front of the building.

I'm turning off the last of the lights in the office. The day is finally over and the weekend is about to begin. Hallelujah. Dr. Olman and Sally are up front, conversing in lowered voices, and Phoebe is following me around like my more perfect shadow, bombarding me with questions.

"He really asked you to go to his parents' party? Like, he asked you on a date?"

I flip the light switch off in the examination room. "No. Not like a date. He was talking to Dr. Olman and said we should all go."

"Even me?"

I look at her. "Yes. Even you. He said to bring his staff. That includes you."

Phoebe smiles widely. "Oh. Wow. How cool. Want to go together?"

I walk the length of the hallway and end up in the reception area. The inflatable organ is limp and falling to the side. I place my hands on my hips and scrutinize it, aware that Dr. Olman and Sally both fell silent when I entered the vicinity.

"Sure," I absently tell Phoebe, knowing without even looking that she's hovering over my left shoulder.

"Are you two going to the anniversary party?" she asks Sally, totally unaware of the undercurrents in the room.

Dr. Olman straightens from where he's practically folded over the countertop in an attempt to get closer to Sally without actually going around the desk. She sits upright in her chair, too straight-backed and frozen to be natural—or comfortable. They wear identical expressions of guilt. I almost want to tell them to knock it off and quit acting all mysterious 'cause I already know what they're up to. But I don't. It's too much fun watching them nervously jump around and fumble about trying to cover up their tracks. Stealth-like, they will never be.

"What do you mean by that? By us two?" she asks suspiciously.

Phoebe looks confused. "Because we're all invited."

"Yeah, the four of us. Are we all going to show up together or…in pairs?" I raise one eyebrow and stare at them.

My boss straightens his tie, avoiding my gaze.

Sally looks like she's torn between glaring at me and ignoring me all together. She thinks I might know, I can tell. She's more astute than her lover boy. She flips her feathered hair and states, "Let's *all* meet here at 6:30. Then, the *four* of us, will ride together. How's that sound?" Her blue eyes bore into mine.

I smirk. "No can do. What if I get lucky? We'll need to take two cars. Phoebe might have to hitch a ride home with you two." I'm completely joking, but apparently they don't know this.

Phoebe gasps.

Sally's eyes narrow.

And Dr. Olman, well, he looks like he's having a hard time swallowing.

"I was so kidding," I tell them when the silence gets awkward.

Phoebe giggles nervously.

Dr. Olman gives me an injured look, like, how could I joke about such a thing?

Sally does glare at me this time. "Not funny," she clips out.

"Sorry," I say, still smiling. "But we probably should have two cars. In case some of us want to leave before the rest."

"Good idea," Phoebe agrees.

"All right. Have a good night," Dr. Olman says.

"See you tomorrow," Sally adds.

They're obviously waiting for me and Phoebe to hit the road. Fine. I can take a hint. Phoebe, not so much, I realize, as I drag her from the room. I wonder if they're gonna get it on in the office after we leave. I shudder. *Please, no.*

"Why are you in such a hurry?" she asks, pulling her arm out of my firm grip.

The sun beats a warm path on my head and I squint. It's gotta be about ninety degrees out. I like it. I close the front door and look at her. "It's Friday."

She perks up. "Oh, yeah. What are you going to wear tomorrow night?"

We walk to our cars, mine a blue Ford Focus; hers a black Jeep Cherokee. Her vehicle is much cooler than mine. An ABBA song about money flitters through my mind.

"I don't know. Probably a sundress or a skirt. You?"

She ponders my question, taking it way seriously. "I have a black mini skirt I've been dying to wear and a new silver wraparound halter tank top. Oh! And these black open-toed stilettos that I haven't worn yet. What do you think?"

I *think* I want to groan. But I don't. She can't help that she has long, tanned legs and a Skinny Minnie frame that will look sexy as hell in an outfit like that. I should be happy for her. I almost snort. Yeah. Right.

"I think you will look amazing," I tell her.

"Really?" She gives me a blinding smile, looking pleased. Wow, I'm actually a pretty nice person. I had no idea.

"Really."

"Do you want me to stop over and help you pick something out?"

She's trying to be nice, knowing there's no way I'll pick an outfit out even close to being as cool as hers, but I am not a charity case and I do know how to dress myself.

"Come over at six and you can give me your opinion on what I'm wearing." And then I'll most likely keep wearing whatever it is I'm wearing.

"Five or five-thirty would be better. To make sure we have enough time," she says in all earnestness.

I squint my eyes and negotiate. "Five forty-five."

She jumps up and down in excitement, much too worked up about this. "Cool. I can't wait! This will be so much fun. We haven't gone out together in *forever.*"

The last time I puked. "Yep. Should be fun." Hopefully not as much fun as last time.

"Oh, it will be. See you then!"

"'Bye."

With a little wave, she gets in her car, blares the stereo system, and peals out of the parking lot.

Mine is a much more subdued exit.

I'm fretting about Graham's brother, whom I should meet in about two minutes. The inevitable confrontation was in the back of my mind all day—as Graham always is. There's not enough room in there for two Malone boys. It made my head hurt. I don't like this at all. I chew on my lower lip as I park my car. He better not be a punk. 'Cause if he's a punk, I am so saying the word red.

It's about five o'clock and I'm mentally exhausted from work, which usually transmits to physically exhausted as well, since the two seem to go hand in hand. I need to exercise, though, so I tell myself to suck it up. I haul my purse out of the backseat, lock the doors, and trudge up to the entrance of the apartment building. It's a brown, rectangular-shaped structure with thirty apartments in it. We lucked out, or I should say, Graham lucked out, when he filled out an application for the apartment. You open the door, turn to the right, and voila! There's our apartment. It rocks.

I steel myself for video game noises and a voice hitting puberty but am surprised to hear neither. I close the door, and take in the living room. A stranger that is so obviously not Graham's brother sits on the couch. He is leaning forward with his head bowed, elbows on his knees, moving a beer bottle back and forth between his palms. Something about his pose tugs at me. He looks despondent. I am not a nurturing person by nature, so he must look really pathetic to get a reaction out of me. He appears to be Graham's age and has shaggy hair so dark it might be black. He looks up and I suck in a really blatant deep breath, then outwardly, yes, *outwardly*, cringe. Subtle I am not.

But, *his eyes*. I've always been an eye gal. I'm drawn to them, eyelashes and all; the color, the shape, the expression in them. The eyes really are the window to the soul. And this guy's eyes are way intense. He's stabbed me in place with one glance and I can't move. I force myself to take in the rest of him. His brows are slanted low over those expressive gray eyes, his nose is hawkish, cheekbones carved by a knife, his lips are on the thin side, and there's a cleft in his chin. I'm usually not attracted to clefts in the chin, but his fits. The guy's pale too, like he hasn't been out in the sun enough. He's like a sexy (possibly vampiric) bad boy with a deep soul within.

Holy guacamole, I'm spouting poetry.

From what I can tell, with him slouching and all, his frame's lean and long, and covered in a black t-shirt that says 'Nirvana' on it with worn jeans gracing his legs. I cock my head, thinking he seems familiar, but knowing I've never met him before.

"How's it going?" he murmurs in a deep, quiet voice that has a slight derisive cast to it, like he really isn't the greeting kind of guy.

I hear him perfectly well, but feel like I need to strain to hear him anyway. I straighten, unaware until now that I'd actually been leaning in his direction. I bet I looked really dumb too.

"Hey." I nod. "Who are you?"

A smile quirks half of his mouth and I find it oddly attractive. "I'm Blake. You're Kennedy?"

"The one and only." I feel like I should strike a pose. But I don't. I glance around the room, knowing Graham's not in it, but double check anyway. "Where's Graham?"

"He's in the shower."

I nod again. "Okay then. Nice meeting you."

The almost smile makes another appearance. "You too."

I have an intense urge to whistle as I leave the room and just barely restrain myself. I get into my bedroom, slam the door shut, and lean against it. Graham didn't decorate this room—which is why it's an eclectic mess of colors and clothes. I don't really have a theme, unless you count the three winter-ish landscape paintings that Graham got me and the silver and plum curtains that match my bedspread. Otherwise, it looks like a rainbow vomited in my room, in the form of clothes and accessories.

My knees are weak. No idea why. I take a few deep breaths—loud ones—and try to get myself under control. I must seriously be overly hormonal right now. Graham, Nathan, Blake. Attractive men are doing funny things to me lately and I swear it's because I'm the oldest virgin alive. Possibly. Okay, so not the oldest, but one of the older ones, for sure. Although, I mean, I just plain love Graham. To death. Forever and ever and until the day after infinity. He's it for me. Really. I know this.

But Nathan is available and likes to flirt with me, which makes me feel good and is also awesome for my ego. He would definitely be a fun time, if I was of the mind to have an uncommitted-not serious-wouldn't last long fun time. That is, if I could not envision myself making out with his toes as I was kissing him.

Of course, I just saw this Blake guy for the first time ever, but he seems like he could induce some heavy, deep, passionate, soul-searching feelings.

And what would Graham think of that? I tilt my head as I ponder this. Would he be jealous? He probably wouldn't even notice. I frown. Plus, he might be pissed if I messed around with his friend. And why hasn't he ever mentioned this Blake guy before? Maybe he just started working with him or something.

I'm sure all my current thoughts are the product of the fact that I haven't had sex, like, ever. Except for the deal with Graham—the infatuation with him is real.

I shrug out of my work clothes and leave them in a pile on the floor near my dresser. Where the heck *is* Graham's brother? Did he not show? I can't say I wouldn't be slightly, okay, ecstatically, happy to learn this is the case. I pause with my black workout shorts halfway up my legs. Am I a bad person? Nah. Maybe less than good. But not bad. I nibble my lip. But if I have to keep asking myself this, it's not really an encouraging sign, is it?

I finish pulling my bottoms up, squeeze into a purple and pink tie-dyed shirt, and dig my running shoes out of the closet. I tighten the ponytail holder in my hair and am ready to exercise, after I find my iPod and earbuds, that is—which I do in record time.

I open my bedroom door, which is directly across from the bathroom door—and I squeak. There stands Graham, with nothing but a towel around his waist. Steam billows out of the bathroom behind him, surrounding him like he's a magician and just appeared out of thin air. And he could be. 'Cause he's got me mesmerized. Hypnotized. Feeling magical. Under a spell. Blah blah blah. You get the point. I feel a *zing!* in my stomach and slightly lower. I want to lick the water from his body. Run my hands up and down his stomach and chest. Press my body against his and never move away—my *naked* body.

His hair is wet and clings to his scalp as rivulets of water make a trail down his neck. My eyes follow them to his chest—his tanned, nicely sculpted chest. I swallow with difficulty and jerk my eyes back to his face. He's watching me with a quizzical smile on his lips. Like he's wondering what I'm doing. Good question.

"Hi," I croak.

His smile turns blinding and I almost choke. "Hi, Ken. Going for a walk?"

I'm about to demand how he would know such a thing until I realize what I'm wearing. "Yeah."

"Cool. You want to get a pizza with me and Blake when you get back?"

I stare at him.

"You met Blake, right?"

"Yeah," I answer slowly. "Are you two hanging out tonight or something?"

It's his turn to stare at me.

"What? Why are you looking at me like that?"

"Yeah, remember? He's staying here for the next couple of months, so yeah, we'll be hanging out tonight. And many nights to come."

My brows lower. "Um. What?" I'm just not grasping what he's trying to tell me. Why would his friend be staying here? What about his brother?

Graham grabs at his towel and my attention is drawn down to the fabric unraveling at his hip. I couldn't be so lucky. "You feeling okay?"

Does he know what I'm thinking, that I'm anxiously anticipating the complete slip of his towel to show me all his naked glory? My eyes snap to his face. No. He's adorably unaware, as usual. Or annoyingly unaware. Whichever.

"Yeah, I'm fine. I just...where is your brother? Did he decide not to come?"

He lets out an incredulous laugh, jams a hand through his hair, and then lunges for his towel as it loosens up more. He leans against the doorframe, one hand tightly clasping the two ends of his towel together. Pity, that.

"I think we're having a miscommunication," he tells me, looking amused.

"I'm not following."

"I realize that."

"Okay." I wait.

"Blake is my brother."

I blink at him. "Say what?" I blink some more. What is he *talking* about?

"He's my brother."

I laugh. "No he's not."

"Yes."

"Nuh-uh."

He leans close to me and gazes into my eyes. I can smell his shampoo and soap and it's a wonderful moment. "Blake is my brother. Blake Malone, same last name as me. My brother."

"No way. Your brother is, like, sixteen. You said *younger*," I accuse.

He straightens. "He is younger."

"How much younger?"

"A year."

"How is that possible? How can you only be a year apart?"

"Well, you see, when a man and a woman..."

"He looks nothing like you!"

Graham presses his lips into a thin line. "Yeah, well, he's my half-brother. Same dad, different mom."

"But...but," I stutter as he patiently waits. "I didn't even know your parents were divorced. I just assumed you had a mother and a father and that they are married—to *each other*. I feel like I don't even know you!" Okay, slightly melodramatic, but it's true. How could I not know this?

Graham's mom lives in Texas, having moved there after Graham graduated from high school, so I've never actually "met" her, but we have skyped plenty of times. She's a feminine version of Graham, so of course she's beautiful and lovable. (She loves me. Obviously.) I can't believe I never realized there's never been a guy on her end of the screen. I am so ignorant. How can I call myself Graham's friend and not know this significant detail of his life?

He gives a slight smile. "You don't know everything about me."

"I should know that." Maybe I shouldn't, but I really feel like I should. Graham's pretty much the most important thing to me; I should at least know his family history. He knows mine. Well, most of it. Some of it. Enough...

"Now you do. Are we done? I really need to put some clothes on."

"But...you said he was in school," I finish lamely, my voice dropping to a whisper.

"He's in college."

I scowl at him. "You purposely led me to believe that your brother was some pimply teenager who was going to mooch off you for the remainder of the summer, not...not..." I jab a finger in the direction of the living room.

"Not what?"

"Not some hottie!" I blurt out, and then wish I hadn't.

Especially when Graham rears back and gets a funny look on his face. "You think my brother's hot?" His voice is even, but his eyes look weird. Like, angry or something. A thrill goes down my spine at the thought of my comment having that effect on him. Could he be *jealous*?

"Yes." I nod firmly.

"Huh." He looks away.

A dash of regret has the audacity to chase the little thrill away. I wonder if I've upset him, but then decide I haven't. Why would he be upset? Unless he doesn't know I think he's hot too. So I figure I should tell him. It would be rude not to.

"You're also hot."

He gives me a look; part incredulous, part I don't know what. "Thanks," he says faintly.

"Yeah." I start to feel dumb about pretty much the whole conversation. "Okay. 'Bye."

"'Bye."

I glance back at him. He is staring at me with a frown pulling his mouth down. "You should put some clothes on."

"Right."

I enter the living room. Blake is studying a fake plant in the corner of the room, which pretty much confirms that he was listening to our complete word exchange. Wonderful.

He glances up as I pass. I see some teeth with this smile. "We'll wait till you get back to order pizza. If you want."

Yeah, like I could endure an evening with the Malone men, feeling awkward and ridiculous, knowing they both know I think they're hot.

I make a sweeping gesture with my hand. "Uh, no thanks. You guys go ahead." I avoid his searching eyes and race from the apartment.

I cannot believe *what a fool I just made out of myself,* I think as I walk the circular length of the high school track. (Isn't a sign of insanity doing the same thing over and over expecting different results? *Why* am I walking in a circle? Even better question: why do Nascar drivers do it?) There is no breeze and the air is damp with humidity, making me think I should have foregone the whole walking thing today. Surrounding the track is a fence, and beyond that is the high school and trees—lots of trees. Trees cause humidity, therefore, at the moment, I loathe trees. Never mind that they also produce oxygen, which, ya know, we all need to breathe. It's a moot point.

I don't really care that I thought Blake was going to be young and obnoxious and found out he isn't. What I care about is that Graham thinks I'm a moron and Blake most likely does too. Well, really, it's not my fault. So I assumed something and was wrong. Big deal. My face feels like it is on fire, telling me that, yeah, it is a big deal. I start lap three. The music in my ears is doing nothing but annoying me so I turn the iPod off.

They're probably sitting at the apartment, drinking beer, eating pizza, and laughing at me. I scowl. I know Graham implied that the guy was a kid and still in high school. Didn't he? *Didn't* he? I search my brain. Crap, I can't remember. By lap twelve I'm tired and feeling slightly better about the whole situation. I'll just pretend like that bizarre conversation never happened. Everything will be fine. Really.

I walk the seven blocks back to the apartment complex, my legs wobbling like Jell-O. It's a good feeling. I pass by familiar houses and establishments, feeling like I'm at home in the town I've lived in since I was five. Lancaster is sort of lame, coolness-wise. Don't get me wrong—it's a super awesome decent town, it just…what is there to do in Lancaster? Not much, that's what.

On the plus side, there are more women than men. Wait. Maybe that's not a plus side? Either way, there's more women than men living in Lancaster. 2% more, to be exact. There are also two historically noteworthy facts about the town that are not lame.

1. The town received the first ever Civil War monument dedicated in 1876.
2. Pleasant Ridge, located on the edge of town, was a home for free slaves and one of the first integrated schools in our nation.

So there's that.

I stop outside the apartment building, eyeing it like a potentially deadly disease is waiting inside for me. I'm sweaty and smelly and self-conscious about it. I'm also breathing funny. I usually just hightail it to the bathroom before Graham can catch too much of a whiff or glance of me, but now there's two of them to look out for. This really sucks. How am I going to survive like this for the next few months? I'm not, that's all there is to it. I'm going to have to stay at my parents' or something. Or not. Only a life or death situation would take me back to my parents' doorstep. And this, so far, is not that dire. But it could turn into that. Oh, yes, it could.

I throw the door open before I lose my courage, relieved to find that the living room is empty. I'm almost disappointed—all that near hyperventilating for nothing. My eyes take in the off-white couch with the light green blanket on the arm of it, the matching chair, the TV that is off, and the stereo system that is silent.

Where are they? I distinctly remember seeing Graham's black Dodge truck in the parking lot. I tiptoe to the kitchen and dart my head around the doorframe, finding it devoid of human life as well. Only the three empty beer bottles on the counter signal they were ever in this room. I sniff the air for signs of food cooking and smell nothing but the coconut air freshener Graham likes. I frown. No pizza boxes. Hmm. I whirl around to the right and peer out the patio doors. Nothing. I'm starting to get dejected. I do one more sprint and leap into the living room, but there's still no sign of life.

"What are you doing?"

I whip around so fast I bump into the end table by the couch. I curse, rubbing the tender place on my thigh. Graham is in the hallway, unfortunately dressed in dark blue jeans and a gray and red striped t-shirt. He has a curious look on his face and his head is tilted, like he can't figure me out. And he can't. I already know this.

"Uh...nothing." I put my hands behind my back and try to look innocent. "Run, wine, run!" I blurt out, thinking fast on my toes.

He walks into the living room, coming to a stop at my words. "What the hell was that?"

I shrug, avoiding his eyes. "Tears of a wine? To the world you may be wine, but to me, you are wine. To you, with wine. To infinity and wine." I clamp my own hand over my mouth to shut me up.

Graham laughs, shaking his head. "You're trying to distract me."

"I was doing nothing," I remind him.

"It didn't look like nothing." He glances behind me. "It looked like you were trying out for one of the 'Mission: Impossible' movies."

I give a nervous laugh. "Don't be silly." I pause. "Those are done now." I mean, otherwise I would so get the leading role if I ever deemed it worthwhile to try out for it.

He waits, watching me in that studious way of his.

I glance down the hallway. "Where's your brother?"

A scowl appears on his face. "Why?"

Whoa. Can we say overreact? "I stink. I need a shower. Is he in the bathroom?"

"He went for a walk."

"Oh."

"Apparently, he needed some fresh air. Doesn't like to be cooped up indoors for too long. His words, not mine." He shrugs, like the notion is inconceivable to him even though he needs to be outside so much he got a career where being one with nature is a given. In the fall, he helps cut and stack wood for various buddies who have wood burning stoves. In the winter, he slaps a plow on the front of his truck and rescues locals from snow. Basically, he's outside as much as he can be, no matter what time of year it is—also, talk about ginormous heart.

"Huh. Did you get your pizza?"

"Blake offered to get a couple on the way back from his walk."

"Oh."

"Pepperoni and mushroom. And I knew you'd be hungry, so your favorite too. Vegetable." He wrinkles his nose. "Mmm-mmm. Delicious."

Graham loves meat. Vegetables, not so much. He'll drink vegetable juice and have pizza sauce and spaghetti sauce for his vegetables. Me, I prefer vegetables to dead animals. We all have our flaws. But his thoughtfulness redeems him time and again—it also doesn't hurt that he's nice to look at.

I give him what I hope is a sweet smile and he blinks. "Thanks, Graham."

He smiles back and it's my turn to blink. Man, he's beautiful. "No problem."

"What's his deal with not being inside for too long? One of his manias?"

He shakes his head of messy blond locks and I desperately long to smooth his hair from his forehead—or grab it and yank his face to mine to do some lip lockage. Either would do.

"I guess. I don't know that much about him and I feel bad about that."

"Yeah, I'm confused about the whole thing."

One corner of his mouth lifts.

"And don't you dare say it doesn't take much for that to happen. Or something similar," I warn.

"I would never," he states, putting a hand over his heart.

"You're so full of it." I walk into the kitchen and sit at the table. He follows. "I don't get how you have a brother that's only a year or whatever younger than you and you barely see him and you don't know much about him. What gives?"

He sits down opposite me and drums his long fingers on the tabletop. "It's complicated."

"Really?" I raise an eyebrow.

"Really."

"Explain."

"I will. But not right now. Later." At my unconvinced look, he adds, "I promise."

"All right. But I won't forget."

"I know. You're tenacious. Like a dog."

"Or a mountain lion."

"That was my second choice."

I stand up and stretch my back. "I'm going to take a shower. Save me some pizza."

He doesn't answer and I shoot him a look. He looks away from what I think might have been my chest. Huh. It's not like there's much to look at. I double check, just to make sure. Nope. Still the same size as they were when I got up this morning.

"Graham?"

He meets my gaze. "Yeah?"

"Save me some pizza, okay?" I repeat.

He nods, eyes trained on a spot behind my right shoulder that is so obviously not my chest it becomes apparent he really was looking at my bosom a moment ago. I wonder if that was the first time he's ever checked me out. Somehow I doubt it. I'm pretty much a sexy beast. Reow.

"That's your cue to make some comment about how I don't have to worry."

"You don't have to worry," he says with absolutely no inflection at all.

"Some people," I mutter and make my way from the room.

"You really think he's good-looking?"

I freeze, unsure what the correct answer is. I slowly turn around and look at my roommate. He's chewing on his lower lip in that way of his that signifies something is puzzling him and he needs to figure it out. Do I deny it or admit it? Didn't we already discuss this? What gives? He must need some reassurance or something.

So I say, "I said *hot*. I think he's *hot*."

Okay, so I like my confrontations, and annoying Graham. If I can't have him to hug and kiss and love on, I might as well harass him, right? I see I've accomplished the whole annoying thing when his eyes flash a darker shade of green. There's tightening in his face that if I didn't know better, I'd think he was super pissed. But I know he's not, so I just ignore the look and leave.

Picture a cream-colored couch. Now visualize one brooding dark-haired sex machine (I'm assuming, but I have a strong feeling about this) sitting on one end and one golden being of near perfection on the other. Then there's me, in the middle, literally squished between two yummy smelling men, and...I just want to escape. The pizzas have been demolished (I ate half of one myself) and now an awkward silence has descended. It doesn't help that I keep thinking of pornos and threesomes. I am honestly waiting for corny seventies music to start.

I was here first. I don't feel like I should have to be the one to move. But I'm awfully uncomfortable. There are other places to sit in the room; a recliner even. Ya know, super comfy, so comfy you can *recline*. So one of them could move to that. I almost think they're enjoying this. Like, they're having fun at my expense because they know I think they're hot.

Why did I blurt that out?

"So, what's with the name Kennedy?" Blake wonders in his deep timbre that doesn't really sound like Graham's, but reminds me of him all the same.

I turn my head to the right, careful not to move any other body part, and meet his challenging gray eyes. He's, like, two inches away. So close I can see green flecks in his eyes. I think he's a little too amused by my predicament, if the upward curve of his mouth is anything to go by. One inky black eyebrow lifts as he waits.

"It's my name." I raise a single eyebrow back. *I can do that too*, the look says.

His smile deepens. "Yeah, but, what were your parents thinking? Kennedy? For a girl? And technically it's a last name."

My eyes narrow. Oh, so it's to be like that, is it? "So is Blake," I retort and give myself an imaginary pat on the back. "And Graham," I add triumphantly.

"Leave me out of this," Graham states from my left.

I notice Blake's shirt reads 'blink-182', and unfortunately, I have to give him more props for that.

"Did your parents have a thing for the Kennedys?" Two eyebrows go up this time.

I get my mental pistols ready—it's obvious there's going to be a showdown. I straighten my spine. "What do you mean by a thing?"

My, totally in this moment one hundred and forty-nine percent resented, roommate groans.

He shrugs one broad shoulder. "You know. An infatuation. An unhealthy obsession. Fanaticism. A thing."

"You really shouldn't have started this," Graham intercedes, leaning around me to give his brother a look.

My face is on fire and my hands are in tight fists in my lap. I stare at the television, which is on and no one's paying attention to, and say very softly, "I'll have you know, the Kennedys were, and are, an iconic family. I feel it an honor to be named after them."

Blake grunts.

"Do you deny it?" I ask the TV.

"Nope. I just wondered about *your* family."

I jerk my head around and give him a look full of venom. "We will not discuss my family."

He holds his hands up in surrender, but there's a gleam in his eyes. What is *wrong* with this guy? "Easy there, Ken."

I growl.

Graham sighs beside me.

"Don't call me that," I state through gritted teeth.

He looks over the top of my head. "Touchy, isn't she?"

Graham's head slumps against the back of the couch.

"So, Blake," I begin in a sweet voice, "what's up with you and *red?*" I go still, holding my breath. Did I really just say that? That was so not nice. I wait with anticipation and dread.

Graham stops moving on the other side of the couch.

Blake stares at me, his lips parted. Then he looks at his brother. "What's she talking about?"

My about to be annihilated roomie makes a sound of dismay.

I twist around to glare at him. He looks like a young boy who just had his hand caught in the cookie jar; guilty and disappointed that his fun has been halted.

"Don't say the word red, huh?" I jump to my feet and back away until both men are within my line of vision. "You know what?"

They both look at me, obviously not knowing what.

"This means war!" I jab a finger in the air to emphasize this.

I think I hear Graham make another incomprehensible noise as I stomp to my bedroom and it's obvious Blake finds the whole situation amusing, if his low chuckle is anything to go by. I close my bedroom door, unable to keep from smiling.

What an exciting Friday night this turned out to be. Not wanting to strain my brain for quick-witted comebacks (and I have a feeling that's all I'll do around Blake), I've banished myself to my bedroom. He's like a kindred soul of sarcasm. Possibly. I'm gathering from our one verbal encounter (the first encounter didn't count, as I didn't know what a nuisance he was yet and we barely exchanged words) I have to be at my mental best to spar with him. Now, not so much the case. Work and exercise and hormones and men have exhausted me.

I'm lying on my queen-sized bed, nothing but the glow of a lamp for light and…I'm reading another smut book. I know, I know! But I can't stay away from them lately. They're so informative—and unrealistic. At least there is an actual story to this one; it's not just sex. Well, some of it isn't sex.

"Hey, Dad," I answer as soon as my cell phone rings.

"Mosquitoes are bad."

I smile. "Are they? I'm inside, so I wouldn't know. Walls are good that way."

"Cock suckers. I got bit at least fifty times today." He pauses. "Caught some fish though."

My smile fades. "Good for you."

"Going to bed now."

I say good night and end the call, knowing he only mentioned going fishing to rub it in that I don't go with him anymore. A soft knock on the door alerts me to a visitor. I glance down at my clothes; red and pinked striped shorts and a white t-shirt with hearts on it. My PJs. They'll have to be adequate 'cause I refuse to move from my current position.

"Yes?" I aim a pointed look at the door and wait.

It slides inward, revealing Graham. He's in his PJs as well, which consist of gray athletic shorts and a yellow shirt with cut-off sleeves. I got him the t-shirt, hence why it reads 'Ken and Barbie For Life' in pink cursive letters. I love that shirt. Proof that he loves me in some form is the fact that he wears it.

He has a sheepish look on his face. He's been wearing similar facial expressions a lot within the past few days. "Hi." He ambles into the room, closes the door, and sits down with his back against it.

"What's the matter? Bored with your brother already?" Do I sound snobbish? It's possible. I feel dethroned as his hang-out buddy. Which is really just wrong anyway. I don't *want* to be his buddy.

"He wanted to go out."

I tense.

"But I didn't."

I relax.

"So he went by himself."

This arches my eyebrows. "He went to the bar by himself? How…alcoholic of him."

"He didn't say that was where he was going, but I don't know. I guess I don't know him well enough to say. I hope not." He shrugs.

I toss my book aside. "And why is that, exactly?" I rest my arms on my knees and prop my chin on them, waiting.

Graham's eyes catch mine. He laughs. "Okay, okay, I can take a hint. Time to air the dirty laundry, right?"

"Past time. It reeks."

He grins, wiping a hand over his face, then looks at me. "Okay. It's like this—my mom and dad never married."

"Bastard," I gasp.

He shoots me a disgruntled look. "Yeah, if it was the 1800s. Anyway. Can I continue?"

I sweep a hand across the air. "By all means. I'm waiting with bated breath."

"Blake's mom and my dad were married for a couple years before I came along. And still are." He waits for me to grasp something.

I squint my eyes and sit upright as I figure it out. "Ooooh."

"Yeah. My dad was messing around with my mom while married to another woman."

"Ooooh," I repeat. "Positively sinful. Does the debauchery have no end?"

He gives me a look of exasperation. "Would ya quit?"

I put my hands up, trying to look innocent. "What?" The devilish glint in my eyes may ruin it though.

He gives a snort of laughter. "You know what is so appealing about you, in a twisted, messed up way?"

"What's that?"

"You have no idea how tactless you are."

"Well. I have *some* idea," I grumble.

His laughter becomes full-fledged.

"Was that a compliment?"

"Do you see it as one?"

I cock my head and think. "Yep."

There's a twinkle in his eyes and I'm glad I put it there. "Then it's a compliment."

"Do you want a hug?"

Before he can respond, I'm off the bed and on my knees beside him. Any excuse for physical contact. Although, that probably really did suck growing up. Poor kid. I wrap my arms around him and pull his head to me. Fortunately, or unfortunately, however you want to look at it, his face is pretty much smothered by my breasts. But he doesn't complain, nor does he pull away. So he must like it, at least a little bit. I suppose there is the possibility that he just can't breathe, but…eh.

"I'm sorry. And you know I'm kidding. You're not a bastard, even if you would have been in the 1800s. I would totally kick the ass of anyone who ever called you that, FYI." I take a much needed breath of air. "Was it awful as a kid?"

His response is muffled, but sounds like, "I survived."

The stubble of his jaw scrapes the tender flesh below my neck and above my chest. I pull away and look down at him. He's got a dazed look on his face and I'm hoping it's from the carefully placed position of my girls directly in his face.

"Do you have any other half-brothers or half-sisters?"

He shakes his head, his gem-like eyes clearing. "No. I didn't really know what was going on until I was much older." He smiles, but there's a twinge of sadness to it with a healthy side of bitterness. "Apparently, from what my mom's told me, my mom and dad were in love, but they broke up for a while, he got Blake's mom pregnant, she miscarried, but not until after my dad felt duty bound to marry her. I came along a few years after that. And then there was Blake after me. No other kids for either mom. My mom by choice and Blake's mom from too many miscarriages."

"Your dad married Blake's mom because she was pregnant, she lost the baby, but he stayed with her after that even though he only married her because of the baby she was no longer carrying? Am I getting this right?"

The corners of his luscious mouth tighten and I want to kiss his pain away. "Right."

"And your mom was, like, his mistress, but he really loved her and not Blake's mom?"

"Supposedly."

"Your mom was okay with that? With being his woman on the side?"

A grimace steals over his features. "No. She wasn't. But she loved him. I'm sure he had all kinds of flowery words and promises to keep her hanging on. I was twelve when she finally ended it. My mom was fed up with my dad, told him to stay away from her, told me the truth because I didn't understand why she told him to leave and never come back. I mean, my dad is a dick, but he's the only one I have. I didn't want to lose him, no matter what he was or wasn't."

"Dads," I say in commiseration.

Graham swallows, looking down. "Yeah."

"That's awfully young to try to understand something like that," I say, placing a hand on his forearm. The muscles constrict beneath my touch.

He looks into my eyes, then glances away. A prolonged silence follows. "I guess. After that I only saw my dad when I had to, once a summer for a two-week stay, which stopped when I turned sixteen."

"What about every other weekend and holidays?"

"My dad and his other family moved to North Dakota, so that was impossible. I think it was Blake's mom's idea to put the extra distance between my mom and dad. She knew about everything, but she couldn't stop it. Blake and I—we didn't know what was going on until we were older. We knew we were brothers, but we didn't understand the logistics of it."

"That is all seriously messed up."

"I know."

"Why did you stop going?"

He gently rubs his forehead against mine, back and forth, smooth skin on smooth skin. I close my eyes. "Because I wouldn't go anymore. My mom tried to make me, my dad demanded I go, and I wouldn't. I said I'd run away if she tried to make me go and she believed me. My dad was furious and pretty much hasn't talked to me since I went against his wishes. *He's* the bastard." He takes a deep breath.

I open my eyes and pull back to look at him. "Was it so terrible there?"

He shrugs, avoiding my eyes. "I was the outcast, the interloper, the one who didn't belong. Blake's mom hated me. My dad acted like I was a possession more than a son. My dad wants to control everyone and everything around him. Blake had his own problems dealing with it all."

I nod. "Oh yes, the mental issues and suicidal tendencies." I pause. "What's that all about?"

He rubs his face, looking agitated. "The first summer I didn't go there he tried to kill himself."

Uncomfortable with that admission, I shift my position. "How? What happened?"

"Took some pills, had to go to the hospital to have his stomach pumped, counseling, all that fun stuff. My dad blamed me."

"What a prick."

He smiles wanly and pats my arm. Really? The arm? Why not get crazy and go for the shoulder? "Said it was my fault for staying away when my brother needed me."

I feel my face droop in sorrow. "Graham. That's awful."

"It's fine. It was a long time ago."

"You know that's not true, right? About it being your fault?"

He shrugs. "I guess. But I still feel responsible. I did stay away. And Blake probably did need me."

I grab his face, his unshaven skin rough but welcome to my fingertips. "Look at me."

He does.

"You know I wouldn't lie to you, right?"

He nods, the faintest of smiles on his face.

"It wasn't your fault," I state slowly.

He stares into my eyes for a long time, then oh so slowly, nods. This time he gets it.

I let go of his face and clasp my hands together in my lap. "What else?"

He examines my features. "How do you know there's a what else?"

I grin. "I just do. Call it intuition."

He sighs and straightens his back against the door. "All right. This doesn't leave this room, right? As far as Blake knows, unless he tells you himself, you have no knowledge of what I'm about to tell you. Right?"

I shiver in excitement. "I love secrets."

He gives me a look.

"Okay, okay. Right. I know nothing."

"I never thought I'd hear you admit *that*."

"Funny." I resituate myself so that my back is against the bed frame. I put my feet on Graham's legs and motion for him to continue, holding completely still so as not to spook him away when his thumb absently draws a circle into the top of my foot.

"He got into drugs when he was seventeen. Had to go to juvenile detention until he was eighteen for numerous petty thefts and to be rehabilitated. I don't know if going there helped at all. I don't think it did, but I don't know a lot about what was going on then and he's never said much about it. It's hard to get him to talk about any of this. I guess he was in love with this girl, they were drinking, he was driving, they wrecked, she died."

My mouth drops open.

"He gets into drugs again."

"Do these drugs include alcohol? 'Cause, you know, he was drinking here earlier, and he did maybe go to the bar by himself. Aren't you worried?"

He drops his head against the door, eliciting a *thud* from the wood. "Yeah. But he's a big boy and he doesn't need or want me looking out for him."

"Right." I don't know if this is true or not, but whatever. "So he gets into drugs again and?"

"He overdoses."

"What the hell?" I exclaim, ready to jump to my feet in frustration. "Does he never learn?"

"He says he didn't mean to that last time."

I snort, showing what I think of that.

"To make a long and sad story short, he checks himself into a private rehabilitation center, stays clean, and goes to college. The end. Those beers you saw him drinking? They were non-alcoholic."

"Yeah right."

"They really were."

I lean forward and give him the evil eye.

"What?"

"The whole red thing? Not very nice."

Graham winces. "Sorry about that. You're just so obtuse about, I don't know, human things sometimes that I can't help but pick on you a little."

"There you go, complimenting me again." I roll my eyes. "Keep it up and I'll think you like me."

"I do like you."

My smile falters. Yeah, as a big brother would like a kid sister.

"You're not seriously pissed, are you?"

"No. I'm not. But I have to get you back. It's a law."

"Really, Kennedy?" He sighs. "A law?"

"Really. It's in my book of laws."

"I'd like to see that book. Fine. Knock yourself out." He unravels his lanky frame and stands. He holds out a hand and helps me to my feet.

"I can't believe you never told me about any of this before."

"It's embarrassing."

"Dysfunctional might be a better word."

"Thanks."

"Sure."

"Want to make some hot cocoa?"

I look at Graham; my best friend, my roommate, the love of my life, and something inside me melts at the sort of, maybe hopeful, look in his eyes.

Obviously he needs comfort, he doesn't want to be alone, and he's asking me to be with him.

"Of course. But only if there's marshmallows."

"Well, yeah." He gives me a *Duh* look and I fear I may be rubbing off on him.

"And popcorn."

"You can't have hot cocoa without popcorn."

I follow him into the hallway. "Not the microwave kind. The stove top kind."

"For you, anything."

"You can't have popcorn and hot cocoa without a movie. It's just wrong."

He laughs. "Definitely."

"Oh, and one more thing."

Graham turns and waits, both eyebrows raised.

"If I ever see your dad, I am so going to punch him in the face. Just so you know."

He looks at me for a moment, then nods, smiling a sweet smile. "I would expect no less from you."

"Just so we're clear."

"Yep."

"Good. Because I mean it."

He reaches into a cupboard, pulling two mugs the color of pumpkins out. "Kennedy?"

"Yeah?"

"Will you shut up now? Just for a minute?"

I sit down at the table and prepare to watch him make magic in the kitchen. "Okay."

chapter four

t's three in the morning. Graham went to bed a while ago, but I couldn't sleep, so I stayed up and watched 'The Golden Girls' for a while. One of Graham's flaws is that he refuses to watch this epic show with me. It's a good thing he has so many other good qualities.

I turn off the TV and lamp in the living room, scowl at the blanket and pillow Graham set out on the coffee table for his elusive brother, and creep into the kitchen. I fumble around in the dark until I find the light switch on the wall, blinking in the sudden brightness. I feel dumb tiptoeing around to see whether or not Blake is drinking, especially in my own place. It's not my problem. None of my business. But like either of those details has ever stopped me.

I open the pantry door and direct my gaze down. The recycling bin is where it should be and so are the beer bottles. I snatch one up, sniff it (I don't know why), and examine the label. O'Doul's.

There's a clicking sound to the right of me and I spin that way. Blake is standing on the inside of the patio doors he obviously just shut, a closed expression on his face. "What are you doing?"

"Nothing. Why?" I feel guilty. I *hate* feeling guilty.

He nods his head down one time.

I follow his motion and look at the non-alcoholic beer bottle in my hand. Son of a! I almost let go of it, realize it's glass and will break, and very carefully, slowly, put it back in the recycling bin. I'm hoping when I turn around Blake will be gone.

No such luck.

I go on the offensive. "What are you doing?" I gesture toward the patio, like it's off limits and he was doing a terrible thing by being on the deck. Anything to direct the attention away from my misdeed.

"I was sitting outside, smoking."

"Smoking what?"

His eyes narrow. "Cigarettes. Is that okay?"

"I suppose."

"What were you doing with that beer bottle?"

"What were you doing with that beer bottle earlier?" See how I turn everything around? I'm suave in unimaginable ways.

"Uh, drinking it."

"You were drinking a beer bottle?" His silence confirms he doesn't want to laugh too hard for fear of never stopping. It's okay—I get it. "How long were you outside?"

"How long were you and Graham making googly eyes at each other and flirting?"

I straighten my spine. "Excuse me? What were you doing, spying on us? Weren't you supposed to be at the *bar*?" I crinkle my nose, like that's the last place I'd ever be, even though I plan on being in one tomorrow night.

"You're really something, you know that?"

It doesn't sound like a compliment, but I decide to view it as one regardless. "Thank you."

Blake shakes his head, looking incredulous.

I stare back at him, crossing my arms over my hearts.

He takes a step closer, bringing the scent of tobacco and his body heat with him. "Why would I want to spy on you? *Kennedy?*"

I take a step back, trying to appear nonchalant, but my heart is pounding really fast and I feel just a smidge too warm. "Because you're lame?" I offer up.

He stops moving, his gray eyes roving up and down my face, and then dipping past my neck. I shift uncomfortably, wanting his eyes away from my womanly parts so as not to confuse them into thinking they like his blatant perusal. Of *course* they don't.

He laughs, sounding surprised. "You *are* something else," he says again, softly, but this time his tone is different.

"Yeah. That's me. Something else."

Blake cocks his head, causing his too long bangs to partially cover the upper part of his face. Somehow, it makes him look even sexier. "Why aren't you in bed?"

I blink. I swear he said, "Why aren't you in *my* bed?", but no, he didn't. "Why aren't you?"

"Insomnia. Plus I didn't want to break up your touching scene with my brother."

"How long have you been back?"

"Long enough to know you two are more than just roommates."

I will not even bother to comment on that. "We're just roommates who happen to be good friends. It's allowed. Not that it's any of your business." I guess I will comment on that.

He is somehow closer to me than he was a moment ago and I stumble back.

"How good of friends? The kind with benefits?" he murmurs, his voice a sinful caress against my frazzled nerves.

I clamp my lips together so I don't respond. "No! Just friends." Okay, so that didn't work.

"Hmm." He dips his head, eyes intent on my face. "Prove it," he whispers, his lips too close to mine.

I know he's going to kiss me. Why is he going to kiss me? I've known Graham for over a year and he's never tried to kiss me on the lips. Blake shows up and in one day is already putting the moves on me?

Why can't this be Graham?

He goes still. Something must show in my expression because he pulls back and puts distance between us. He runs a hand through his hair of disarray, not looking at me when he says, "You got a thing for my brother, huh?"

My silence is my admission.

He turns to look at me. "But let me guess, he's clueless?"

I chew on my lip and stare at my purple-painted toenails.

"He always was slow to figure things out," he says, sounding amused and disgusted as well.

My head shoots up and I glare at him. "Graham is one of the smartest people I know."

"Graham's a damn genius," he agrees.

I gaze at him, full of wariness. I don't understand him at all. Granted, I just met him, but still, I should have an inkling of some kind about him, right?

There's nothing. He's like a blank canvas and I am without a paintbrush. And again with the poetry?

"Good night," he says as the silence intensifies.

I scowl at him as I hurriedly walk from the room. Dismiss me, will he? Obviously he will, because I'm walking to my bedroom at this very moment. My steps slow outside of Graham's bedroom and my fingertips lightly trail across the door. Longing stabs me. I swallow and pick up my pace.

Once inside my room, I take a deep, calming breath. I turn on the light and move to the dresser to stare at the face in the mirror above it. It's flushed with shining eyes. I enjoyed that. I mean, Graham's fun and I love him to death, but he is not mine to have. With Blake—I felt like I was with an equal tossing insults back and forth. Am I so fickle in my feelings to quickly overturn my emotions from one brother I can't have to the other I probably can have? Of course not.

I think…

"Hi."

I halt in the perusal of my closet and look at Graham. As always, a buzz goes through me at the sight of him. "Hi."

His hair looks windswept and there's fine stubble on his face that accentuates his cheekbones, making him look even more delicious. He's got on straight-legged jeans with a couple tears in them, a red shirt, and gray Pumas. He's dressed down, but looks better than most men at their best. And he smells really, really, really good—manly, but also sweet. So good I want to sniff him all over.

He shoves his hands in the pockets of his jeans. "What are you doing tonight?"

"I got invited to a wedding anniversary with the gang from Dr. Olman's. How about you?"

He walks into my bedroom more. "Actually, I was too. At the golf course country club; the Mezeras, right?"

"That'd be it, yes. Why are you going?"

"John Mezera is one of my students."

"Oh." One of his legitimate ones.

"Why are you going?"

I fiddle with a hanger. "Well..." I don't want to mention Nathan. Why? Because, I don't know, it seems like I'm betraying Graham. Which is ridiculous—I do know that much. Doesn't stop the way I feel. I toss the hanger on my bed. "Do you know Nathan, their son?"

"Yeah. What about him?"

"He invited us."

He looks taken aback. "The whole office?"

It is my turn to nod.

"Why?"

"Um...he likes us?" It seems like I'm asking him if Nathan likes us and that's not what I wanted to do, but whatever.

"Huh."

I go back to searching my closet for something to wear. I want to look hot tonight. I'm thinking trashy—only I don't own anything trashy. I whip another hanger onto the bed in frustration.

"You okay?"

"Yeah, sure," I mumble, staring into my closet like a killer outfit is going to magically appear. Maybe if I stare long enough...

"I was going to invite you to come along with me and Blake, but I guess I'll see you there."

I glance at him, too distracted by my lack of clothing to get worked up about spending the evening in the same vicinity as his brother. "Yeah, okay." My eyes flicker to the clock. It's almost five. There's no way I have time to go anywhere to try to find a worthy ensemble. Why didn't I do this sooner? Like, five hours ago.

"Kennedy?"

"Yes?"

"Would you look at me?"

I turn around and frown at my roommate. "What is it?"

He opens his mouth, closes it, and then shakes his head. "Never mind. I'll see you there, okay?"

"Sure."

Two minutes later, there's a shout from the bathroom. "Really!"

I smile. Apparently Graham just looked at the sink countertop full of (unopened, of course) tampons and pads. Score one for me.

I will never admit it out loud, but I am seriously ecstatic when Phoebe shows up at 5:15, even though I told her to be here much later. I need help. Desperately. She looks smoking hot with her teeny tiny clothes on her teeny tiny body and I'm instantly envious. I sigh and show her to my bedroom.

She claps. "Oh, I'm so excited! This is going to be so much fun. What do you have picked out?"

"Nothing."

Her smile disintegrates. *Poof.* It's gone. "But…it's almost time to go. You don't have *anything* picked out?"

I give a helpless shrug. "I can't find anything. I want to look good, really good, and all I have are boring clothes." I grab her hands and stare into her large eyes. "I need your help." That sounded melodramatic, but she doesn't seem to mind.

She presses her lips together and nods firmly. "Yes. You do. Go do your makeup and hair and I'll find something. Go on, go." She shoos me from the room.

Thankfully I have good skin, so all I need to apply is a bronzer to give my somewhat already tan skin a healthy glow. I put on glittery purple eyeliner, mascara, and peach lip gloss. And I'm done. I'm just not fussy about makeup.

My hair, now, that's another matter. The thick layers hang halfway down my back and usually have a mind of their own; flipping this way and that and never in sync. My hair requires a lot of attention. I brush it out, pull the sides and front back and give them a poof (bouffant-like). I insert two dozen hairpins into my hair and spray it with a couple gallons of hairspray. When I'm satisfied it won't be going anywhere, I head back to the bedroom.

Phoebe is sitting on the floor, surrounded by pretty much all of my clothes. She looks up, her teeth sunk into her lower lip. "I just…I don't know, Kennedy. I can't seem to find anything. I mean, you have nice stuff, but nothing flashy." Flashy…trashy—same thing.

"You gave it your best shot," I tell her. "Chin up, soldier."

That seems to spark some determination back into her. She puts her shoulders back and starts digging in the clothes with renewed fortitude. "There's …got…to…be…something."

"It's okay, Phoebe, really." I'm getting concerned as clothes start flying everywhere.

"Ah ha!" She stabs her arm in the air, looking triumphant. Off her finger dangles a skimpy hot pink stretch dress that I will never, ever, *ever* wear. I bought it on a whim once and have forever regretted it. There's nothing to it. It is way form-fitting and strapless and short. I can't believe I ever bought it. I think I was drunk shopping at the time. It happens.

"I don't know how I missed it before," she murmurs, brows lowered.

"I do. It's microscopic. I can't wear that."

Her face transforms into something scary. "You're wearing it."

"No. I'm not."

She takes a menacing step toward me. "You're wearing it and you're going to look hot and you'll thank me when Nathan asks you out on a date. Put it on." She tosses it toward me and I catch it, disturbed by the fanatical gleam in her eyes.

"All right, just calm down."

"I am calm." She smiles sunnily. "I'm gonna go smoke."

I look down at the flimsy material in my hands and sigh. *Go out of your comfort zone and into your slutty zone.* Right-O.

I self-consciously tug at my dress, for which Phoebe rewards me by slapping my hand. I give her a look.

She gives me a look back, but she's smiling. "Stop messing with your dress. You look amazing."

"My ass is almost hanging out." I point my leg out and look at my strappy three-inch silver open-toed heels. "Although, I really love these shoes and have been wanting to wear them for forever."

She draws on her cigarette and squints at me through the smoke. "Your ass looks hot. Trust me."

I sigh and nod. This is what I wanted, right? I just need to suck it up and not think about it. Have fun. But it's hard not to be self-conscious when I feel like I'm baring all and I don't like the feeling. This dress is like a second skin against my curves—and lack of. I added a wide black belt to feel not quite so naked, but you know what? For some reason, it didn't help too much, probably because it's a *belt*.

She puts her cancer stick out and weaves her arm through mine to pull me inside. "Where'd Dr. Olman and Sally go?"

I look around the country club. It's filled with drinking, laughing people, but I don't see anyone I know. My boss and the receptionist are most likely off in a corner necking. They pretty much deserted us the second we got here. Which is fine 'cause if they hadn't ditched us we would have ditched them; if for no other reason than what my boss is wearing. FYI: red and green striped shirts and navy blue pants do *not* go together.

There's a DJ playing, so we have to shout to hear one another. "I don't know where they went. Do you see Nathan?" I ask loudly, feeling majorly dumb when the song stops just as I say 'Nathan'. I avert my eyes and hope no one knows I was the one shouting his name.

An elderly lady is casting a censored look my way and I jerk my head toward an unsuspecting Phoebe and mouth, "It was her." I even add in a shrug when her eyes narrow.

The country club, generically called Lancaster Country Club and Golf Course, has a large banquet room, which is what we're in. The lights are low, tables and chairs are set up around a dance floor in the center of the room, and the bar runs along the whole far wall of the joint. The place is packed and it's hard to make heads or tails of any particular person.

"No. Oh, hey! There's your roommate." She waves, smiling prettily. Almost immediately, she grabs my arms and squeezes painfully. "Who is that super broody yet crazy attractive guy next to him?" Her voice got really high and breathless as she said that.

I stare at her for a minute, wondering where those intelligent words came from before I follow her gaze, already knowing who she's talking about. My eyes land on Graham and my stomach flip flops. He's talking to some pretty chick I imagine he gives lessons to. I want to be jealous, but try not to think about it, since I have no right to be. He's a good-looking man. We women like good-looking men. I just have to deal. Plus, you know, he's not mine or anything.

Then I shift my attention to Blake. He's staring back at us. Or rather, at me. I feel my face heat up under the directness of his smoldering eyes. I swear he knows what I'm thinking at all times just from looking at me. He's wearing a gray t-shirt with the 'Ghostbusters' logo on it, faded jeans, and black boots. It's annoying that he keeps wearing shirts that appeal to me. It's like he *knows* me or something.

I turn away from his gaze. "That's Blake. He's Graham's younger brother." I carefully extricate my arm from her fingers.

Her mouth is a perfect O. "Why haven't I heard of him before? Where does he live? What does he do? You have to introduce me."

"He's staying with us for the summer and working here with Graham. I don't know where he lives and I guess he's in college. For what, I don't know."

"Mommy likey."

I give her a look, but she's engrossed in her eye candy.

Hands cover my eyes, smelling faintly of cologne. I go still, wondering if I should be alarmed or not. "Guess who." The voice is male and deep.

"I don't have a clue."

"Come on, guess."

"Nathan?" I pull the hands away from my face, turning around to see exactly that person's smiling face.

"Hey, Kennedy. Wow. You look great." He nods, his eyes going up and down the length of me.

"Thanks," I say breathlessly. I sound a lot like Phoebe did when she was drooling over Graham's brother. I don't like it. And should I be feeling good about him singling me out of the crowd and approaching me? Because I do.

His hair of unruly waves is especially messy tonight, but it looks good. His brown eyes twinkle at me and a dimple says hello. My heart races in response as my eyes coast over the length of his muscular body, taking in his blue and white striped buttoned down shirt, khaki pants, and end at his brown shoes, then go back up to his eyes. Visions of calloused feet swim in my head and something inside me dims. I feel I should admit defeat—I'm just not getting over that.

"Thanks for coming." He looks amused, like he totally knows I was checking him out.

"Thanks for inviting us!" Phoebe trills next to me, flashing a megawatt smile his way.

Nathan's dimple deepens. "Hey, no problem. How are you, Phoebe?"

"Wonderful!" She's practically hopping up and down, she's so wonderful.

He turns and searches the room. "Where's your boss and the secretary? Did they come?"

I shrug. "Yeah, they came. But I have no idea where they went."

"We'll find them."

"Do we have to?"

He laughs. "I guess not, no. You ladies in for some dancing tonight?"

"Definitely!" Phoebe exclaims. Does she have to be *quite* so excited?

He blazes me with his chocolate eyes. "What about you? You gonna dance with me?"

I give a nervous laugh. I can't think when he's looking at me like that, mostly because his head just turned into a big, dry foot. "Sure."

"Don't sound so happy about it."

"Okay." I almost groan. Sadly, I'm not even *trying* to sound sarcastic.

He laughs again. "I know you can't wait. I can tell. Can I get you ladies something to drink?"

"Are you playing host?" I ask, smiling. There, that's better. I didn't sound quite so ridiculous.

"Sure. Come on, the bartender's a friend of mine." He places a hand around my wrist and gives me a gentle tug. Phoebe, not wanting to be left out, attaches herself to my remaining arm. Our three person train weaves through the throng of people and ends up at the bar.

Nathan looks at me expectantly.

I'm a picky drinker. I like wine and a few mixed drinks. The only beer I drink is Leinenkugel's. But I don't like other people making my drinks because they usually mess them up and I like fruity wines, which are hard to find at your everyday establishment. Therefore...Leinenkugel's it is.

"Leinenkugel's Berry Weiss?"

His full lips curve up. "Good choice." He turns to Phoebe. She simpers at him. "What would you like?"

She strikes a pose and announces, "I would like a Cosmo." I mentally roll my eyes.

"Cosmo it is." He talks to the bartender, who is red-haired and gorgeous. I can tell they're flirting. She must be a *good* friend.

I pull my co-worker toward me. "Have you ever even had a Cosmo before?"

"No. But I've always wanted to try one. Have you?"

I shake my head.

A hand snakes around my waist and I'm pulled up against something hard. I look up and am staring into green eyes. "Hi, roomie."

My heart sighs. "Hi. Having fun?"

He releases me and takes a drink of his beer. "Sure. You?" His eyes go from me to Phoebe to Nathan's back.

"Yep."

Graham's eyes scrutinize me from head to toe. "You look..."

I smile expectantly.

"Different."

I scowl. "Gee, thanks."

He rubs the back of his neck, laughing. "Sorry. You just…I didn't know it was you at first when I saw you across the room. You normally don't dress like this."

I clench my jaw. He is so not making it any better. "Like what?"

He silently gestures to Phoebe.

"Hi!" She frantically waves her hand in front of his face.

"Hey, trouble. What's new?"

She glows under his attentive eyes. "Oh, well, I'm thinking of getting a tattoo."

His eyebrows lift. "Really? Where?"

What did he mean by that—that I look different?

"There's this new place in Platteville a friend of mine went to. I think I'm gonna go there."

A faint smile crosses his lips. "I meant on your body."

What's wrong with my clothes?

"Oh!" Phoebe tosses her head and smiles coyly as she juts out a bony hip. With a finger pointing to her rump, she says, "I'm thinking just above here. What do you think?"

Nathan hands me a drink, momentarily distracting me. "Thanks," I murmur, taking a healthy swallow.

"You're welcome." He nods at Graham in greeting. "Graham."

"Nathan." He gives a singular nod back. Am I imagining it or is he tight-lipped and Nathan's grin slightly mocking? Doubtful.

I go back to my silent fuming. At least *Nathan* appreciates the effort I made to look good.

"Kennedy!" Phoebe smacks me on the back and I choke on the beer I was attempting to swallow. "We should go together. That would be so much fun."

"Go where?" Nathan wonders.

I'm coughing too hard to answer. Nathan thumps me on the back. "Thanks," I croak.

"To get a tattoo!" she practically shouts.

Graham laughs. "Kennedy's not into that kind of thing."

He gives me a knowing look, and I decide, in this moment, that maybe I am into that kind of thing. And plus he pissed me off with his comment about my wardrobe choice. What is up with that? So maybe I am exactly the kind of person that would get a tattoo. I halfway listen to the conversation going on around me, surprised to find my bottle is empty.

"I've got three of them," Nathan's telling Phoebe.

"What about you, Graham?" she purrs.

Gag me.

"Nah. None for me," he responds.

A beer magically appears at my elbow. I look up. Blake gives me a fleeting smile. I take the bottle. "Thank you," I say somewhat stiffly.

He shrugs, setting my empty bottle on a nearby table. "You owe me." I'm pretty sure my eyes are flashing as I give him a glare. He just grins and it has a sardonic twist to it. "Looks like everyone's having a blast," he murmurs close to my ear.

I take a sip from my beer. "It sure does."

"Except for you," he adds.

I pause with the bottle to my lips. "One way to rectify that." Then I chug about half of it.

His eyes narrow. "Never drink to feel better; drink to feel *even* better," he says, taking the bottle from me.

"Hey," I protest halfheartedly.

"Let's go."

I stare at him. "Go where?"

"Anywhere. You game?" There's a challenge in the stormy depths of his eyes.

I find myself responding. I've never been one to back down. Call it stubbornness, call it stupidity. Butterflies go through my stomach. I glance at Graham, Nathan, and Phoebe. None of them are paying the slightest bit of attention to Blake and me. They're still engrossed in their tattoo conversation.

"Sure."

He grabs my hand; his is firm and dry, and pulls me from the room and into the dark and quiet of the night, immediately releasing his hold on me. "What's there to do for fun in this town?"

"You're looking at it," I respond, not realizing how that sounds until I glance at him.

He's staring at me with one eyebrow raised.

I open my mouth, close it, open it again, and then shake my head. Not even going to try to correct that.

With a smirk, he lights a cigarette, the hard planes and angles of his face momentarily illuminated. It's an intriguing face. He inhales deeply, the smoke curling around him. "Want one?"

I open my mouth to decline, then shrug. "Okay."

I catch a glimpse of one of those half smiles he must be famous for. "No, you don't."

"I do," I say, crossing my arms.

He squints his eyes at me. "You sure?"

"Positive." I even nod my head to show how positive I am. "I need to try new things. I think I'm going to start smoking, maybe get a dozen tattoos, try out a pink Mohawk."

Blake laughs. The sound is raspy, like his funny bone is rusty from disuse, or he hasn't had much to be amused about in his life. "You think you're going to start smoking, huh?" He hands me a cigarette. "Well, then, don't let me stop you."

I take it and stare at it. I put it between my lips. "How do I look?" I mumble around it.

"Like you shouldn't have that in your mouth."

"Nonsense. I'm a professional."

"Have you ever smoked a cigarette before?"

"Of course."

"Would you like me to light it for you?" He is close, the warmth of his body radiating over to me. He raises an eyebrow when I don't immediately respond.

"Yes, please."

He cups the side of my face with one hand and lights the cigarette with the other. "Inhale," he commands softly.

I look up, the cancer stick forgotten. His eyes…they're so…something.

"You going to inhale that thing or just keep it hanging out of your mouth all night?"

I quickly inhale, cough, and exhale.

"Atta girl." He chuckles.

I inhale again, this time not managing to scorch my throat. I still cough though—a hacking, totally unattractive sound.

"I thought you've smoked before?"

"I have, but I've never been any good at it," I tell him, disappointed.

He laughs again. "Here. Give it here." He motions with his hand. I reluctantly give up my nicotine. So much for that.

"What made you decide to stay with Graham for the summer?"

He doesn't answer; just flicks the cigarette to the ground and starts walking. I have no option but to follow or be left behind, all alone. I follow.

"I'm moving after I finish college," he finally answers.

"Okay." Don't get it.

Blake hops on one foot, removing his boot and sock.

"What are you doing?"

He goes to the other foot and does the same. "I'm taking my socks and shoes off." He rolls up his pants legs.

I decide not to ask him the obvious question of why. "Where are you moving to?"

"Out of the country. Australia. Maybe for a year, maybe longer, maybe forever."

"Oh."

He looks at me. "Ah, don't be sad." He gives me one of his mocking smiles. "We'll always have the summer."

I'm not sure if he's joking or serious, so I say nothing.

"I figure I won't be seeing too much of Graham after that. And I haven't seen much of him in the past ten years anyway." He shrugs. "We can bond for the next few months and say our goodbyes and all of that mushy stuff." If I wasn't paying attention, I would miss the sadness in his eyes.

"Why Australia?"

His eyes meet mine. "Why not? You might want to take your shoes off."

"Why?" He doesn't answer, so I go about removing my high heels. I sigh in relief once they're off my feet. Stylish shoes are not always comfortable shoes— something we tend to forget when the pretty ones call to us.

"You're dressed up tonight."

I stiffen. "Yeah, so?"

"Any reason why?"

"Nope."

"You look good."

"Thanks," I say softly, surprised.

"In a slutty kind of way." He smirks.

I laugh.

Blake grabs my hand. "Come on." He pulls me along, into the dewy grass.

"Where are we going? Blake?" I have to trot to keep up with him or be dragged behind him. "What are we doing?"

On and on we go, until there's nothing visible around us but grass. The country club and its occupants are just a blip on the sunset, the sound of music a faint pulse on the night air. I twirl in a circle, feeling exhilarated. It's like we're all alone in the world and it is ours.

"Look up there." He points to the sky. I tip my head back and stare. The moon is full, partially covered in clouds, and twinkles of light seep through the wispy clouds filling it.

"Isn't it beautiful?" I sigh at the cosmic wonder of it.

"Yes." His tone is deep and husky. I look over at him and find him staring at me. He leans into me, the hardness of his body just barely touching mine. My pulse is racing and for some reason my brain is not working properly with him so close to me.

He lowers his head, his lips inches from mine. Something cold hits me and I'm instantly wet from head to toe. I shriek. Blake rears back, blinks, and then laughs. I look around at the sprinklers saturating the ground (and us) with water. I give him an accusing look, but he just shrugs.

"Might as well enjoy it," he says and proceeds to run through the sprinklers, whooping as he goes.

I watch him for a moment, biting my lip. Then I do the same.

The ride back to the apartment is interesting, to say the least. First of all, because Blake has a motorcycle. Visualize a woman in a skintight spandex-like dress trying to straddle the body of a motorcycle without flashing the world a view of her nether regions. Yes. That's presently me.

He removes my helmet, his dark eyes set on me. I shake wet hair out of my eyes and grin at him. He pauses with a cigarette almost to his lips. I wonder what he finds so interesting about me all the time, why he's always watching me. Then I think, why wouldn't he?

"That was awesome!" I exclaim, allowing him to help me off the bike. I pull my dress down and attempt to stay upright. My legs are wobbly, especially with my non-practical shoes supporting me. The ride partially dried me off, but I'm still uncomfortably damp and chilled. I really want to take a shower and put on warm, fuzzy pajamas. But first the adrenaline rushing through my veins has to abate.

He chuckles. "First time?"

I nod, too exuberant to be my usual cynical self. "No one ever told me a bike ride could be so much fun."

"It's better during the day, going on a day trip." He lights the cigarette. "You wanna go sometime this week?"

My first inclination is to say no, just because I typically would. But I want to go. Not sure why. "Sure."

"Tomorrow?"

Sunday is reserved Graham and me time. Every Sunday we go out for breakfast, go for a walk if the weather is nice, and cook supper together, or something along those lines.

"Or not? Is Sunday no good?" He watches me, a strange look on his face. Like he wants to be hopeful, but is scared to be. "You probably got plans with Graham, right?" He gives me a self-deprecating smile. "I should have known."

He needs someone to care about him. I go still. Where did that unlikely thought come from? I mull it over, deciding it's probably true. And furthermore, Graham will survive one Sunday without me. And maybe then he'll realize how much Sundays and I mean to him.

He looks down. "Some other time then?"

I draw in a noisy breath and give myself a mental shake. "Tomorrow would work."

He looks up, his eyes meeting mine. "Really?" Pleasure makes a fleeting appearance in his expression.

I nod, smiling. "Really."

"Okay. But you gotta wear that dress again." He gives me a lopsided smile and it is so freaking adorable and so unlike the Blake I've so far seen that my customary acerbic tone thaws.

I laugh. "We'll see."

He nudges my shoulder as we enter the apartment building. The first thing I notice is that Phoebe is sitting on the couch, gnawing on a fingernail. Then I take in Graham, pacing back and forth before the couch, his hair sticking up like he's run his fingers through it repeatedly. Blake gives me a push from behind and I stumble into the room, glaring at him over my shoulder. He stares innocently back.

The soft click of the door behind him is the only sound for a moment.

Phoebe looks up.

Graham stops moving.

I cease breathing.

He is pissed to the point that the features of his face are twisted with it and his body is wound tightly enough I suspect the least provocation will make him explode. I've never seen him look this enraged in all the time I've known him. Okay, so it's only been a year and some months since we've been roommates, but that's over three hundred and sixty-five days for him to be out of control with anger. And it's never happened.

"Where the hell were you?" he says quietly, evenly. He's not looking at me, but beyond me.

Blake pushes my shoulder, propelling me farther into the room. "Why don't you go change, get into some dry clothes?"

Graham's face darkens. "Don't tell her what to do."

I look at Blake in confusion, not really sure what to do in a situation like this. Probably 'cause I've never been in one before.

He raises his hands, eyes on his brother. "Relax. We got wet and Kennedy needs to change."

Graham finally looks at me and I wish he hadn't. There is disappointment in his eyes. Like I let him down; like he doesn't know me. It hurts, seeing that look on his usually untroubled face. But I didn't do anything wrong. Besides, screw him. I can do what I want with whomever I want. This revelation doesn't make me feel any better.

He looks away, as though dismissing me. "Why are you wet? Where were you and what were you doing?" he asks his brother.

"What business is it of yours?" Blake replies.

Graham clenches his jaw. "Because it's late, you two just took off without letting anyone know where you were going or what you were doing, and I was *worried*. So was Phoebe."

She vehemently nods her head, but doesn't speak.

The younger Malone crosses his arms. "Kennedy, go change."

Graham stares at his brother. "Stay where you are, Kennedy."

My eyes go from one Malone to the other; it's almost comical how similar their stances are in their misguided showdown. But I don't really find it funny how they both act like they can just boss me around.

"I think I'll go outside and you two can throw your testosterone around without me as a witness." I look at Phoebe. "Want to come with me?"

She wordlessly jumps to her feet and follows me from the room.

I stomp through the kitchen with gritted teeth, fling open the patio door so hard I'm lucky it doesn't slide right apart, and throw myself into a chair on the deck.

Phoebe slowly slides the door shut and looks at me.

"What?" I snap, and then feel bad. It's not her fault I live with an idiot and have another visiting.

She briefly chews on her lower lip before sashaying toward a chair and siting down. "What's going on?"

I throw my hands in the air. "Nothing! Why does everyone think something is going on?"

A pack of cigarettes and lighter magically appear out of some part of her skimpy clothing. "Well, it's odd that you took off with a guy you met, like, one day ago. Right?" She looks undecided about this.

I shift in my seat. "Maybe."

"And you were gone, for, like, hours, and..." She motions toward me. "You're wet."

I look down at the dress clinging to my skin. "It's mostly dried," I grumble.

"We were just worried, that's all."

"Really? Graham looks more than worried."

She exhales smoke from her lungs. "Yeah, I thought he was going to smash something or have a heart attack when we couldn't find you guys. He was seriously upset. I offered to come back here with him to wait, to make sure you made it home okay. He tried calling your cell, but then I remembered you left it in my car. I put your purse in your room, by the way." She flicks ashes from her cigarette. "Graham was about ready to call the cops. If you weren't back within ten more minutes, he said he was."

I straighten my spine. "That's ridiculous! He knew I was with his brother. Why would he call the cops?"

Blake = former problems with drugs.

I push the needless reminder away. It's not fair to judge someone now on how they used to be. I blink. Did that thought just come from my brain?

"I guess to make sure you weren't in a wreck or anything. You'll have to ask him."

Not flipping likely.

"So what happened?" she asks. Is there a spark of excitement in her eyes? Yes, yes, there is.

I shrug, laughing self-consciously. "Nothing. We went for a walk out on the green and the sprinklers came on, then he gave me a ride home on his motorcycle."

She watches me through her cigarette smoke. It's unnerving. I mean, doesn't that sting her eyes? "He's definitely hot. I personally wouldn't say no to him."

I narrow my eyes. "What do you mean?"

She leans forward in her chair, saying excitedly, and much too loudly, "You totally had sex, didn't you?"

I open my mouth.

"You did! How was it? I bet it was amazing. You can just tell it would be with someone like him."

Okay, so, she doesn't know I'm a virgin. If she did, she wouldn't assume I'd just have sex with someone I just met (I think). Also, Graham is standing in the doorway, his stance one of granite.

She looks up and sees him. "Oooooh." She winces and mouths, "Sorry," to me as she gets to her feet. "I better go. Promise you'll call me tomorrow?" She winks at me. "Details!" Then she sways her hips from side to side as she makes her way past Graham. Harlot.

He shoves his hands into the front pockets of his jeans and looks out into the darkened night. I shiver, suddenly chilled. "You want to explain to me what happened tonight?" His voice is quiet, clipped.

My shackles instantly rise. I tell myself to be calm and rational, neither of which I am very often. "I didn't have sex with him, if that's what you're asking. Not that it's any of your business."

His back stiffens even more, if that's possible. "*I know*—" Graham takes a shuddering breath and begins again. "I know you didn't have sex."

"How do you know?"

"You wouldn't do something like that with someone you barely know."

I purse my lips. He's right, of course. I feel like I'm a doll on a shelf tagged under the name Kennedy and every little detail about me is bottled up neat and nice, easily readable with just a glance from Graham. Of course, I'm not going to have sex with someone just to prove to him wrong either.

"So? You gonna talk?"

I sigh. "We just weren't into the whole tattoo conversation like the rest of you. So we went for a walk, got wet from the sprinklers at the golf course, and rode home on Blake's motorcycle. That's it."

"*We*, huh? Not you and Blake, but we?"

"Yeah. So? What's the big deal?"

"The big deal is," he says roughly. "I was out of my mind with worry. I didn't know where you went, what happened to you, if you were okay, if you were hurt, if something had happened with Blake. I didn't know anything. And suddenly you're a *we* with a guy you just met?"

I don't understand his problem with the whole "we" thing. It's just easier to talk that way.

"My brother and I—we're two different people, who've dealt with problems differently, and frankly, I don't know him that well, not as an adult—not enough to feel comfortable with him being responsible for your well-being. I was frantic, practically going *insane* wondering what was going on."

Okay, now I feel guilty. I didn't want him to worry about me. But really, why would he? I'm an adult. I'm nothing more than a friend to him—maybe his best friend—but a friend nonetheless.

"You're not my keeper." Slick.

He whirls around, fury etched into his features and stance. He stalks toward me with menace in his eyes. I jump up from the chair and race behind it even though it is flimsy and plastic and doesn't offer much protection.

"What...did you...say?"

"You're a keeper?" I reply meekly.

"How long have we known each other?" His voice is soft, but not even close to being gentle. It's constructed out of steel—sharp; and when wielded just right—deadly.

"I'm not really sure the exact—"

"Kennedy."

I sigh, releasing my grip on the poor excuse for a shield, and straighten. "Over a year. Which you know."

"Have you ever acted so irresponsibly in all that time?"

"Really? You're asking me this? Must I count the ways?"

"I always knew—" He bites off, clenching his jaw. "I always knew you were safe, no matter what stupid, outrageous thing you were doing."

"Thanks."

"Tonight...tonight I didn't know you were safe." He swallows, averting his gaze. When he lifts his head, there is fire in his gaze. "I don't want you around my brother."

"Why?" I demand.

"I don't trust him."

I cross my arms, shivering in the cool air. "Well, you don't get to tell me what to do. Sorry. And you're sort of acting like a jerk, in case you feel like apologizing. Go ahead, I won't stop you."

His head snaps up and my mouth goes dry at the expression on his face. It's menacing and…freaking *hot*. Graham's brows are swooped low and his jaw is tight, his mouth a slash of displeasure. I almost want him to do bad, bad things to me. No, really, I do. *Show me what a wicked boy you can be.* Is it strange that I'm thinking sexual things about him when he most likely is thinking of all the many ways to dispose of my body without getting caught?

He kicks the patio chair out of his way to close the distance between us. So much for that barrier. Those ten dollars were a waste.

Before I know it, my butt is against the railing and Graham's got an arm on either side of me, barricading me in. There is no escape and I'm okay with that. The air between us is a live spark, ready to flare up and cinder us both. I have to be imagining this. Only there is scalding heat in the space between us and I swear I can hear his heart thundering. My whole body is liquid fire and aching. His mouth is near my forehead, and I feel it graze my temple. I am having a hard time breathing; the air leaving my lungs is gaspy and unattractive, and my heartbeats are in overdrive. If he took me now I would so be a willing participant. Only, sadly, he won't.

"You're mine, not his."

My head falls back so fast I fear I have whiplash as I stare wide-eyed and confused at Graham. Did he really just say that? And what did he mean by it? Green eyes, steady with conviction, watch me.

"What?" I croak.

Shutters fall over his face as he backs away, running an unsteady hand through his hair and mussing it up. His muscled back is taut as he turns around and my fingers itch to touch him, to soothe the agitation from his bearing. "You're my friend, not his. That's all I meant."

Grinding my teeth, I fist my hands. "I'm only allowed to have *you* as a friend, is that it?"

"No, of course not." He faces me, looking weary. "Just…not him. Okay?"

"I'm not promising that and you're stupid for thinking I ever would."

"Wow, don't be so gentle with my emotions, please."

"You're being ridiculously lame right now. I hope you realize that."

"No, really, tell me how you really feel."

I snap my lips together, but not before, "You're being annoying," escapes.

"Again with the coddling."

"Good night, Graham," I say stiffly, moving toward the sliding glass doors.

A hand, warm and firm, catches my wrist. "Don't make me compete."

"Why would I ever make you do that?" Okay, so maybe I would, if it meant knowing where I stand with him. If it meant maybe having a chance with him.

"Because I will," he adds. "Only you might not like it."

I have no idea what he is talking about and yet I am strangely turned on. He's being insane and mildly unlike my roommate. I like it. Every girl wants a guy who's willing to fight for her. But Graham? Psssh. Like that would ever happen. I tug my wrist from his grip and he releases me. I leave him alone on the deck to brood or whatever it is he is going to do—maybe plot his brother's death.

Blake is in the kitchen, standing against the wall with his arms crossed over his chest. His dark eyes bore a hole into me, seeing things I probably don't want him to see. "Maybe he's not as clueless as I thought," is all he says.

chapter five

Snarky much, is my first thought as I enter the kitchen the next morning. I pulled my hair up in a messy ponytail upon leaving the bedroom and didn't change from my blue and white shorts and red tank top I wore to bed the night before (Go, USA!). The shirt is tight and the shorts are short, but I'm completely comfortable. Graham is presently glaring at me like he doesn't like me too much, so I'm thinking he is not comfortable with my outfit— or he still isn't over last night.

I don't think he's ever been so angry with me before——well, except for maybe that time I *accidentally* put salt in his girlfriend's coffee instead of sugar.

I pour myself a cup of coffee, showing him my back. And I wait. He doesn't make me wait long.

His voice is brittle as he snaps, "Do you have to dress like that?"

"I always dress like this. You never seemed to care before." I give my behind an extra wiggle just to irritate him. I know I've succeeded when something thumps loudly against the tabletop.

"I think you should dress like that more often," Blake immediately replies.

"Did anyone ask you?" is Graham's hotheaded comeback.

"In fact, I think you're wearing too many clothes. You should remove some."

A low growl leaves Graham.

When I finally face the Malone boys, it is to find them staring one another down from across the small table. Graham's wearing a white t-shirt and black shorts; his brother is in jeans and a brown shirt. Their coloring is so different, as are their features, but they are both striking in appearance, and their expressions currently mimic one another's.

"Graham, you're being an ass," I calmly inform him.

He grabs a piece of toast off his plate and whips it at me. I duck and it lands in the sink. To say I'm surprised would be an understatement. Toast throwing now? This is what our friendship has resorted to?

"I will not live with someone who throws toast at me in anger," I announce, setting my untouched cup of coffee on the counter.

Blake snorts, covering his mouth with the back of his hand as he turns his attention to the world beyond the sliding glass patio doors. Graham blinks at me, like he doesn't understand what I just said or maybe he doesn't understand what he just did. Either way, I grab my mug and stride out of the room and down the hall to my bedroom. I'll drink my coffee in peace, away from the toast throwing.

Only peace is not to be mine.

The door immediately opens after I close it, and there is Graham, staring at me, his head cocked, his expression unnamable.

"This coffee is hot," I warn, holding the white mug out. "You wanna be a toast thrower then I can be a coffee thrower. Just saying."

"Put the coffee down."

"No."

He takes a step toward me. "Come on. Please."

"You threw toast at me," I point out, in case he forgot.

"I don't know why I did that," he mumbles, looking down. When he lifts his eyes to me, they are pleading. "Please?"

With a sigh, I comply. I am putty in his hands—or I *could* be. I keep the mug within reach on the dresser, should I need it as backup. As soon as I let the cup go, I'm pulled against his hard chest, his strong arms wrapping around me, his chin on the crown of my head. His scent cocoons me; a mixture of soap and Graham, and I inwardly sigh.

He should throw toast more often if this is the end result.

"I'm sorry—for last night, for the toast. I don't know what's wrong with me." His arms tighten.

"You act like you're my parent," I mumble into his armpit.

He pulls away. "I do not." He looks insulted. The guy is so dense at times. It's adorable. Well, sometimes it's adorable. Other times it is just really annoying. "I just—" He turns and rubs his neck, his back tense. "You're sort of my best friend—"

"Sort of?" This is not what I want to be. I mean, I do, but that's not all I want to be.

"You are. For a girl. Anyway, I care about you. And I worry about you. That's all." Yep. That's all—dismally.

"Okay." It is so not okay.

He blinks. "Okay? That's it? Okay?"

"Yeah. Now leave. I need to get dressed." I don't look at him as I say this. And I may be pouting, but I am not sure. I glance in the mirror above my dresser. I try to school my features into blankness, but instead my face takes on this garish, totally unattractive look instead. I become aware of how quiet it is and look up. Graham's staring at me with his usual quizzical expression he reserves just for me.

I *am* an enigma.

"What are you doing?" He sounds like he really wants to know. That's the thing about Graham; he is always interested in why I do the things I do. He's extremely thoughtful toward me, or maybe it's just concern for my unstable mental state. Either way...

"Don't ask such difficult questions."

Frowning, he says, "You're acting strange. Stranger than usual."

"And you're acting grumpier than usual."

"I'm sorry. I'll stop. What do you want to do today?"

I freeze and unconsciously make that garish, unattractive look again. I wonder how often I do that without even knowing it. "I have plans."

It's his turn to go still, only his face darkens along with the whole freezing thing. He tries to straighten his expression and I don't feel quite so bad as I watch him struggle to appear nonchalant when he is anything but. Clearly I am not the only one who has an out of control face. Maybe some muscle relaxers would help with that. An image of a drooling, moaning zombie flutters through my mind. Then again, maybe not.

"Oh. With who?" His voice is even, but roughness underlies it.

"Some...one. Don't ask such difficult questions," I snap again in a really ingenious way.

"Blake?" he asks incredulously.

"Maybe. I mean, I think that's his name. I could be wrong. It's all a blur."

"You just met him Friday."

I pat his cheek. "You're so observant."

His jaw clenches. "Sunday is our day. We've spent almost every Sunday together since you moved in."

I ignore the little stab of guilt in my chest. "So? Blake asked me to go for a bike ride and I agreed. We'll always have next Sunday."

It's amazing how fast he moves. One minute he is in front of me and the next he has the door slammed shut with his back leaning against it. "You are not going on a bike ride with him. You just met him and you know nothing about him."

"I'll get to know him today."

"I don't understand. Who *are* you? This just...what is going on?" he asks with furrowed brows. He looks so confused, like he is looking at a version of me he didn't realize existed

"This is me—all real Kennedy and whatnot. Move away from the door."

He crosses his arms, looking belligerent.

"Are you seriously trying to keep me barricaded in?"

"I...*no*...yes. I don't know!" His face is comically frustrated and I feel bad for him at the same time I feel exasperated and irritated. It's amazing all the many emotions I can feel within a span of seconds in his presence.

"Then you better plan on entertaining me," slips out in a totally pre-Blake Kennedy way.

The strangest look passes over his face. It's surprise and ferocity and something I can't name all spun into one. He moves for me and I brace myself, trying not to appear too wanton, although the way I immediately melt might contradict that. "You know what I like best about you?"

"Aside from my amazing sense of humor and fabulous good looks?"

Half of his mouth lifts. "Yeah. Aside from that."

I shrug, feeling like I'm going to hyperventilate if he doesn't move away soon. I strive for cool and collected as I answer, "I make all your secret fantasies come true with just one glance?"

"You're deceptive."

"Um...not exactly what I was going for."

"Look at you." He slowly walks around me, the air between us warming as he moves, yet I feel chilled. He stops before me once more.

"I can't. You're blocking the mirror."

Green eyes pierce me, locking me in place. "You look like this sweet, angelic girl. I mean, you've got the pretty brown eyes and the pretty blond hair. You're amazing to look at—and then you talk."

"And you realize how much more than that I am, right?" My face feels uncomfortably warm. I don't know if he's ever alluded to my looks in a positive way before. And—should I be offended about the talking bit?

His head tilts. "Yes, actually. Your voice is still sweet, I'll give you that. But the words...the words that come out of your mouth don't fit your exterior at all. You're completely improper and unladylike. Rude, even. Blunt. Self-centered at times. Sarcastic. Tactless. Possibly—no, you *are* immature."

"Stop. I'm blushing."

"Funny. Honest." He touches a lock of my hair, his fingers sliding down the length of it and causing tingles all the way up to my scalp. "Loyal. Unique. There is no way to like you *in spite of* all that you are, because all of those traits make you *who* you are. I never know what you will say or do next and...even so, you are innocent in a way. You are naïve." He steps away. "And because of all of that, I will not let my brother take advantage of you or hurt you, no matter what."

"Well." I cross my arms because I don't know what else to do. And really? Talk about awesome comeback right there. I also don't know whether to feel insulted or...whatever. Graham and I don't really do the baring of souls bit. I'm shockingly speechless from what he just told me.

I recover quickly enough with, "It's a good thing you're not spending the day with your brother and me then. You won't be around to try to save me every time I do something you don't approve of. I'd hate to put that burden on you. Now leave before I get naked in front of you."

I swear he considers staying, but then he leaves with an unhappy glare aimed my way. "We're not done talking about this."

"Yes, we are, because in case you didn't notice, you just walked out of the room, hence the ending of the conversation!"

He comes back to say, "It will be resumed at a later date."

"I'm calling in sick that day."

And once more he returns to gift me with a steely-eyed scowl. "I'm just trying to look out for you."

"Now, if you said you were just trying to look *at* me, well, that would be an entirely different matter altogether."

"You never stop, do you?"

"Why stop when I am overflowing with coolness?"

His lips tighten into a thin line. "One day, Kennedy, one day all your little quips will come back to bite you."

"Don't promise something you can't deliver."

He leaves without another word, which is just as well as I can barely stand from the shaking of my legs. Wouldn't want to fall to the floor before him. He'd think I was worshiping him or something. I do enough of that in my head—he doesn't need to *see* it. My heart is racing and I feel sick. I put my hand against the door and lean forward until it softly clicks shut. Then I rest my head against it and take deep breaths. Am I dying? It feels like I'm going to have a heart attack. No, that's just the aftereffect of my roommate.

I turn around so that the back of my head is resting against the door and try to figure out Graham's bizarre behavior. I wonder if it's a territorial thing? Like, I'm Graham's friend and roommate. He knew me first. Blah, blah, blah. Kind of caveman-ish, but also kind of...not Graham. I like not Graham. He's way more interesting than regular Graham. I mean, I love regular Graham, don't get me wrong. But regular Graham doesn't seem like at any minute he could toss me over his shoulder, throw me down on his bed (or mine, I'm not picky), and ravish me. Not Graham has a combustible element to him that is super attractive.

A banging commences behind my head and I shriek, lunging away from the door. That didn't really help with the whole 'feeling like I'm going to have a heart attack' moment.

"Kennedy? You indecent?"

I open the door.

Blake's eyes rove up and down the length of me. "What a shame. You still have pajamas on."

"Yeah. I haven't gotten dressed yet."

"Which means you haven't gotten *un*dressed yet."

I tilt my head as I digest his words.

"Are you going to bail on me?" Something flashes in his eyes, like he knows I am going to tell him I've changed my mind and he is steeling himself with an air of indifference to hide how my words truly affect him. Yes, I got all that from one glance at his face. What can I say? I'm abnormally observant.

"Are you going to make me wear a dress?"

His stance relaxes. "Not if you wear something tight and revealing. Either will do."

"Hmm. I'll see what I can whip up." I mime cracking a whip.

Leaning forward, he purrs into my ear, "I like rough, dominant women. Don't hold back on my account."

I laugh shakily and pull back. Maybe I'm out of my league with Blake. Although, inspiration strikes and has me saying, "I don't think you can handle me."

"I'd sure like to try."

Oh no, he didn't.

"You need to get out," I say abruptly and point a trembling finger at the door.

His lips lift in a slow, seductive smile. "Don't make me wait too long."

When the door is once again closed, I stumble to my bed and plop face-down on it. My whole body is tingling and I feel like I just ran twenty miles, or rather, how I *think* I would feel after running twenty miles, as I've never actually done that before. Running that far would mean death for me and I kind of like myself.

I flip onto my back and stare at the ceiling. What am I doing? What are *they* doing? Is this some sibling rivalry bit and I am the one they decided to be stupid over? Although, I know Graham loves me in a totally platonic, aggravatingly innocent way, so whatever he does or says, at least he has concern for me spurring him on—or jealousy. (I can only hope.)

His brother, on the other hand, could have some devious plot formulated for the ultimate revenge against Graham. Blake I know nothing about, other than he is cynical, has a troubled past, and likes to flirt. So maybe I know a lot about him, but all of that is surface stuff. I don't really know him. Maybe if I, like, spent a day or something with him, I could get to know him better. Hmm. If only I had made plans with him. Hmm.

I jump from the bed and hurriedly fling clothes on.

"I'm going to puke!" I scream, but I think my laugh takes away the seriousness of that comment.

"Face away from the bike!" he yells over his shoulder.

I laugh even harder, squeezing my legs and arms tighter around his hard body. Maybe it is the combination of cigarettes and his deodorant, but Blake smells like cloves. I like the smell of cloves, hence I like the smell of him.

I don't want to know how fast the bike is going. In the daylight, I noticed it was black, close to the ground, and said Harley Davidson on its side, which was enough information for me. The bike is loud and my whole body is continually jarred from the power of the engine, but *I love it*. I've never done anything like this before. The most exciting thing I can recall participating in is going on a week-long RV trip with my mom and dad when I was fourteen, and yeah, that was pretty lame—especially in comparison to this.

Speed is sexy, I have determined.

I let go of his waist and hold my arms out at my sides with my head back. The sun is warm on my face, the air around us cool and strong. I close my eyes and let my mind go blank, simply enjoying the moment of freedom. Oh yeah. I am a rebel. I should totally get a shirt saying that. Then everyone would know with just a glance at my chest how badass I really am—and how small my breasts are, I guess. Maybe I should rethink that.

The hours merge and seem endless on the bike at the same time they are over too quickly. He pulls the motorcycle into the parking lot of a diner, the engine abruptly cutting off. It is unnaturally quiet after listening to it roar for the past how many hours. I slowly get off the bike and remove my helmet.

I brush tangled wisps of blond hair from my mouth and grin at Blake. "I like how you're more concerned with the bike getting vomit on it than you."

"I got my priorities straight." He lights a cigarette, looking like a hot biker dude with his dark hair, sunglasses, and black jacket, which—I suppose he is. His hair is windswept and chaotic, which is alluring as heck.

"Have you heard of this place?" I ask, taking in the red building with a wall of windows and a worn-looking metal sign that reads 'Betsy's'. A lone forest green car sits in the parking lot.

Blake squints as he takes in the run-down restaurant. "Nah. But, ya know, gotta take risks and all that."

"Not with your *food*," I point out.

He flashes a grin. "I'll eat the food if you do."

"Are you challenging me?"

"Are you scared?" The smoke from his cigarette curls over to me, its wispy tendrils connecting us in a smoke-infused haze. Usually turned off by the smell of cigarettes, I am strangely *not* by his. Although, it could just be him.

"No. Only clowns scare me. What kind of cigarettes are those?"

"The bad kind. Why? You gonna give it a go again? Reactivate the bad habit?"

"You just never know. I wasn't born a quitter." I begin to walk toward the building, deciding today is a day about living on the edge, even if that edge is covered in unknown food substances.

"You're scared of clowns?" he asks as he joins me.

I scowl. "Don't you dare tell anyone."

"Never crossed my mind."

A bell chimes as the door opens and I am instantly covered in the scent of fried food. "How far are we from Lancaster anyway?"

I wasn't paying attention to the direction we were going or the towns along the way, too wrapped up in feeling like a swashbuckler (I love that word) to note such insignificant details. But now, as I take in the scary-looking man sitting at the table across the room, I am thinking maybe I should have. If we need to run, it would be nice to know how far. The man's face is grisly, like he has dirt caked into the wrinkles of it. Greasy brown hair and an unwavering gaze completes his panic-inducing persona.

Blake gives me a small shove when my footsteps falter.

"You need to stop with the excessive force," I grumble at him as we slide into the booth farthest away from the other occupant in this fine establishment.

"You need to not stare."

The waitress appears, sporting a purple shirt and black pants. Her curly hair is dyed fire engine red and the nametag on her shirt reads 'Marsha'. Her blue eyes are outlined in black and there is a sardonic twist to her lips.

I jump when she slaps two black and white menus on the table, averting my eyes from Blake's grinning face.

"What can I get you to drink?" she sort of demands in a rough voice.

"Lemonade?"

"Are you asking me or telling me?" she says as her eyes shift to me.

"Uh...telling?" She's scary. I think it's her unflinching eyes more than anything. How can someone stare that long without blinking?

Blake says, "She'll have lemonade and I'll take a strawberry soda."

Marsha, if her nametag is correct, leaves without another word.

"I think we should go," I say, my gaze going back to the man across the room. Of course he is watching me. I jerk my eyes away and return them to Blake. "This place is giving me the creeps," I whisper loudly.

"Do you see any clowns?"

"No." I sit back and cross my arms, totally knowing where he is going with this.

"Then you have nothing to fear."

"I also fear murderers."

He rolls his eyes. "Well, when someone comes at us with a hatchet, I'll cue you."

"What if it's a knife? Or a gun?"

"I'll still cue you." He produces a pack of cigarettes from a pocket and lights one up.

"You can't smoke in here!" I hiss.

He nods his head and I follow his gaze. Marsha has her back to us as she prepares our drinks, a cigarette dangling from the side of her mouth, smoke swirling up from it. I really hope she doesn't ash in our drinks. Well, mine anyway. Blake is on his own.

"What's with you and clowns anyway?"

I stiffen. "I don't want to talk about it."

"Come on. I'll tell you something I'm scared of if you tell me why you're terrified of clowns."

"I didn't say I was terrified." I am.

He patiently waits.

With a sigh, I say, "My mom and dad took me to the circus when I was five. I wasn't feeling well, but I didn't want to tell them because I really wanted to go to the circus and I knew my mom would make me stay home if I told her." I pause—even now my stomach is getting knotted up thinking about it. "We went into this tent where all of these clowns were performing. They did this bit where they picked a kid out of the audience to help with something—I don't remember what. They picked me.

"So there I was, standing in the middle of the ring, with all of these clowns smiling at me with their painted faces, weird hair, and crazy outfits. I remember they were trying to talk to me to get me to do something, but I was starting to feel worse and worse the longer I stood there.

"Everything started to spin and their laughter took on this maniacal quality and then I threw up. Everywhere. Not just once. Repeatedly. I could tell they were angry, because, I mean, who wants to be puked on? Not even clowns, apparently. The crowd got really loud, in a really bad way. I was mortified. My mom rushed out to get me and they took me home. My dad was upset that I didn't tell them I felt sick. I think he was embarrassed because his kid puked all over the circus clowns. It was horrible. I've never gone to a circus since then and I never, ever want to see a clown again."

"So you associate clowns with a humiliating part of your childhood. You aren't necessarily scared of them. They're just connected to a bad moment and that's why they repel you."

"Wow. You're smart." I sound disbelieving, but luckily he just laughs.

"I never said I wasn't."

"Like, brain study person smart."

He shrugs, looking uncomfortable.

I straighten. "Okay. Your turn. Tell me something you're scared of."

His expression tightens. He looks down, sighs, and says, "All right. I'm scared I am not worthy of anyone's faith."

Whoa. Talk about deep and meaningful. I talked about clowns and he talks about that.

He looks up.

"What do you mean?" I ask cautiously.

He puts the cigarette out in the ashtray and takes a sip of his drink. I test the lemonade. It is good—equal parts sweet and tart. I didn't even know she'd brought our drinks. It must have been during my traumatizing confession.

"My life is one screw up after another. I just wonder if anyone should keep thinking someday I'll be okay."

Oh no. I go soft. Like, everything melts inside me with those words. Of course, he can't know that, so I hope my voice is even as I say, "That isn't really for you to decide."

He tilts his head.

"Whether or not people should continue to hold out hope for you or not. That's their choice, not yours. You just have to deal with it."

"If you knew the circumstances, you might think differently."

I do know the circumstances, or at least a variation of them, and it doesn't make me think less of him—only I can't tell him that. So I say, "I don't think that matters. If people care about you, they won't give up on you, no matter what you've done in the past or what you do in the future. We aren't programmed that way. We're made to find hope in the most hopeless of places and in the people that seem the least likely to deserve it, because they really need it the most, and something in us knows that, at least subconsciously. It's what makes us human. No one is unworthy. Not even you. If people want to have faith in you, let them. And really, you can't stop them. It's not up to you." I totally pulled those words from my basket of awesomeness.

His expression shifts as he stares at me. Blake doesn't speak, but in his gaze he says so much. I watch him, sweaty-palmed and feeling asthmatic. Never taking his eyes from mine, he leans over the table and softly presses his lips to mine. It is a feather light kiss, a gentle caress of lips against one another—a thank you. Neither of us closes our eyes, and really, it happens so fast there is no time for that. Our open-eyed kiss has a sweet poignancy to it, and when he sits back, I cannot seem to look away from him.

"Ready to order?"

I jump at the sound of Marsha's voice, hastily ordering a grilled cheese sandwich and French fries. I don't even know if those are on the menu, but she doesn't say anything, so they must be. Blake gets a cheeseburger and onion rings. Once again, she departs.

"How long have you known Graham?" he asks. His manner suggests we didn't just kiss, and even though I am reeling from the fact that we *did* just kiss, I decide to act like it never happened as well.

"Over a year. He was looking for a roommate and I answered the ad in the paper. Apparently he thought I was qualified enough to live with him." I smirk. It seems like I just met him at the same time it seems like I have known him forever. I suddenly miss Graham and take a large gulp of my drink to hide it.

"You two seem pretty close."

"We are. He's probably my best friend, even if he is a guy. For some reason, I don't have a lot of friends that are girls. Actually, I think Phoebe is the only girl I really consider a friend and I don't know if we would be if we didn't work together." I frown. I'd never really thought about my lack of girlfriends before.

"That makes perfect sense to me."

"What's that mean?"

"Nothing bad. You're just unconventional."

I squint my eyes at him. "So?"

He shrugs. "So nothing."

Our food arrives.

I chew on a French fry, probably overthinking his words, but I don't think I am because Graham said something kind of the same earlier. Apparently today is the day I get to learn about all of my flaws.

"Do you think I'm likable?" Why am I asking him this? I answer myself immediately—because he won't lie.

His lips curve up. "I like you. Does that make you feel better?"

"No. Not really." I shove another fry into my mouth.

Chuckling, he says, "Do you really care if people like you or not? You don't seem the type."

I tilt my head, considering his words. "Generally, no. But if it's someone I like, I want them to like me back."

"Well, we both know you like me and I just told you I like you, so I don't know what else you need to worry about." He takes a large bite of his cheeseburger, leaving residual ketchup on his upper lip. I don't tell him 'cause it's good for his arrogance to be taken down a notch, even if he is unaware of it.

Marsha later ruins it for me when she brings the bill, immediately telling him about the ketchup on his mouth. He gives me a long look, but doesn't comment, paying the bill and leaving a tip even though I try to pay for my half. We leave the restaurant and the creepy guy behind, the thought of wrapping my body around his for the return trip making me feel not completely grossed out.

chapter six

lake drops me off at the apartment, saying he has errands to run. I don't know what kind of errands he would have to run in a town he is only temporarily living in, but I don't ask 'cause it isn't any of my business. Maybe he needs to pick up mouthwash or something.

As I head for the door to my apartment, I am besieged with apprehension. I feel guilty that I ditched Graham for Blake and it's annoying that I feel guilty. Since when do I feel wimpy emotions like regret? I'm also nervous. How will Graham act when he sees me? We were gone a long time. We left before eleven and it is now almost six in the evening. I am also irritated with myself for everything recently thought or felt. We're just friends—roommates even. Right? Right.

He is reading a book in the living room. My heart melts. Even him reading is attractive to me. Although, reading *is* pretty hot. I check the cover of the book to see if it is one of my smut books, but alas, it is John Saul. I shiver. I read one of his books once—'The Right Hand of Evil'. Never even thought about reading another one. I had nightmares for weeks. I even slept with Graham the first few nights afterward. Of course, it was totally unproductive. All we did was sleep.

I feel like a rebellious teen trying to sneak in after curfew and instead caught by their parent. He doesn't look up. He doesn't acknowledge me in any way. I should probably leave him alone. Instead I plop down on the couch and rest my head in his lap. I feel him stiffen, but otherwise he acts like I am not even here. So I grab the book from his hands and chuck it toward the end of the couch.

"If you get scared tonight, you can sleep with me. Or even if you don't."

Lowering his head so that our gazes collide and hold, he stares down at me. The expression on his face isn't necessarily unfriendly, but it isn't exactly loving either. If I was smart, I'd get up and walk from the room without further antagonism toward him. It is obvious he is not happy with me. As I watch, a lock of golden hair falls onto his forehead and I gently brush it aside. It feels like satin. His eyes darken, but otherwise there is no indication my touch affected him in any way.

"You're offering your bed to me?" he murmurs quietly.

Something about the way he says this—a dangerous vibe to his deep voice— makes me rethink my choice of words, but I am not one to dwell too heavily on what I say or should have said instead, so I move on. "Are you saying you want to be in it?" My heartbeat quickens as I wait for his response.

Seconds turn into minutes as we silently watch one another, and all the while, I am struggling to breathe. Why do I feel scared, like something monumental and irreversible, is about to happen? Why do I feel like if we do not connect in some cosmic way, I will not recover from the disappointment that will follow? Why am I asking myself questions when a superbly good-looking guy is staring down at me?

His fingertip trails down my cheek. "Not this way."

And the spell is broken.

I abruptly sit up. "I was kidding." Wasn't I? Where is my snappy comeback? And since when do I have to tell him when I am kidding—or even feel the need to? What does he mean, not this way? The moment is too serious, too full of unspoken wants, for me to sling back one of my retorts like I normally do.

"Did you have fun?" The words seem innocent enough, but there is discord imbedded in them.

I glance at him from the corner of my eye, feeling confused and angry and even confused that I am angry. "Yep. Best time ever. I've never had so much fun in my life." There is a taint of wrongness on my tongue at the words. I've had more fun lots of times—all aforementioned fun times spent doing anything at all with Graham; even doing nothing at all, but with Graham.

"Good. That's good. Glad you and Blake are getting along so well." He pauses. "Can I have my book back?"

"Yeah. Sure." I take the paperback and throw it at him, jumping to my feet as he catches it against his chest. "I hope you have horrible dreams, and just so you know, the invitation has been retracted." I huff off to my room before he can say anything, not that he probably wants to anyway. Maybe that was immature, but according to Graham, I *am* immature, so that was in character for me.

Two minutes later I am back in the living room. "I'm sorry," I say as I gaze at him sitting on the couch. "I don't really want you to have bad dreams."

He hasn't opened the book yet; it is resting undisturbed on his lap. There is a bemused look on his face as he studies me. "You know what?"

"What?" I ask worriedly. What if he announces he is sick of my lack of maturity and kicks me out? He can totally do that. He has that right.

Graham stands up, tossing the book to the couch. The air around us warms as the space between us closes. One side of his mouth lifts. "Let's do something for supper. What sounds good?"

"You?" I blink, the word totally spewing forth of its own admission. But he just laughs, which makes me relax. I blow out a breath. "I mean, whatever you want to do is okay with me."

He gives me a look, like he isn't sure what to make of my amendment. "Let's go somewhere. Forever Blue okay?"

Forever Blue is a small diner with blue and cream as the color theme, a limited menu of sandwiches, soups, and salads, and Oldies music. They have delicious homemade pies and always-fresh coffee. It's kind of our place.

"Yes." I smile. "I would love to go to Forever Blue with you."

Graham smiles back and it is like the sun gracing me with its presence after years of being without—stunning, warm, and thoroughly missed. "You want to walk or take a vehicle?"

"Walk. But I need to change quick."

His eyes rove over my black form-fitting jacket and dark skinny jeans, landing on my knee-high black boots and finally stopping on my eyes. "You look good." He sounds surprised, like he never noticed my apparel until now.

"Yeah, I know, the casual frumpy look is usually my thing, but I had to dress appropriately."

"You have dressed in many unusual variations of clothing, but never have you been frumpy," he denies immediately.

I pause, not sure what is going on. "Are you feeling okay?"

The smile that grazes his lips is anything but cheery. In fact, it looks sort of sickly. "Yeah. Never better."

"Okay. So I'll go—"

"Don't change. I mean, change if you want to, but…you don't have to. Unless you want to."

Graham is stumbling over his words in a non-polished sequence that befuddles me. I openly stare at him. I can't help it. Although, even if I could help it, I'd still be staring, 'cause, ya know, he's nice to look at. But since when does he blush and act like he is nervous around me? Since Blake showed up, that's when. Everything has been twisted into an unknown mass of disorder and I am not really sure why. I hate not knowing things. It makes me feel incompetent.

"What is with you?"

Closing his eyes, he takes a deep breath. "Nothing is with me," he answers as his eyes open. "Were you going to change?"

"No." I unzip my jacket and throw it onto the couch, revealing a tight hot pink shirt with a silvery star on my designated boobage area. "I'm fine like this. If you're fine with me like this?"

Again with the eye closing. "Don't ask me that," he says with difficulty.

I shrug. "Okay. Let's go."

The sun decides to be evil and blinds me as soon as I step outside, so it really isn't my fault I don't notice anything is amiss until I hear Blake's rough voice. I guess maybe the stiffening of Graham beside me could have been a clue, had I chosen to acknowledge it.

"Out for a moonlit stroll?"

I squint at him through the glaring rays of sunshine. "That doesn't even make sense. It's daytime."

He shrugs, lifting a cigarette to his lips and lighting it. Smoke forms a blurry shield between him and us. He's still got his aviator sunglasses on and his black hair is messy from the wind continually running its fingers through it, which totally works in his favor. "I couldn't very well call it a sunlit walk, could I? I think you'll agree it doesn't have the same clandestine punch."

"What do you care what we do or don't do?" Graham demands.

Blake turns to his brother. I think he's looking at him, but it's hard to tell with his sunglasses on. He could have his eyes closed and no one would know. That would show us. "I don't. Just making conversation." He pauses to inhale nicotine and chemicals. "I decided I won't be staying with you for the summer."

"Oh? When did you decide that?" Graham's tone of voice is pleasant enough, for a snarly tone.

"About thirty minutes ago." He turns his head in my direction. I'm about ready to snatch those sunglasses from his face. "That was the errand I had to do."

"Are your eyes open?"

"What?"

"Are you looking at me right now?" I wave my hand in front of his face. His brows lower.

"I think you should take your sunglasses off." I laugh, but it sounds sort of scary. "Take them off!" I snap when he doesn't move.

Blake shoves the sunglasses to the top of his head. "Better?" No, because now I can see how strangely he is looking at me. "Maybe you should add sunglasses to your list of fears."

Graham turns to me. "He knows about the clowns?" He looks hurt, like I told a fatal secret and now the end of his life is inevitable.

"Maybe. The details are hazy. What was your errand?" I ask to distract the Malone men from my odd behavior. I move into the shade of a tree to better see my surroundings, since we don't appear to be leaving them anytime soon. And why are they looking at me like that?

Blake recovers first. "I found a room to rent while I'm in Lancaster."

"Why did you do that?" Graham asks slowly, staring the younger Malone down.

His eyes remain locked on me as he answers, "I came to the conclusion it would be for the best."

My breath hiccups as his heated gaze continues to sear me.

"Meaning?" Graham prods.

He finally drags his gaze from me to gift his brother with a sardonic grin. "Meaning I intend to date your roommate. You don't mind, do you?"

The fist flies forward before I can blink, clipping Blake's jaw hard enough to snap his head to the side. I haven't even digested his words or Graham's reaction before he is fighting back. His features twist and he rams into his brother's gut head-first, propelling them into a tree. A grunt leaves Graham at the contact, but it doesn't take him long to land another punch to his brother's shoulder. At first I just stare with my mouth open, but as they continue to pummel one another, I feel it is only necessary to intervene, especially 'cause cops could be called at any point. And, ya know, *awkward.*

"Stop!" I shout, running for the pair. "Stop it. Both of you!" I grab for Blake's arm and his elbow jabs back, right into my collarbone. The pain is instantaneous, sharp and hot, and a gasp leaves me as I stumble back. I trip over something and fall onto my rear, the impact jostling me. Gritting my teeth, I carefully move to my knees, glaring at the large rock that just kicked my butt.

Somehow Graham is paying enough attention to notice what just happened, and with an animalistic snarl, he shoves his brother back hard, immediately storming for me. The fierceness in his face clears as he stares down at me, his eyes lowering to my shoulder I am gingerly touching.

Dropping to his knees beside me, he gently moves my hand aside. "Are you okay?" His voice is low, strained.

I can tell he is fighting to steady his breathing by the way his chest heaves up and down. Sweat trickles down the side of his face and a lock of hair is sticking up. His lip is bleeding and my stomach not only turns queasy at the sight of blood, but also that he is hurting in any way, however small it may be. I want to fall into his arms, but I can't because he is stupid and I don't hug stupid people.

I slowly stand, shaking my head when he reaches for me. With a confused look, he drops his hand and stands up, backing away. I glance toward where Blake is standing by the tree, his features drawn with regret. Anger wraps around me as I eye the testosterone-ravaged men. I have never had men physically throw punches over me before, and I am sickened by it. I am also slightly stunned by this revelation, wondering what is wrong with me that I can't appreciate two of the male species turning into imbeciles on my behalf.

"Kennedy, I didn't mean to—" Blake begins, but I shut him up when I slice my hand through the air.

"What the hell is wrong with you two?" I demand in a low voice, splitting my gaze between the two men. "I am not some possession. I am not here merely for you two to be Neanderthals over. I don't know what is going on with you, or whatever games you're playing at, but I will not be a part of them. You just made me respect you, like, not at all, and I never would have thought that was possible, especially with you." I turn my disillusioned eyes on Graham.

He looks down, swallowing.

Gazing at Blake, I say, "And I don't even know you. You don't just announce you're going to date me without even seeing if I want to date you. And just so you know, I don't. Not after this. Maybe I would have considered it, but you just messed that up."

He looks properly chastised. Good.

I can be serious. And pissed. The combination is not good. I leave the brothers, feeling like an unknown layer is covering me and I can't shake it off, no matter how much I want it gone. It is uncomfortable and heavy.

This, I have decided, is sensibility.

Moodily splashing teal nail polish on my toenails, I fluctuate between seething at what happened and remembering the look on Graham's face—before he struck his brother and after Blake accidentally elbowed me—and I don't know how to feel about it. I swallow thickly as the memory of the possessiveness, the rage, and the protectiveness I saw in his eyes and stance pummels my senses. I recap the bottle of nail polish and draw my knees up to my chin, wrapping my arms around my legs. Sunshine streams in through the lone window of the bedroom, somehow knowing exactly where I am sitting on the floor to blast me with its rays. I think it has something against me personally. The sun always reminds me of Graham, and even now, when I am irate with him, a part of me still needs him. I need his warmth.

The text I got two minutes ago from Phoebe should have annoyed me, and somewhat did, but only because of my bad mood. Otherwise I am suspiciously not concerned about the fact that she and Nathan are going out this weekend. She sounded apologetic and I assured her, about three times, that it is absolutely okay. Maybe it's the visual I get of his toes wiggling at me from the top of his neck every time I think of him, or maybe it's because I simply don't care about him like I do Graham. Whatever it is, good luck to them and all that.

There is a soft knock on the door and then it is slowly opening. A familiar voice, simultaneously rough and lyrical, asks, "Is there toast or coffee in the room?"

"No." I pause. "But there's me. And that's even more terrifying."

The door opens all the way and Graham enters, carrying a Styrofoam container and a serious look. "Hi." His upper lip is split and swollen and I soften at seeing the battle wound, regardless of how unnecessary it is.

"Hi."

His eyes study me, finally dropping to my newly painted toenails and back up. A faint smile touches his lips before quickly fading away. "I brought you supper." He raises the white box in an apparent peace offering. I don't say anything. "I figured since I ruined our dinner plans at Forever Blue I should at least get you something from there."

"How thoughtful of you. Maybe you could have thought of that before you decided to punch your brother in the face. You could have been like, if I punch Blake, that means Kennedy and I won't get to go to Forever Blue for supper, only no, you didn't think of that, did you? And now look. I'm painting my toenails and you're trying to win back my love with bribery. Since when do you punch people?"

"It's turkey and Swiss on cranberry rice bread."

I jump to my feet and snatch the box from him. "Your tricks won't work on me."

"Then why did you just grab the box out of my hands?"

"I'm keeping it safe."

"I also got you cheesy broccoli soup, but I didn't think I should bring anything hot into the room."

It is on the tip of my tongue to respond with, *Then why are you here?* But I refrain. I have to remind myself I am mad at him. So I say, "Good thinking on your part."

But cheesy broccoli soup? Yum. It is hard to stay upset with him when he brought me some of my favorite foods. Of course, I could be enjoying them at the diner with catchy Oldies music playing in the background, so there is that to keep my anger going.

Again a hint of a smile curves his lips before dissipating. "Kennedy," he says in a somber voice. "I'm sorry for acting that way. I'm usually able to stay in control, no matter what. I don't like that I lost it like that, or that you saw it. I feel like an ass."

"Well, you should. And I don't understand you two. Do you hate each other or something? I was under the impression you liked each other, but you haven't really acted like it since Blake showed up."

He shows me his back as he says, "It's complicated."

Grabbing his arm, I feel his muscles tense as I tug him back to me. "It's not, really. You and I have known each other for a while, and I have never seen you behave like that before. Tell me what's going on."

He silently regards me, something tight in his expression.

"Graham, answer me." The air has shifted around us, full of secrets and warm with what-ifs. What if I kiss him? What if I tell him I love him? What if I finally tell him everything he is to me?

"I don't think you're ready to hear what I have to say."

My brows lower. "Meaning?"

A short laugh leaves him as he shakes his head. "Never mind. It's not—I always thought I'd have more time."

"More time?" I am seriously confused, hence my parrot talk.

He shakes his head again, not answering. His fingers gently touch my collarbone, his eyes cast down as he brushes the strap of my green tank top away from the already bruised flesh. A grimace steals over his features. "Does it hurt?"

Air has abandoned me and the breath I inhale is stolen, sounding loud in the quiet of the moment. "Only when you stop touching it." His eyes lift to mine. It wasn't meant to be sexual or flirtatious. It was honest. As his fingers graze the wound, the ache goes away and is replaced with a warmth that pools and grows within me. It flows down my limbs and into my fingertips. Although, that could merely be my reaction to him.

"Can I ask you something?" he murmurs. Without waiting for a response, he continues, "What is it about him that makes him so interesting?"

I blink, the warmth leaving me and coldness taking its place. I step back, setting the container holding my sandwich on the bed. "What?"

He appears to be searching for words. "Like you said, we've known each other for a while. You've known Blake for two days. You've already been with him more than you haven't since he showed up. What is it about him that you find so interesting? Why do you want to be with him?"

I fiddle with the drawstring of my black sweatpants. "The truth?"

"Please."

I don't think I can tell him the truth—not the full truth anyway. I hung out with Blake because I thought it might irritate Graham. That's part of it. The other part isn't so clear. Blake looked like he needed a friend and there are glimpses of vulnerability in him that make me think maybe he isn't as tough and arrogant as he wants everyone to think he is.

I settle with, "He's fun."

"He's fun," he repeats slowly, like I talked in a foreign language. Which, I don't know any so that is a non-issue. I barely passed my two years of required Spanish and have forgotten just about every single word of it.

"Anyway, isn't he here so you two can spend time together before he goes to wherever it is he's going to after he's done with college? Why don't you go kiss and make up and hang out together or something?"

"I don't think that's possible."

"Why?"

"He left. But even if he hadn't, things are tense between us."

"Because of me." And probably because they just tried to kill each other—which, I guess, is also because of me. "Where did he go?" He didn't even tell me goodbye, although, if he had tried, I would have ignored him anyway. That's beside the point. It's about effort.

"Wherever he got a temporary residence at, I'm guessing. And our inability to get along is not just because of you. Things have been strained between us for a long time. I told you about that."

"Since you stopped visiting during the summers and he had all his issues."

"Yeah. We just haven't been close since all of that. I mean, we really don't have anything in common. Or, we didn't," he adds.

I frown, not sure what he means by that. "I don't want to be the cause of any problems between you two. I know you're trying to protect me and you think his intentions toward me are whatever, but I can handle myself. Really. Blake is harmless. You don't have to punch guys on my behalf. You don't have to be all brotherly toward me and—"

"You think I'm being *brotherly* toward you?" he interrupts, his voice incredulous.

I nervously reach for the drawstring of my pants again. "Well, yeah—"

"Would you *stop* doing that?" He sounds like he is in pain.

My hands still. "Stop doing what?" Again with the parrot talk, but really, Graham is being extremely perplexing.

He closes his eyes and tips his head back as he inhales slowly and deeply. Somehow I find the act to be exceptionally erotic. I dig my nails into my palms to keep them from roaming over all parts of him.

"I'm going to go now. We'll...we'll talk later, okay?" And then he just leaves me.

"Yeah. Okay," I tell an empty room. I turn my gaze to the bed. Well, I guess I'm not completely alone. I have my sandwich.

chapter seven

i 'm sitting in the living room, staring at the television. It isn't on, because it would take more energy than I presently have to pick up the remote, aim it at the TV, and push the button. Graham went to the gym to work out, as he does almost every day. There's a pile of unfolded clothes on the couch beside me and a bag of cheese puffs in my lap. I love it when he goes to the gym, if only because I can be the massive sloth I naturally am in peace. If he were here, he'd be eyeing up my laundry and staring at the edible garbage in my lap and on my fingers, internally freaking out over the possibility of powdery cheese getting on the furniture.

One hand in the bag, one hand wrapped around the stem of my wine glass— this is my idea of perfection. 'Girls Chase Boys' by Ingrid Michaelson is presently keeping me company from the stereo system. When my phone rings from where it resides on the back of the couch, I jump and send the bag flying. Orange confetti falls to the floor and I swallow, knowing I am so dead if Graham walks in the door right now.

"What?" is my less than friendly greeting.

"What'd you do?"

How does he know me so well? I guess because he made me. "I just let off a bomb of cheese puffs. Although, technically, I'm blaming it on you since it was your phone call that scared me into dumping the bag over."

"Your mother is knitting again."

Eyes glued to the orange blobs on the pale carpet, I reply, "Oh? I'm sure it's marvelous, whatever it is." Are they seeping into the carpet as I watch, even now becoming an irremovable part of it? Graham is going to majorly freak out over this.

"Looks like a yellow condom."

I choke on nothing. "I have to go, Dad."

He grunts a goodbye. I fling the phone away and dive to my knees, hurriedly scooping up the abused deliciousness into my hands. Of course this is when Graham decides to come home—when my ass is in the air facing the door and I look like I'm eating processed food off the floor. I groan and let my head fall forward, smashing a cheese puff with my forehead. He doesn't say anything for a really, really long time, and I refuse to move or look at him, so it gets sort of awkward.

"Never thought I'd come home to this scene. Ever."

Just to rile him up, I shove a cheese puff in my mouth and chomp away.

"I can't believe you just ate that!"

I get to my feet as I pop another into my mouth. "Mmm."

Graham's face is twisted with horror, his backpack dropping to the floor. Sweat clings to him in a delicious way, his hair damp with it. "Do you know how dirty the carpet is?"

"You clean it almost every day. It can't be that dirty."

"I don't get everything out of it!" he exclaims, slapping the remaining puffs from my hands. "Go brush your teeth. No. Wait. Induce vomiting. Immediately."

I look at him and laugh. "You're crazy."

"Just...go drink water or something. I'll clean this up."

"I am perfectly capable of cleaning up my own messes."

He just looks at me.

"Okay, so not as well as you, but still."

He remains mute.

"Fine." I toss my hands in the air and carefully walk over the splotches of orange beneath me. As I leave the living room, I pause by a framed photograph of a lemon tree, sliding it off-center on the wall.

"I saw that," he calls after me.

"Just giving you something to do!" I smirk as I saunter into the bathroom.

"I'll give you something to do."

I cock my head at that, wondering if that was meant to be sexual or not. I'm thinking not. I flip the light switch up in the bathroom and scream. Even with the distance between us, I can hear him laughing. The mirror is covered in what looks like blood, spelling out R – E – D. I put my face close to it and sniff. Ketchup. What a waste of a good condiment.

"Not funny!"

"*So* funny!"

My breath leaves me in a whoosh as I slam upright in bed. Sweat causes my clothes to cling to me and the overactive thundering of my heart is slightly worrisome. Swiping damp hair from my face, I force myself to relax. The room is bathed in black and the evil red numbers on my clock boast that it's just after two in the morning. I wrap trembling arms around my midsection and close my eyes. It was just a dream. I know it was just a dream. Even so, I did not enjoy it. Not at all.

In my dream Graham disappeared. I don't know if he died, but it felt like he did. There was so much grief inside me, so much emptiness. The dampness on my face isn't only sweat, I realize as I sniffle. We were walking and laughing and then he was just *gone* and I knew I would never see him again. The thought of living in a world without Graham causes a painful ache in my chest. It feels suffocating, ever-growing, and endless. The compulsion to know he is okay is undeniable and I know I won't be able to sleep again until I see firsthand that he is breathing.

Tossing the blanket off me, I stumble from the room and down the short hallway to his. The door is closed and I lightly press my forehead against it, telling myself to go back to bed, telling myself he is okay. But the fear won't dissipate. I quietly push the door open and am enveloped in the scent I associate with Graham—clean clothes and faint cologne.

The bed is king-sized and located in the center of the room with a large window directly behind it. Our apartment building is located on the edge of town, so there isn't much civilization surrounding it. Because of this, Graham's window gives him an awesome view of small hills in varying shades of lime and emerald—my bedroom window gives me a view of the parking lot. Yeah, I totally got shafted that way. On the plus side, I'll be the first to know if anyone ever tries to steal my car.

He told me once he doesn't like walls on any side of him; that it makes him feel claustrophobic. I also know that he likes light colors in his room because he doesn't like the darkness, and when it is nighttime, everything seems black to him, which is why his sheets and all the furniture in the room are either white or pale wood. I know it took a lot for him to even tell me those details, so I never pushed to know more. But I wonder, a lot. What happened to him to make him fear those things?

I can hear the faint sound of him breathing, even and steady. "Graham?" I whisper, not wanting to startle him too bad, although I suppose entering his room in the middle of the night may be the wrong way to go about that.

He is sleeping on his stomach with his arms hugging his pillow to him, his face in profile to me. The white of the moon spotlights him. He looks so young—peaceful. I watch him rest, longing to caress his cheek. I realize I can't keep standing here staring at him. Imagine if he woke up and caught me? I am thinking he might be creeped out. I can't seem to force my limbs to take me from the room either. I don't want to go, and I know if I do, I won't be able to sleep, not unless Graham is beside me.

Unsure of what to do, I move to the other side of the bed and slide into it, the sheets soft against my skin. They're the expensive kind, with the bazillion thread count or whatever. I place my head on his pillow and feel safe next to him. If I could be with him every night like this, I know I could keep whatever demons he has from the past out of reach for him. I should write up a proposal saying exactly this. I could give it this catchy title: Why You Should Allow Me to Sleep in Your Bed. That wouldn't seem odd. Not at all.

"Kennedy?" he mumbles, feeling behind him.

I clasp his hand and squeeze. "Who else would be crawling into your bed in the middle of the night?"

"Good point. You okay?"

"Bad dream," I whisper back. "I'm okay now."

He immediately rolls toward me and gathers me into his arms. I go still, my breathing turning uneven. His arms are hard and warm around me, the bare skin and muscles of his upper body flush with me. A feather light kiss is pressed against my temple and I can almost convince myself that this is normal and natural for us. Because, intimacy between us actually has always been comfortable. A touch here, a hug, an absent kiss—not on the lips, of course, but we always seem to be physically aware of one another in some way. Maybe that isn't the proper protocol for roommates to have, but then, do I care?

"What was it?" he asks sleepily.

"Hmm?"

"Your dream. What was it?"

I press my cheek to his chest and squeeze him close to me. "Nothing." Only the tears that trickle from the corners of my eyes call me a liar.

His voice is suddenly alert when he demands, "Are you crying?"

"No!"

He moves away and the room is alive with light. Graham faces me, his lips turned down. The cloud of slumber still clinging to him in the form of half-lidded eyes and tousled hair adds a seductive element to him that makes me think of sex. Although, everything about him sort of does that.

"You never cry."

"Just because you don't see me cry doesn't mean I don't," I grumble, sitting up.

"What was the dream about? What happened in it that has you so upset?"

Stupid eyes. I dash a hand against them to halt the flow of the waterworks. "I lost you," I whisper.

The bed shifts and he is closer to me, the heat of his body scorching me. "What do you mean, you lost me?"

I look up and want to cry all over again. The tenderness on his face pulls at me at the same time it shreds me. "It's stupid. We were walking." I shake my head. "You were with me and then you weren't and I knew something terrible had happened to you. I didn't see you die or anything, but I just knew I wouldn't see you again. It's lame, I know," I say, taking a deep breath.

"It's not. Dreams can seem very real at times." His fingers trail down the side of my face and my eyes close as peace wisps through me, blooming in my veins. "Sometimes they are more real than we think they can be, or than we want them to be. But that's all they are; just dreams. You're okay. I'm okay. And…you're not going to lose me."

A half-smile takes over his mouth, but there is a tinge of sorrow to it. "Not unless you want to." He's staring at me, his eyes edged in a shade of green dark enough to be mistaken for black. He looks so serious, mature in a way only a person who truly understands themselves and their emotions would be able to pull off.

"I don't. I never want to lose you," I say with soft conviction.

When I notice the stillness to him, I think maybe I have said too much, but then his arms are around me again, hugging me tightly, and I think I said exactly the right thing.

The only time he lets me go is to turn the lamp off, and then I am cocooned within his arms once more. His chin rests on the top of my head, his strong arms holding me to him. Our lower halves don't touch, and I am not as saddened by this as I would have thought. It is okay for us to just be like this. It feels like he is gathering strength from me, or that I am his lifeline in a storm of black. I know, I really should have been a poet instead of a podiatrist's assistant. Why am I only figuring this out *now*?

"You know what I thought the first time I saw you?"

"That you couldn't believe someone as gorgeous as me existed?"

His grip tightens. "That I couldn't believe I'd gone so long without knowing you."

Every part of my being sighs. A contented smile takes over my lips as sleep beckons. "You know what I thought the first time I saw you?" I mumble under the lull of slumber.

"That you couldn't believe someone as gorgeous as me existed?"

My smile deepens. "Yep."

His soft laughter pulls me the rest of the way into the nothingness of sleep.

Sunbeams and the scent of java awaken me. I open my eyes to the sight of Graham and a cup of coffee; two of my favorite things. Slowly sitting up, I attempt to smooth down my hair and then give up. It is too thick and heavy to cooperate. I eye him, not understanding how he can get up so early every morning *and* be happy about it, but here he is. His work ensemble is in place and his hair is artfully out of place. Today he is being a rebel and wearing a white polo shirt. And the shadow of stubble on his jaw? Totally thigh-clenching.

I didn't hear the alarm clock go off, but that's because he never sets it. Graham subconsciously knows when it's time to wake up. It's almost weird, like, vampire-ish weird, only in reverse. The sun comes up and so does my roommate.

"Hi," he says, as he customarily does.

"Hi." I feel like maybe I should get out of his bed, but I don't really want to. I like it here. Only thing missing is Graham. Plus he doesn't seem too upset about me being in it, I would like to point out.

The coffee mug is outstretched toward me. "Did you sleep okay? No more bad dreams?"

"Yes. No. Thanks." I salute him with the cup before taking a sip. It is hot and smooth.

"Am I fun?"

His question surprises me enough that I choke on the coffee I was about to swallow. "What?" I gasp out once I can breathe again.

He shrugs, not looking at me. "You said you wanted to hang out with Blake because he was fun. Am I not fun? I mean, do you have fun with me?" When he raises his eyes to mine, they are darkened with insecurities that make my chest squeeze.

I set the mug down on the nightstand with a hand that has a tremble to it. "Of course you are, and I do, yes." Fun is a frivolous word, and while it is important to enjoy the time you spend with someone, there is so much more needed in a relationship than how entertained you are in someone's presence. There has to be a connection; an understanding.

Whoa. What has *happened* to me?

"But?"

I frown, still stuck on how reasonable I am being lately. "What?" I ask, blinking at him.

"I'm fun and you have fun with me, but?" The look on his face is one of determination, like he has convinced himself he can take whatever I am about to tell him.

With a shrug, I say, "But it isn't everything. It's good to have fun, don't get me wrong, but that can't be all there is. I mean, fun is good for a while, but even that will get boring after so long."

"How can fun get boring?"

"I don't know. Don't argue with me. Don't you have to go to work or something?"

Graham laughs. "Yeah. So do you. Are you doing anything afterward?"

"I thought I'd get my walk in and then vegetate."

"Want to do something after your walk, instead of being a slacker?"

"Only if it's boring instead of fun. And I'm good at being a slacker."

"Like, staring at a curtain blind kind of boring?"

"Exactly. That would be super slacker-ish. We should do that. Or we could contemplate why an ocean is called an ocean."

"We could stare at the fake plant in the living room."

I grin. "What about cleaning? That's always dull."

"I like cleaning."

"I know," I say with a sigh.

"Or we could go roller-skating."

My mouth opens and closes. A grin curves my lips. "That would be really boring, but I don't know if that qualifies as slacking. It might mess up my non-productive vibe."

"Sometimes you have to step out of the slacker box. You up for it?"

I squint my eyes and nod. "Yes. We should do that. I can take one for team and do something that requires physical movement."

He smiles back. "See you then." Pausing near the door, he says, "You look good there."

"Where?"

"In my bed."

Duuuuude.

The beat of my heart and my breaths take a little while to get back to normal after those parting words. I flop onto my back and stare at the ceiling, not sure how I am supposed to take what he just said. I mean, obviously he meant it—*how*, exactly? I am just full of answers this morning. A glance at the clock shows me I'm going to be late for work if I don't start moving my butt.

Forty-one minutes later, I walk outside into sunlight and heat, slipping sunglasses on to protect my eyes from my nemesis. Don't get me wrong—I love the sun; I just don't love it blinding me all the time. My hair is pulled up in a messy bun and I got black scrubs on today 'cause I'm badass like that. I chomp on an apple and wish I'd had time to eat something with more substance to it—like a doughnut. I could really go for a gooey, sugary, chocolate cream-filled one. Too bad I don't have time to stop at a gas station or I would so stock up. I take another bite of my apple as I cross the parking lot to my car, trying to trick myself into believing it is a delicious ball of carbohydrates and goodness. It doesn't work.

The sight of Blake leaning against my car falters my steps. I swallow with difficulty, although the chunk of apple in my mouth could be partly to blame—I really should have chewed that up better. He certainly knows how to make an impression; even the curl of his upper lip is a perfect mix of sardonic and sexy. The white t-shirt and dark jeans that mold to his muscular frame make me think he may have time-traveled from the fifties or sixties. A trail of smoke weaves up from the cigarette dangling between his lips, caressing his facial features like the loving hand of all that is naughty. Must he be so attractive? He shouldn't be, especially when he has a cancer stick in his mouth, but he manages to pull it off anyway.

"Kennedy," he greets, flicking his cigarette to the ground.

"That's littering."

"I'm a bad person. I litter."

"You know, you're really not."

He straightens with one dark eyebrow lifted.

"You want people to think you're a bad person, but it's all an act."

"You've learned this from knowing me all of two days?"

"It's closer to four now, and yes, I have. I also learned that you like to antagonize your brother—and apparently you don't know how to add." I cross my arms. "You don't want to date me. You're not even all that interested in me. You just want to piss Graham off for whatever reason and you're using me to do it."

"Now, see, that's where you're wrong. I mean, yeah, maybe I do like to muss up perfect Graham's life with his perfect behavior and perfect perfect, but I am interested in you. A lot."

"Perfect perfect?" I remark, my head spinning from his comment about his interest in me—his "a lot" interest in me.

He shrugs. "Maybe if I was as perfect as my brother, I would have come up with a better word."

"Why do you want to hurt him?" I ask in all seriousness, knowing I need to get going so I am not late for work, but desperately needing to know why the brothers are the way they are.

"I just told you he's perfect. Isn't that enough of a reason? And I don't want to hurt him," he answers slowly. "I just want to—I don't know."

"Get him to lose control? Aggravate him? Annoy him? Piss him off?"

"Maybe. I guess."

I hold out my hand. He gingerly puts his rough, warm one in mine. I shake it once before releasing it. "Congratulations. You accomplished what you set out to do. He lost control. He punched you. Now maybe you can move on to the next step of your evil brother plan."

"Evil brother plan?" His lips twitch and humor flashes briefly in his steel-shaded eyes.

"Or just, you know, try to get along while you're here. I mean, did you even really come here to spend time with Graham, or to just make him miserable for a few months?"

"Why not both?"

My lips thin. "What did he ever do to you? I'd really like to know."

"Nothing. Not enough. That's the problem." He steps back. "Anyway, I wanted to apologize for that." He gestures toward my collarbone. "The last thing I wanted was for you to get hurt."

I wave his apology away, more pressing matters than my health at hand (I know, I'm always sacrificing myself for those around me). Namely, letting him know how unfounded his views are.

"It was over ten years ago. You were a child. He was a child. You can't blame him for what happened. It wasn't his fault. If it was anyone's fault, it was your dad's. That's who you should be pissed at. Graham didn't stay away because he didn't want to be with you; he stayed away because he couldn't stand to be around your dad," I tell him heatedly.

His expression closes. "He told you about that?"

I shouldn't have said anything. It isn't any of my business. My protective nature toward Graham just went into growly status and now Blake is glaring at me because I opened my big mouth when I shouldn't have. I shift my feet, the heat of the sun and my own conscience making me uncomfortably warm. That could also be the black garbs I smartly decided to wear on such a blistering day.

"What else did he tell you?"

"He only told me parts. I just know parts. That's all."

He mutters, "Unbelievable," and shows me his taut back.

My eyes, of course, have to look down and admire his rear. They have a will of their own, clearly. A will not intelligent enough to look away before he turns, showing me what's on the other side of his body in the same spot. My face burns and I jerk my head to the side, tearing my eyes away from where they want to be.

"I know, it's impressive."

I want to die. My eyelids slowly slide shut.

"I didn't decide to get my own place because of Graham. That was all you," he finally tells me, starting to walk away as I force my eyes open again.

"What does that mean?"

"You'll find out."

"You're confusing!"

"You're hot," he calls back.

"You don't know me!"

"I will."

112

Flustered, I clumsily unlock my car door—meaning I fight with the key to get it into the lock and scrape my knuckles on the door handle—and fling my purse and half-eaten apple inside, not seeing where the fruit lands. I want to shout out that I love his brother, but I have this suspicion he'll just say he doesn't care. I notice an elderly lady from two apartments down watching me with avid interest, her rheumy eyes flickering to Blake and back to me. She's standing near the apartment building entrance, wearing a yellow and brown checkered housecoat and nylons. I turn away, really hoping that isn't me when I am her age. I could see myself being that lonely, nosy old lady with no fashion sense. As if I needed that thought to make my morning any better.

Being a Monday and all, the day wasn't terrible. The highlight was when I opened the cleaning supply closet and caught Dr. Olman and Sally making out. Busted! At least they were clothed, so I don't think there will be any long term trauma to my brain or eyes. At least, I can say I wasn't instantly blinded, so that has to be a good sign. I guess I won't really know until I attempt to make out with a guy, preferably Graham, and see if I am bombarded by visions of old people groping or not. I should ask him to be my guinea pig and test it out.

It was kind of funny when Dr. Olman said Sally got locked in the closet and he was trying to help her get out, but then he got locked inside too. There is no lock on the door. And even if there was, how would he first enclose himself in the closet and then lock it? I suppose it depends on what kind of lock there is, but still, it is a moot point, as *there is no lock on the door.* I tried telling him that and then he said the door must have somehow gotten stuck. Yeah. And then they just decided to pass the time by making out. Makes perfect sense. It's what I would do in the same situation. Well, if Graham was nearby.

My cell phone buzzes as I get into the sauna-like atmosphere of my car. I keep the door open so I can at least breathe and pull the phone from my purse. With a groan, I answer. "Hey, Dad."

Phoebe waves as she heads for her vehicle and I nod in acknowledgment, waiting to see what awesomeness my father is about to bestow upon me.

"Have you seen the TV remote?"

Now, this would be a strange question to ask someone that doesn't live with you and hasn't been to your house in over a week, but this is my father we're talking about. Nothing with him surprises me.

"Why would you think I would know where your remote control is?" Exasperation has put an implied sigh in my voice.

"You used it the last time you were here."

"Haven't you used it since then?"

There is a pause. "Maybe."

I rub my perspiring forehead and crank the AC higher, grudgingly shutting the door so all the cool air doesn't seep out whenever it decides to become cool. The fake cherry smell of the car is potent, reminding me of cough syrup, and I eye the cherries swaying from the rear-view mirror, seriously thinking about ripping them down and putting myself out of my misery.

"So then it would make more sense that you would know where it is," I explain slowly.

"Maybe Graham knows. He was here with you."

"I have to go now. I need to go walking."

"Walking. Walking is overrated," he scoffs.

"You're right. We should all never walk again. That'll show our legs."

"Stop by when you're done and see if you can find the remote. Bring Graham."

"I have my own plans with Graham after I go for a walk."

"What are you two doing?"

"Roller-skating."

My dad laughs. "See you after your walk."

He just assumes I'll pick him over my walk, like he's more important. I mean, sure, his sperm helped create me, but it isn't like my fitness isn't important too. Tightly clenching the phone in my hand, I force a calming breath and remind myself all the reasons I have to be thankful for my dad.

Number one: Without him, I would not exist.

Number two: If I didn't exist, I wouldn't know Graham.

Number three: There is no number three.

I put the car in drive, realize if I hit the accelerator I'll drive through the front door of the office, and put the car in reverse instead. I call Graham as I drive. I know, shame on me. But it isn't illegal! Although, with the way I drive, maybe it should be—for me anyway.

"On your way home?" his voice greets. *Home.* His home and my home are the same home. Deep sigh.

"Yeah, but I have a favor to ask."

"Okay." This is so like Graham—ready to do anything needed of him without hesitation.

"It's sort of bad." I pull out in front of a Nissan and wave when they honk at me. It isn't like we crashed.

He laughs. "I doubt it's that bad. What do you need?"

"My dad called me. He wants us to come over."

"All right." Answered immediately and without any snark. He is a good man.

"I'm supposed to find his remote while you get to endure his worshipful eyes admiring your every move."

"I can handle that."

"I know. My dad loves you. He wishes you were his son instead of me."

"I don't think that's it." He pauses. "And you're not his son."

"Oh. Right. Silly me. How could I forget that?"

"It'll be fine. I promise."

I nod even though he can't see me, feeling better just from our short conversation. "We'll probably be there a while. I don't know about roller-skating tonight. I'm sorry. I suck."

"You don't suck." *Do not respond to that, Kennedy.* "I like your family," he adds.

"I know. You're weird."

"I like you too."

"Exactly my point."

I pull the car into the parking lot of the apartment building and turn it off. Only the key won't turn off. I glance down at the gear shifty thing and note that it isn't in park. Muttering to myself, I put it in park and it shuts off.

"What was that?"

"I forgot to put the car in park again."

His laughter washes over me and I find myself grinning. "I take it you're at the apartment?"

"Yeah. Where are you?"

"I'm pulling into the parking lot now."

I get out of my car just as he pulls up beside me. His smile is wide and unburdened. It is the usual Graham smile. I have missed seeing it. Honestly, I have missed him during the time we have been apart. I can almost delude myself into thinking we are dating, in love, and this is a normal happy day for us. But I am not that far gone, so I have to accept that the dream is not reality.

He bumps his shoulder against mine as he reaches me. His cheeks are tinged red from being outside all day and he smells like sunshine. "I'll get ready while you go for a walk. Want me to pick anything up from the store to bring?"

"Well, my mom will probably make something for supper."

"I should get something then?"

"A whole meal would be nice."

We walk toward the apartment building. I am hoping to get inside before I melt.

"Do you think she suspects?"

The door opens, cool air flowing out and coating me in a layer of bliss. "That she is a terrible cook and we get out of eating her food by bringing our own food all the time?" I tilt my head and watch as he unlocks the apartment door. "Nah. I mean, if she was going to figure it out, she would have at some point during my teenage years. I was never hungry when she asked 'cause I'd always already eaten. I lived on popcorn and fast food."

"While I'm thinking about it…there's this thing at work and I wondered if you wanted to go." Graham tosses his keys in the red square dish on the kitchen counter, not looking at me.

"A thing? What thing?"

Rubbing the back of his neck, he says, "Like bring a date for a fun-filled day of golfing and drinking extravaganza thing."

I blink at him, but he still isn't looking at me. "Date?" I echo.

Graham is *blushing*. I have never been witness to such an occurrence before. "I mean, yeah. That's what it's called, but we're just friends, so…it won't really be a date. But I thought you might have fun. I know you've never golfed before and I could teach you some things. You might like it. Plus there will be drinking and I know you like drinking. I don't want to go alone and you're the only one who will make it bearable, the only one I can imagine having any fun with. If you don't want to go, I understand. But it's mandatory for me. I can ask someone else—"

"I'm going," I practically snap at him. There will be no other female companion for Graham, not if I can help it.

Relief transforms his features and his shoulders relax. "Thank you. It's next weekend. Sorry for the short notice, but I just found out about it today."

I turn to leave the kitchen. "Sure. No problem. It's a non-date date."

A strong hand wraps around my bicep, halting my steps. "You were crying last night."

116

I go still, unable to face him, not when he just threw that at me. "Yes."

His hand drops from my arm as I face him. "For me."

"Yes."

"No one's cried over me before." His green eyes are dark with emotion.

"Do you *want* people to cry over you or something?" I'm not sure where this is going.

He studies me, then shrugs. "It's not that. I just don't think I've ever mattered enough to anyone for that to even be an issue."

"You've had lots of girlfriends," I argue.

"Nothing serious."

"You have a mother."

"Mothers don't count. They have to love you."

"Not necessarily."

He just looks at me.

"Come on," I scoff. "You're a great guy—good-looking, you have a huge heart, you're funny, you are an extremely likable guy—and loads of people care about you."

"You think all of that about me?"

Crap. I said too much, revealed too much. I shift my feet and say, "Not just me. Lots of people."

"I only care what *you* think about me," he says softly. His hands move up to cup my jaw. I watch him watching me, his face so close. I focus on the dip of his full upper lip, wondering what it would feel like pressed against mine. "I am constantly confused by you, always surprised, and continually shown why you are so very special to me."

"Because I cried over you?"

"Because you care enough about me *to* cry." His eyes search my face as he steps back. "Sometimes I feel like we're trapped by our own fears and doubts. Do you ever feel that way?"

Fricking right I do. "No. Never." I smirk so he knows I am not being serious.

The smile he reciprocates is faint. "You should go, get your walking in while you feel like it."

"Right. Because, as we both know, that feeling won't last long. I'll see you soon."

He nods absently, already turning away from me.

I walk to my room to change my clothes with an impossibly heavy pressure on my chest. Dare I have a trickle of hope that Graham possibly cares about me the same way I do him? I don't know if I can allow myself to do so. If I am wrong, my heart will be broken, and even though I have never endured that before, I have this feeling it will be unpleasant and sort of unlikely to move on from. Like, if the world ran out of coffee, devastation.

I slowly undress, tugging on black stretchy shorts and a red top. I don't know if there is true love for everyone, or soul mates, or that one person who is your perfect match. I don't know if I believe in any of that, but I know that there is a bond between us that I have never had with anyone else. Graham will always be there for me when I need him to be. He will support me and any decision I make; whether it is a good one or a bad one. He understands me and all of my quirks and he still wants to be around me. I tighten the rubber band in my hair and get my shoes. I waited twenty-one years and some months to meet someone like Graham and the thought of being without him is unbearable.

When I get to the living room, Graham is waiting for me, grinning. He holds up a hot pink t-shirt and my eyes drink it in, warmth spreading through me. It reads 'Wine-oceros' and has a cartoon rhinoceros standing on its hind legs holding a wine glass. My eyes sting and I lunge for him, squeezing him to me.

"I take it you like it." He hugs me back.

"I love it," I whisper. "Did you have it made up yourself?"

"I did."

I blink my eyes against the possibility of tears as I pull away, staring at my roommate. "You totally tossed all of my wine sayings out the door with this shirt. You know that, right? You are the king. I gladly admit it."

His smile widens, his face shining with it. "'Bout time." He brushes hair from my face. "Go on. I'll see you soon."

I nod, quickly hugging the shirt before setting it on the couch. "Thank you."

"Have a good walk."

"Don't tell me what to do," I say by the door.

Graham shakes his head, a grin holding to his lips. "Was that necessary?"

"I don't know, is Kim Kardashian necessary?"

"Good point."

As I walk, I can't keep a smile off my face. He knows me like no one else does. And I'm glad of that. I wouldn't want anyone else to get me the way Graham does. I realize I understand what he said last night about going so long without knowing me. It feels like we have always been, though we have only been in each other's lives such a short time. But time does not define emotion.

And I cannot imagine my life without him, no matter how far into the future I look. I inhale deeply.

That is a terrifying thought.

chapter eight

"**a**re you stalking me?" I demand as I head toward Blake. After my walk, I hopped in my car and boogied over to the bank to deposit a paycheck I'd forgotten about. Strange how something like that could happen. It isn't as if I have loads of money lying around. I'm blaming it on the polluted air, messing with all of our heads and stuff. It could be true. You just don't know.

He straightens from the wall of the stone building known as a bank. He is wearing his usual plain clothes, but today he livened up his ensemble by wearing a dark blue shirt instead of his customary non-colors. "I saw your car. Knew the plates were yours."

I don't even know my own license plates. "Right. You're stalking me. Should I be worried?"

"Why would you be worried? I'm cute. Cute guys are always harmless."

"Cute guys are the most lethal, and who said you were cute?"

"You did. With your eyes." His voice is purposely low, just the hint of seduction to it.

I roll said eyes, giving him a gentle shove. "Yeah. My eyes are always getting me into trouble." As opposed to my mouth. Yes. That's it.

"I live across the street." He nods toward a brown two-story house. "Upstairs. It's an efficiency apartment, but it works."

"Could you even say it's efficient?" I lift a single eyebrow.

"Adequate, actually. I like adequate."

I nod in understanding, though I am faking it. I don't really get anything about Blake. He's sort of weird—more than me, even. "Where do you go to college at anyway?"

"University of Illinois."

"What are you going for?" My tone is brusque, but I don't know much about Blake, and I guess the only way I'll find anything out is by being demanding. Why I want to know about him so badly still isn't completely clear to me.

"Why?"

"Call me nosy." He really better not.

He hesitates. "Child psychology," he finally answers. "I, uh, had a pretty messed up childhood, as I'm sure Graham was nice enough to inform you of, and I want—I want to help kids if I can, help them so they don't make the same mistakes I made, or maybe help them to understand why they do."

I just stare at him as a barrage of emotions hit me. Sadness for the boy he once was and the errors he made and can never undo, respect that he is doing something so worthy, and empathy that he felt the need to waver before telling me.

"You should be proud of yourself," I say when the silence gets too uncomfortable.

"Oh, I am. Can't you tell?" I wonder if he ever tires of the mocking tone. But then, do I?

Jiggling my keys, I search for something else to say, something not quite so serious. "How was work? You're at the golf course, right?"

"Yeah. First day. I got to watch a really boring movie and follow people around. Best time ever. Most of the day I was actually considering stealing a bottle of booze from the bar just to counter the dullness of it all. Which, hey, I might as well confess all my evil deeds, right? I'm sure Graham told you about that too."

I don't answer.

He runs a hand through his dark hair before returning his eyes to me. "What are you doing tonight?"

There is bleakness to him that pulls at me; restlessness to his bearing that warns of possible danger—not to me or anyone else, but to him. I wonder if it is a daily struggle to stay away from alcohol and drugs. I wonder what thoughts he has and how he manages to overcome the temptation. And I know he needs someone, because in spite of his tough exterior, there is a noticeable crack in it.

"I have to go to my mom and dad's. My dad lost the remote and seems to think I know where it is."

"Want some company?"

He isn't my responsibility to entertain or keep out of trouble. If anything, he is Graham's, but because of their bullheadedness, they aren't exactly hanging out together like they should be. So what do I do? Do I tell him to come along, and if I do, do I tell him about Graham going as well?

Spinning the situation around in my head, I come to a decision. It entails me remaining in my workout clothes and possibly smelling bad, but if that is what it takes to get the brothers together and talking, then I am willing to forfeit my hygiene for the greater good—just this once.

"Yes. I do. You can ride with me."

"Let's go."

Grinning, I send a text to Graham asking him to meet me at my parents' house instead of me picking him up because I have girly errands to run later—like buying feminine products and whatnot. He replies that he'll leave now. I laugh, knowing he never wants to be in the feminine product aisle of a store ever again. There was an emergency once and he actually had to go to the store to buy me stuff. He was horrified, but put a brave face on and did it anyway. He had to text me pictures to get the right kind. It must have been awful for him in the store. He mentioned people giving him odd looks as he snapped photos of pads and tampons, but did he complain? No. Now that is a man to be admired.

Once we're settled in the car and on our way, it doesn't take Blake long to comment, "You're a terrible driver. Has anyone ever told you that? You didn't even stop at the stop sign."

"I paused." So I am not the most cautious, law abiding, observant person. I did, however, get my driver's license on my first try, unlike the majority of girls in my class. And, has anyone died yet while riding with me?

No.

"You swiped the curb when you took the last turn."

"The road was narrow there!" I turn the volume up on the radio as 'What Now' by Rihanna plays. I actually do like this song, but I also want to drown out my driving instructor's criticisms.

I glance at him to find him grinning.

"You totally just coasted through that stop sign. Again."

"The stop was implied. And would you be quiet? I can't concentrate when you keep critiquing my driving skills."

"What driving skills? And if I shut up, will you suddenly acquire some?"

Luckily for Blake, we are at my parents' house. Or not, because a scowl darkens his face when he notices his brother's truck. "You forgot to mention Graham was going to be here."

"Did I?" I tilt my head and try to look innocent.

He narrows his eyes at me, but says nothing more, getting out of the car and shutting the door more exuberantly than is warranted.

"Hey. Only I can abuse my car." I meet him at the sidewalk and point to the sage green house with white trim. "Home sweet home." There is even a mat in front of the door saying exactly this.

As we walk to the door, I look over my shoulder at him. "I wouldn't eat any of the food, just to warn you. Unless it comes pre-made from a store, that is. And even then, proceed with caution."

He stares back at me.

"Kennedy!" My mom engulfs me in flowery perfume and fleshy arms as I walk through the door. I am used to the decorating theme of the house, but I imagine it may be a shock for Blake. I don't look back to check. He doesn't want to see the den, I already know this. It's covered in Kennedy men and women, pure proof that my father is fanatical about the famous family.

I hug her back, spitting curly blond hair out of my mouth. "Hey, Mom."

My mother is affectionate. My dad—not so much. He nods at me in greeting as I disengage my arms from the woman that birthed me.

I wrinkle my nose. "Is something burning?"

"*Shit.*" My mom turns her head in the direction of the kitchen as she hollers, "Graham! Can you get the chicken from the oven?"

"On it!" comes from the kitchen. The oven door bangs shut and a curse word rings through the air. Apparently both of the brothers have a thing with slamming doors today.

"You didn't injure yourself, did you, dear?" she shouts next to my ear.

I step away with a ringing ear and introduce Blake. "This is Graham's brother, Blake. This is Jim and Alice Somers. I'm going to go see if Graham needs first aid." Or mouth to mouth. It is my civic duty.

"Graham doesn't need you crying over him like a girl."

This from my dad, which I ignore. I don't point out that I am a girl, 'cause he would just grunt like he isn't too sure about that. I don't understand him and don't think I ever will. He pushes me away in some ways, but in others, he tries to pull me back. I wanted Barbie dolls for Christmas and I got tractors instead. I asked for a pretty dress for my ninth birthday and I got a baseball glove. It isn't that I didn't enjoy playing with toy farm equipment or participating in sports, but his view was that I had to choose one, and it had to be what he wanted.

Apparently I was difficult even while in the womb and it was advised that my mom not have more children after me, so this is what they got—me. Maybe my dad plays a large part of why I am the way I am, but that is a serious, deep subject and I tend to stay away from those as much as I can, so I stop thinking about it.

Graham turns as I enter the rose-themed kitchen. He doesn't say anything. He looks at my face and then he gathers me into his arms, pressing a firm kiss to my forehead. He has been around my father and me enough to know the situation. He's seen my old bedroom. I couldn't have purple walls like I wanted or anything frilly in my bedroom, so as a form of semi-rebellion, I had nothing. I painted the walls white and kept anything that would have given the room a sense of being mine out of it.

I went through school doing what I had to do to pass, but I never got involved in any extracurricular activities or excelled at anything—not just because of my dad, but also because I was never bit by the school spirit bug. I did become fluent in sarcasm during the four years of high school and did my share of partying.

That should count for something.

"Did you burn your hand?" I ask, pulling away.

Most people put decorations of fruit in their kitchen, or bright, cheery colors—not my mom. The wallpaper is white with tiny pink roses for the print. The appliances and furniture are white and the curtains that grace the windows are pale pink. It even smells like roses in the room; over the scent of burnt bird, that is. It's...I don't know...it reminds me of movies with insane old people in them that seem really nice, but actually eat children.

"Yeah." He lifts his hand to show the blotch of red on the back of it. "I think I'll live, but there is no saving the chicken."

I glance at the oven timer. "There are two hours left on that thing."

"I brought pizzas."

With a smile curving my lips, I lightly pat his cheek. "Good boy."

"Hate to interrupt, but...did you know there are dead animals on the walls of your living room?" Blake casually asks, leaning against the wall near the doorway.

"What are you doing here?" Graham demands.

"Kennedy invited me."

A dark look flashes across Graham's features as he turns to me. "What the hell?"

Taking a deep breath, I move to stand between the brothers, preparing myself for the speech I am about to give. Obviously it will be a good one. "So here's the thing—you two are brothers. Things happened when you were kids that you had no control over, by no fault of either of you, and you haven't seen each other for a long time, but...Blake's here now. Obviously there was a reason for you wanting to come here, Blake, and Graham, there was a reason you agreed to it."

"You orchestrated us both being here, at your parents' house of all places, so we could hash things out?" His voice is incredulous, as is the look my roommate sends my way.

"Yeah, so?"

"You are such a deviant," Blake murmurs.

"I'll act as mediator," I say, ignoring the younger Malone.

"You really want to do this now? Here?" Graham crosses his arms. "Do you honestly think this is the best place for us to talk about our *feelings?*"

"I hate that word. It makes me feel unclean," his brother adds.

"Foul even," Graham murmurs.

"Feelings is a loathsome word."

"It should be removed from the dictionary."

I look between the two of them, noting the similar way they stand and their perturbed expressions that match so well. "See? You can get along. You just agreed with each other."

"Yeah. About *you*," Graham points out.

"The one thing we have in common."

His expression turning stormy, Graham suddenly asks in a not so nice tone of voice, "How's your arm?"

"About as well as your busted lip, I imagine."

"Whoa." I raise my hands and wave them around. "Stop. Stop with the snippy comments." I rub my forehead, feeling a headache approaching. "Okay, this is what we're going to do...we're going to make the pizzas, find that stupid remote control for my dad, and then we're going to sit in the backyard and talk. No one leaves until something positive happens."

"Something positive would be us not killing each other," Blake informs me.

"Therefore we're already being positive," Graham states.

"Yeah. None of this is really necessary."

"Fine. How's this? If you two don't figure out a way to get past whatever is up both of your asses, I won't be talking to either one of you."

"I love it when you talk dirty." Graham unwraps a frozen pizza and carefully places it on an oven rack. "You'd miss me too much and you know it." A moment later there is a second pizza baking beside the first.

He is so right, but it doesn't matter. "I will somehow find a way to survive," I tell him.

Blake snorts.

"You'd play sappy love songs and woefully stare at a picture of me," he continues.

Maybe. "I'd eat gobs of doughnuts and curse you."

He laughs, reaching out to tug on my ponytail. "How is that different from any other time I irritate you?"

"I'm going to find the remote. I'll be back." My lips are twitching with the need to smile and I lose the battle as I walk past Blake. He watches me with a thoughtful look on his face, his gaze shifting to his brother as I leave the kitchen.

"Such nice men. That Blake boy is as sweet as Graham," my mom tells me. She is, and I am in no way exaggerating, knitting something that looks like a pink bra.

"Yeah. That's exactly what I think. Really sweet guys, both of them." I plop down on the opposite end of the couch from my dad and feel something dig into my behind. "Really, Dad?" I fish the remote control out and toss it toward him.

"What are you making?" I ask my mom.

"It's a scarf." She proudly holds it up for my perusal, her pink-cheeked face happy.

He points the magical contraption at the television. "That remote wasn't there a few days ago."

"You're right. It was probably in your hand."

He grunts, scratching the back of his head. "Which one is your boyfriend?"

My face catches fire. "Um…neither?"

"Then why is your face so red?"

"Is the chicken almost done?" my mom asks, humming a tune that sounds disturbingly like 'The Wheels on the Bus'.

"Oh yeah. It's good and done," I comment. "Who's the scarf for?" I really hope it isn't me.

"Your grandpa Jack."

I decide to point out the obvious. "It's pink."

She shrugs. "He said he didn't care what color it was as long as it kept him warm on the lawnmower. And pink is my favorite color."

Okay, so I should probably mention something—other than the obvious fact that my parents are loopy. My mother's dad can't drive. It isn't that he *can't* drive, but, well, he's been pulled over so many times for driving while intoxicated that he had his license taken away—indefinitely. Maybe forever. I'm not really sure how that all works. I mean, if you get, like, eighty tickets, is there any hope of ever legally driving again? He drives a lawnmower around town year-round, and it gets cold during the winter, but I guess the pink bra-like scarf is going to take care of that now.

Hooray.

"Graham brought pizzas over. I don't understand how that boy can eat so much."

"Apparently he wants to live," my dad mumbles, replacing his empty beer can for a full one from the pack sitting on the floor beside the couch.

"He didn't want to imposition you, Mom," I hurriedly interject, giving my dad a look.

"Such a nice boy. I'm glad you two are friends."

"Yep. We're the best of buds."

"Want to go fishing this weekend?" my dad asks.

"No."

"Maybe Graham wants to go."

"I don't think he does."

"Maybe you could ask him."

"Graham!" I shout.

He comes sprinting from the kitchen, a worried look on his face. "What's wrong?"

"Want to go fishing with my dad this weekend?"

He gives me an odd look, turning to my dad. "Sure. Saturday good?"

"Pick me up at seven."

"All right." He returns his gaze to me. Probably because I am exceptional to look at. "Are you going?"

"No."

"She's being a girl. Used to go fishing with me."

I scowl and cross my arms. "Because you made me. And I am a girl."

"You had fun. Took you all the time during the summer up until you were fourteen and got strange ideas about makeup and clothes." My dad looks at Graham. "Ask your brother if he wants to go."

This perks me up. "That is a great idea." Nothing like the brothers spending quality time with one another and possibly being mutually annoyed by my father—everyone needs to bask in the awesomeness that is Jim Somers at least once in their lifetime. I ignore the glare Graham sends my way and hop to my feet, brushing against him as I enter the kitchen.

Blake is looking out the windowed door that leads to the backyard. "I take it I'm going fishing."

"Are you opposed to it?"

He glances over his shoulder at me, a wry grin on his face. "I can handle it. I haven't been fishing since I was ten. Who knows, it might even be fun." He pauses. "You're right, you know."

"Duh." I wait a beat. "What am I right about?"

Turning around to face me, he tells me, "About Graham and me. I did come here to get to know him better before I leave the country. This is our last chance at being brothers. I shouldn't let anything get in the way of that."

"Right."

His grin deepens. "But it would be so much fun to let it."

I grab oven mitts and finesse the pizzas out of the oven, ignoring that comment and the way my pulse careened from it. "Are you going to the golf course thing next weekend?"

"Are you asking me out?"

Snorting, I reply, "You so wish."

"But you'll be there?"

"Yes." I hand the pizza cutter to Blake. "I always cut myself."

One dark eyebrow lifted, he begins slicing the pizzas. "How do you manage to do that with a pizza cutter of all things?"

I think about it for a minute, watching his arm muscles bunch and release as he cuts away. "You know, I'm really not sure. I'm just gifted that way."

"Did you find your dad's remote?"

'It was up my ass' probably isn't the best thing to say here, so I just nod.

He sets the pizza cutter down and faces me, his stormy eyes drilling into mine. "I know you're attracted to me."

I blink. That's all I am able to do. He did not just say that—only he did.

"I can tell," he goes on. "You watch me. A lot. You wouldn't watch me so much if you weren't interested."

Again no words form. When I open my mouth to deny what he has just said, a squeak leaves me. Then I start to stutter. "That…you…that…"

"If you're so in love with my brother, why are you drooling over me? And trust me, you are."

"I never…" I inhale slowly, deeply, and begin again. "I never said I was in love with your brother," I hiss, eyeing the doorway to the living room. "And you're good-looking. Sorry for noticing."

I move to leave, but his strong hands catch me around the waist and pull me back. Lean, rough fingers slide up the sides of my waist and then fall away. It was the barest of touches and yet it caused flames to ignite inside me.

I whip around to glare at him. "What are you doing?"

He looks much too calm as he crosses his arms. "Just proving a point."

Graham, of course, chooses this moment to reappear. His gaze shifts from his brother to me. "What's going on?"

"I had to save Kennedy from cutting herself. She thanked me with tongue."

My mouth drops open, his words making common sense things like speaking and moving impossible, but Graham doesn't seem to have the same problem. "You asshole," he growls, striding for his brother.

Blake straightens, a satisfied smirk on his mouth. He catches my eye and his grin deepens. "It's just too easy."

Exasperation replaces the shock of seconds ago. I grab Graham's arm. At first he resists, but after a moment, stops trying to get to his brother. "Why must you two turn into idiots every time we're all within the same vicinity? It's getting old. I mean, it's obvious Blake is just saying things to piss you off and it's obvious you're going to react all crazy each time he does. Why can't you figure this out, Graham? Where's your head?"

Blake opens his mouth, but his brother snarls, "Don't even think about saying anything," and he closes it back up. His chest expanding with a deep breath, Graham says to me, "You're right. I don't know why I'm getting so worked up about things lately."

"I do," is his brother's smug reply.

I watch my roommate glare a million wordless threats at his brother before he says stiffly, "I think I'll pass on the brotherly bonding and pizza. I'll see you back at the apartment."

He leaves the room, and after glancing my way, Blake says, "I'll catch a ride with him. And I can't wait for you to see me again."

"He won't give you a ride."

"I think he will." Striding confidently from the room, he poofs into nothingness like he was never here.

I look to the pizza, thinking, *Why am I always left with food?* And then I eat it. Because, I mean, it looks sad sitting on the counter all uneaten and such, and yummy, and you shouldn't waste food.

I get out of the shower and dress in pale purple pajama pants and a lime green top, low playing music reaching me through the thin bathroom door. Graham wanted to keep our bathroom gender friendly, so it's shaded in tans and creams. I brush my hair, trying to pick out the tune. Graham loves music and his tastes are diverse; ranging from country to alternative to rock and almost anything else. Even so, he has never liked a song I didn't like as well. Clearly he has phenomenal taste in music.

My hand pauses and a smile curves my lips. It sounds like 'Wonderful Tonight' by Eric Clapton.

Upon opening the bathroom door, cool air passes over me and I follow the sound of the melody. I stop just inside the living room. Graham stands in the middle of the room, looking down with a frown on his face. His shoulders are set with an edge of weariness. I want to hug him and erase whatever is troubling him.

As I study him, he glances up, some of the darkness clearing from his eyes. The faintest of smiles touches his lips. "Hi."

"Hi."

Silently he holds a hand out to me and I don't even hesitate in going to him. He clasps my left hand within his calloused right, the other hand resting on my waist. I slide my hand to his shoulder and feel it tense beneath my palm. He steps forward as I go back, we move to the side in accordance, and then move the opposite way; moving so smoothly in sync, the dance seems graceful. This isn't ballroom dancing, but it isn't exactly shuffling either.

At the 'blond' reference in the song, he smiles down at me. At the 'beautiful lady' part, he squeezes my hand. Thoughts really aren't forming in my head, but there is this feeling of surreal euphoria. My chest is tight with emotion as his eyes steadily gaze into mine. They do not falter from mine once, and in a way, our locked eyes remind me of our friendship. Unwavering, without doubt, and whole. Well, it used to be anyway.

This is the first time we've danced. I mean, we've goofed around dancing, but this is the first time we've slow danced. This is big to me. Like, having a hard time breathing and accepting this as real, big. I worry I will ruin whatever is happening between us if I talk, so I don't. I move, and I watch, and I feel. The song is over much too quickly and we go still, waiting a beat before releasing one another and stepping away.

Graham smiles. "I feel wonderful tonight."

"Is it because you're drinking?"

The smile widens and touches his eyes. "No. I'm not drinking."

"Really? 'Cause you were swaying back and forth during our really long hug."

"That's called dancing."

I cock my head. "Are you sure?"

He winks at me before turning toward the kitchen. "Popcorn and hot chocolate?"

"And 'Golden Girls'!" I call after him.

Graham halts, turning to give me a look. "Just this one time."

"Times a million."

Shaking his head, he continues into the kitchen and I settle into the couch to watch some awesomesauce old chicks rule from the television screen. As I'm flipping through the channels with the remote, something niggles at me. I frown when I realize what it is. Graham hasn't called me Ken in days, and not just that, but every time he does refer to me by any part of my name, it is the full three syllables. I wonder why?

I get up to help him. Or rather, ogle him and hand him a utensil upon request. The scent of melted butter and popping corn seeds greets me upon entering the kitchen—as does his smoking hot body and gorgeous face. Graham broke out our air popper tonight. I guess 'cause it's healthy or something. It's strange, and probably wrong, how I think of everything as 'ours' and 'we' because, really, most of the stuff here is his, but that's not the only reason. It's more because one day everything I consider 'ours' and warrants a 'we' reference may someday be someone else's to have instead of me—just like Graham.

It makes me sad. I hate being sad. You know what else I hate? Glass ketchup bottles. Those stinking commercials act like it's a glorious occasion to have to bang the heck out of the bottom of one to get a drop of ketchup, but I really just find it a waste of precious seconds better spent on eating.

A smile is sent my way as he heats up milk for the cocoa. I stand beside him, wanting any excuse to be close to him. Our arms are touching and he doesn't move away—I don't either. In fact, there is stillness to him as though he is savoring my nearness. Ridiculous, I know. I can smell his clean scent through the popcorn and chocolate aroma of the room. I have a compulsion to lower my face the few inches it will take for it to reach his chest, but I quickly shove the impulse aside.

I hop onto the counter with my knees next to his arm. Something sweet and gooey flows through me—possibly love, possibly delusion. I swing my legs, asking, "What did Blake want to talk to you about?"

He spoons real cocoa and sugar into the dark blue mugs, not looking at me as he says, "Something I don't want to talk to you about."

My chest stings—or maybe that's my pride. "Why not?"

Mouth pulled down as he glances at me, he stirs the liquid around with a spoon. He does the same to the other cup and sets the spoon in the sink before answering. "Because it was stupid."

"If it was stupid, then why can't you just tell me?"

"Kennedy—drop it."

"Why do you keep calling me Kennedy?"

"It's your name."

I hop down from the counter and pick up one of the mugs. It warms my fingers and I blow on it before taking a sip. I think I could love him for his cocoa making skills alone. It's sugary, chocolaty perfection that is smooth on the tongue and throat as it goes down.

"I realize that," I tell him. "But you always call me Ken."

"I thought that annoyed you." He won't look at me, which is odd.

"Did that ever stop you before?" Too many seconds go by, and as I am an impatient person, I continue. "So? Why haven't you lately?"

"Is this a big deal?" His eyes finally meet mine and there is a serious cast to them I don't understand.

"Well, I think it sanctions proper inspection." Ooooh, big, sophisticated words. I mentally pat myself on the back.

Half his mouth lifts and lowers, humor lightening his eyes before disappearing. "It just..." He trails off, drumming his fingertips on the countertop.

I reach out and place my hand over his, halting his jittery movement. As I look at his profile he looks at our hands; mine smaller and paler than his, but steadier and calmer. "It just what?"

When he raises his head, my pulse skips. "It doesn't fit anymore."

Not knowing what to think of that response, I ask the next one of two logical questions: "Since when?"

"I don't know. It just doesn't."

Most important question: "Why?"

Finally he looks at me full on. I want to say his features are stiff with grimness, but I don't know if that is what it is. Regret would be the correct term, I believe. He looks like he lost something and he isn't sure how it happened. "I think I was seeing you one way when I should have been seeing you another. But it was all I knew, all I expected, and I just couldn't look beyond that."

"You're being extremely vague."

His lips thin. "Blake showing up has changed everything, even you. Or maybe it hasn't. Maybe I'm the one who's changed. I don't know." His eyes lift to mine. "But now I feel like it's too late."

"It is sort of late. Work and everything tomorrow. You know," I agree, purposely being obtuse.

It's like I never even spoke. He stares at me; studying, thinking. "Do you know much I care about you?"

I shift my stance, my body heating up and my brain malfunctioning at the emotion and conviction in his voice. "Sure. Best friends forever." I attempt a smile as I show him my crossed fingers, but it doesn't work. My lips are in rebellion because I don't want to smile.

As he continues to watch me, it's as though he is looking into me—into my heart and head—and he knows everything. He knows my secrets. He knows I love him, and not just as a friend, but as the man I could see myself growing old with—though the growing old part is a minor setback. He knows he means so much—too much—to me. It is all there in his eyes.

"Is that what you want?" he finally asks.

"What?"

"Us being friends. You're okay with that?"

I laugh, but it sounds choked. "Yeah. Of course. I'm glad we're friends."

The space between us closes and warms. "You see, the thing is, Blake and I talked."

"Right," I say breathlessly, staring at his long-lashed eyes. I clear my throat and stand straighter. "You mentioned that about two minutes ago."

"We came to an agreement."

"Agreements are good."

He takes another step toward me and only inches of nothingness separate us now. Lowering his head, the weight of his gaze brands me. "Have you ever thought about us being more than friends?"

My mouth opens and closes but no sound comes out. Why did he just ask me that? How does he know about that? Did Blake tell him his stupid assumptions about me that are completely true, but illegitimate as I will never verify them as fact? That *asshat*! Thoughts in disarray, heart pounding like it will stop altogether any moment, I place a hand to my head and try to think. Then I realize I never answered him. So I do. Quite loudly.

"Of course not!" My voice is shrill as I stumble back to put more distance between us. *Please don't say Blake told you I do.* Oh, and I am so killing Blake if he did. It isn't even up for debate.

Blake = gone.

His features become shuttered as he wordlessly turns from me. With his back to me, he says, "Right. Silly question. You know, I'm kind of tired. I think I'll call it a night. See you in the morning."

Brows furrowed, I watch the doorway he just walked through, wondering what I missed, or am missing, or continue to miss. A glance at the microwave clock shows me it isn't even nine yet. He usually stays up past ten. He is upset and I don't understand why. But I know who probably does.

I dump the hot cocoa down the sink and toss the popcorn out, wash the dishes, wipe the countertop, and grab the keys from my purse in the bedroom. I pause outside Graham's closed door, unconsciously pulled to it—to him. But there is no sound, no light from under the door, and I know he wants to be alone. So I go.

To say Blake is surprised to see me may not accurately sum up his reaction. "What the hell?" he mutters, bleary-eyed with his hair all sexily disheveled.

"I know, right? I ask myself the same thing every day. Were you sleeping?"

"No. I was reading."

I blink at him.

"I know how to read," he states dryly.

"Was it smut?"

"Dean Koontz."

"That's too bad. I was so close to respecting you. Can I come in?"

"Will you leave if I say no?"

"Nope," I cheerfully inform him and push past him into the room. I turn in a slow circle, taking in the white walls, hardwood floors, and sparse furniture. The scent of coffee lingers and the room is cast in dim lighting. "Homey."

He crosses his arms and the fabric of his white t-shirt is pulled tight against his chest. "It's temporary. I don't need a lot."

"You said this was an efficiency apartment?"

He nods.

"Where's your bed? And bathroom? I was expecting a toilet in the middle of the room. You could do some awesome multitasking if that were the case." I sigh. "Alas, it isn't."

"Funny. There's a bathroom—with walls and a door even," he answers. "The couch pulls out into a bed."

"Hmm." I grab the book from the brown couch and see that it is, indeed, Dean Koontz. 'Odd Thomas', even. He's microscopically redeemed himself with his non-reading of smut books. I don't understand the Malone men and their aversion to book erotica.

I decide to cut to the chase. Small talk is not my thing and I want to go home and sleep for as close to a dozen hours as I am allowed. "What did you tell Graham?"

"What time?"

"When you caught a ride with him today. I want to know what you told him. Because he told me you two talked and then he also asked me if I'd ever thought of us being more than friends. What did you tell him? Did you tell him your stupid suspicion about me being in love with him?"

"He did *not* say that," he moans as he rubs his face. Dropping his hands, he says, "He is such a dweeb around you. Seriously. How can you think you're in love with such a nerd?"

"Are you done? Because I'm supposed to be the center of attention here and you're totally mucking it up."

Blake snorts, moving to the couch. He stretches out on it with his hands behind his head, his dark eyes never leaving me. "Carry on, Oh Great One."

I pace the length of the large room. "Did you or did you not tell him how you suspect I have more than roomie feelings for him?"

"I don't *suspect*."

I pause to jab a finger in his direction. "Answer the question."

"No. I didn't."

I narrow my eyes at him. He looks back, all innocent. "You're telling the truth?"

"I'm a lot of things, but a liar is not one of them. I haven't sunk *that* low just yet."

I plop down on the couch beside him, shoving at his legs to make room for me, and stare at the blank screen of the small television. "Then why would he say that? About me and him being more than friends?"

Blake must think it's a rhetorical question because he doesn't respond.

Thoughts form and fade, collide and separate. I turn my head toward him. "Does he want to be more than friends? If you never said anything to him, but he brought it up...or does he just think I want to be more than friends?"

"Is this going to take a while?"

I study the television screen again. Unfortunately, I find no answers in the blackness of it. "I don't understand. What did you two talk about?"

Head dropping against the back of the couch, he says, "We decided not to fight over you anymore."

"Oh." Is that a hint of dejection in my tone?

He must notice it because he gives me a look. "Upset about that?"

"No. I'm glad. Of course I'm glad. That's good. You guys were being idiots for nothing. I mean, you and I...and Graham and I..." Laughter starts in my throat and falls away before it really makes a sound.

"We decided it would be best to cease the mutual antagonism where you're concerned. Or at least, I did. Graham just scoffed at me and called me a moron. Only it looks like he changed his mind after going home. So. Tell me. Has the courtship begun?"

A long, faint noise begins from somewhere in the room. I try to determine what it could be. A hum? No, it's like keening, but not quite that dramatic. Then I realize it's me, trying to breathe.

"I'll take that as a yes. What did he do? Draw you a picture with his toes? No, wait. His Graham superhuman powers wouldn't do something so ordinary. Let me guess. No, no. Don't talk." He smashes a finger against my lips, his expression thoughtful. "He picked up his bed with one finger and spun it around like a basketball. No? How about——"

I shove his finger away. "How about you shut up for once? What are you talking about?"

"Graham and his epicness."

"No. I mean about your discussion."

His eyes get a shifty look in them. "For the record, I would like it noted that I am the one being honest and upfront about this, therefore, it should add points to my score card."

I cross my arms. Score card? As if. I can't even keep track of the points on my driver's license.

"I said instead of us fighting about you, we should be cordial about it and let you decide who you'd rather be with. He said it was a stupid idea and acted like he wanted no part of it, said that it wasn't a competition and he wasn't participating. Clearly he lied."

"Graham doesn't lie," I feel the need to point out. "And why would he even talk about something like that with you?"

"I know you're blond, but..."

"Oh, you did not just say that!" I grab his book and whack his arm with it.

"Ow! Hey! That's the library's book!" He yanks it out of my hand, drops it to the floor, and gives it a kick across the room.

"Way to be gentle with the library book."

He sits up. "Graham's got feelings for you. Either he doesn't realize what they are, or he's in denial, but they are there. You two are dismally obtuse about each other. And me, well, I'm the guy with no hang-ups about dating you. I'm the guy you secretly fantasize about." He grins and my stomach flutters. "I would totally go for me, if I were you."

"Uh-huh. You're also the guy leaving soon. You're the guy who just wants a good time. You're the guy who's supposed to be hanging out with his brother and is instead worried about some chick."

"I'm just a man. I can only do so much." He rubs his lower lip. "You know, if you want my advice——"

"I really don't."

"I would use me to make Graham jealous."

"No." Not that I ever had the same thought on my own. Of course not. Nope. I look away from him in case he sees the guilt on my face.

"You're right. You'd probably enjoy the attention too much."

"What would you get out of that?"

"Kissing and fondling?" he asks hopefully.

"I'm leaving now. Graham is right—that was a stupid idea." I head for the door.

"I'll take you to the fair Friday night."

"Deal," I respond without even pausing.

It isn't until I am outside, staring into the darkness of night, that what I just agreed to hits me. What was I thinking? I walk down the stairs, remembering all the things I was thinking. I was thinking of the Ferris wheel and the cotton candy and the live bands. I was thinking about the tractor pulls. I was thinking about the games and the bright lights and the excited atmosphere. I was thinking about how my dad and mom used to take me to the Grant Country Fair every summer and it was the highlight of the whole year.

It was all too easy.

chapter nine

i sweep my hand through water hot enough to have a layer of steam floating up from it and make my skin turn a nice shade of red. The sound of slicing water is soothing to me and I focus on that. I lift a handful of honey scented bubbles to my face and blow them away, patting the residual soapy concoction on the top of my head. I need this listless nothingness to unwind—and the bottle of wine sitting on the ledge of the bathtub. It's red and the perfect blend of sweet and tart. Cranberry, the favorite of all my favorites.

Today was a killer at work. I'm going to get fired if I continue to have verbal strife with the patients. But, I mean, why would someone request that their toenails be painted at a podiatrist's? Hot pink, even. We are not a salon. When I told the guy that, he got really irate and left. Dr. Olman stared at me for about a second and then wordlessly went to his office, quietly closing the door behind him. I think he was pretending he didn't just witness that—which part, I am still not sure.

I got home before Graham and immediately overtook the bathroom, forfeiting my Wednesday night walk even. Desperate times call for baths and wine. I don't know how long I've been soaking, but long enough that my skin is getting wrinkled and I'm getting a good idea of what I'll look like when I'm old—it is not pleasant.

There's been this strange tension between Graham and me since our 'friend' chat that I really don't like, but I also don't know how to get rid of it. My usual comments don't seem appropriate and whenever he looks at me, my brain empties out. *Poof*—all words, thoughts, anything intellectual at all, is gone. I keep thinking about what he said about us being friends, about what Blake said about us being more than friends, and how I feel about it all.

Confused. I feel confused.

And like I need to blurt everything out to him and deal with the consequences, but *fudge*—what if I lose him? What if I ask him how he feels about me, tell him I'm madly in love with him, and he looks at me with pity? Ugh. I would die. Seriously. I never thought of myself as a coward, but clearly that was an inaccurate assessment.

With a sigh, I determine I have pruned myself long enough and slowly stand, the water sluicing off me as I get to my feet. Dried and concealed in a fluffy pink towel, I open the door and freeze. Graham is standing across the hallway, leaning against the wall with his arms crossed and his eyes locked on me.

I give a weak wave and say hello.

"I've been waiting for you," he says, which isn't really all that significant, but his voice is rough, which makes me think maybe he is talking about more than just needing to use the bathroom I've been hogging for an undetermined amount of time.

"Yeah. Sorry. Rough day. I needed—"

He moves abruptly, reaching for me like a predator snatching up its prey. His fingers slide up the back of my neck and his lips latch onto mine. *Holy shit*, is the first thought that forms from the jumbled up letters in my head, and then I don't think anymore. My whole being sighs, lights up, burns, and sinks into him. The only setback to this amazing kiss is the fact that I am juggling my hold on the towel while attempting to touch him. And then, that is no longer an issue because the pink confection falls from my body. I should feel self-conscious or something, but his lips are still tormenting mine, so I can't even pretend to care.

Graham stiffens, only his body pressing to mine keeping the towel from landing on the floor in a pile. He ends the kiss, his forehead to my cheek as he murmurs, "I know I should act concerned about your nakedness, but I don't have it in me to tell you this shouldn't be happening." He takes a deep breath, continuing with, "You should probably retrieve it while I can still think clearly, and the ability is leaving me even as I am saying this."

"So you're saying I should put my towel back on?"

His face is pained as he nods, meeting my gaze. "Yes. Before I look down. And believe me, I *really* want to look down."

"Just so I understand this right…you kissed me. I mean, you didn't just, like, accidentally fall on me and manage to stay upright by attaching your lips to mine. You actually kissed me. On purpose." I stare at him. "You liked kissing me. You're attracted to me. The thought of seeing me naked turns you on."

I watch his eyelids slide shut as he takes a shuddering breath, and a huge smile forms to my lips. "I turn you on." Graham groans and my body jerks in response. This is a high like I never knew was legal. Knowing all of these little details gives me a sense of empowerment. I almost want to walk around with nothing on at all times just to see how he'll react.

My view on my body is this: it is what it is. I am not embarrassed of the curves or lack of curves I have, nor ashamed, and really, my body isn't going to substantially change no matter what I do or don't, so I might as well be confident about it. Shyness has no role in my world.

"Yeah." His voice is weak. "Yes. It's true. All of it."

"Why didn't you ever tell me?" I whisper. Not a fair question, really. Why didn't I ever tell him?

"Like I said, I was waiting for you." His smile is faint, sadness shining through the beauty of it.

He locks eyes with me as he leans down and carefully, without so much as grazing my skin, retrieves the towel. His mouth—his mouth is so close to my woman parts that I squeeze my legs together and tightly clasp my hands to keep from accidentally on purpose having my lower half fall on his face. His eyes never leave mine, which is either admirable or disappointing, depending on which way you want to look at it. My skin is burning and my heart is thundering and—did his breath just flutter across my thighs?

He slowly stands, moving the towel up with him and around my body. I let him. I mean, if I made a big deal out of this and refused to put the towel back on, it might get strange. I stare at him, noting the way his hands are trembling, and take the towel from him as he continues to fumble with closing it while simultaneously trying not to touch me. Tenderness weaves through me at his chivalry, frustration that he is so decent, and longing so intense my chest hurts with it.

To summarize, I'm in agony.

"What were we talking about?" I blurt out, trying to get my thoughts and emotions in some kind of order. "You were waiting for me? I don't understand." I hate admitting such a thing, but, well, sometimes you just have to.

He rests his forehead against mine and exhales slowly. "I don't know how to say this, but I can't continue to not say it. I should have told you long before now—I care about you. A lot. The timing never seemed right and I didn't think you were ready to know how I felt about you. I didn't know if you felt the same or ever would. I mean, yeah, you joke about stuff all the time, but I figured that's all it was."

He steps away, looking down the hallway as he talks. "Blake's arrival showed me I waited too long. This is all my fault. I was stupid. And now…now it's too late. I feel like I already lost you to him and I didn't even get a chance to *try*." Graham's jaw tightens. "He told me you kissed."

Ugh. Blake is so dead. It was, like, a grazing of lips, not even really technically a kiss. "It was a peck. Not a kiss. It lasted all of two seconds."

The look on his face has me hurrying to move on, as does the burning sensation in my face. "Anyway, who said it was too late? Was it in the paper or something? Did you write something up and have it notarized by a judge saying that by such and such date, it was too late for Graham Malone and Kennedy Somers to be anything other than roommates? I mean, who's in charge of determining this?"

Regret twists the smile he aims my way. "I see the way you look at him, the way you respond to him. I had my chance and I blew it. Granted—I didn't realize it was my only chance. Things are different now. If you won't admit to anything else, you at least have to admit that. I know you're attracted to Blake."

Like a microscopic amount, that's all. I don't think saying this will really help my case. I look down so that I am no longer witness to the lines of pain in his face, but it doesn't matter because I still see them. Discontent rolls off him in invisible tendrils of remorse. Maybe it *is* too late for us. Maybe he waited too long. Why did he wait so long? Why did *I*?

Maybe now isn't our time. *What if it never is?* I swallow, pinpricks of discomfort abrading my skin.

He's right. Something has changed, but I still want him. I also want more of him, more than he is giving me. No matter what, I know I will always want him—just like that song where the chick licks the sledgehammer or whatever it is in the music video. Totally don't understand that, but whatever.

"I don't know what to say," I admit.

He widens his eyes. "Kennedy Jacqueline Somers—speechless. Never thought the day would come," he gently mocks. He turns to walk away, my eyes trailing after him because they can't stand not having some part of him within their view. I open my mouth to say something, anything, to keep him from leaving, but he is already turning around to face me once more.

He tilts his head. "Can I know one thing?"

I slowly nod.

"How long have you known?"

"Known what?"

"That we should have been more than roommates."

I tighten my hold on the towel as I say with complete honesty, "There was something about you, even that first day we met. The way your eyes saw into me—saw more than my embarrassing rambling and awkward joking. You really saw me, ya know? And you were okay with everything about me that usually repels people. That makes you really strange, but it's okay, because I'm pretty strange too."

"Why didn't you ever say anything?"

I shrug, avoiding his eyes. "I didn't want to lose you and I was scared I would."

"And I didn't want to push you away."

"We both suck."

"Yeah." His eyes darken and brackets form around his full lips. "Just so you know...I've always been okay with you, Kennedy, any way you are or decide not to be." He begins to walk away again, shaking his head as he goes.

He pauses to say, "Here's to the fucked up world of waiting for the right moment and then realizing you waited too long."

A moment later the door to the apartment closes and eerie silence becomes my companion. My grip relaxes on the towel as my shoulders slump. My first instinct is to charge after him, but I'm wearing a towel, and also, I sort of feel like this had to happen. I may later regret letting him leave, but right now, it seems like a necessity. Things are all crazy and we both need to think.

A small part of me thinks, *Why didn't he tell me all of this before his brother showed up?* It leaves me with a bad taste in my mouth and the flavor is resentment.

This is what I have to decide: Do I want the short-term thrill ride or do I want the long-term commitment? Why is this even a question? Shouldn't I just know?

I blame my indecisiveness on my inexperience with men. How can I know what I want when I haven't really ever had anything?

But you want Graham. You do know that. I do know that. And if I dabble in the sensuality of Blake, I lose Graham. Even if he says I wouldn't—I would. He would never get over it and I would never stop feeling guilty and it would be the end of us. We'd be a 'might have been' and that is it. Am I willing to chance it?

I suppose maybe I should have decided all of this before Blake showed up to take me to the fair. Because here he is, standing outside the apartment door, looking at me like I should invite him in. I am so not inviting him in. In fact, I feel sick, like I'm betraying Graham. Why did I agree to this? One weak moment and here I am. Damn the intoxicating pull of cotton candy.

I scowl at him in greeting, crossing my arms. "You told Graham we kissed."

He pauses, then shrugs. "I alluded to it."

"I'll give you something to allude to," I mutter.

A smirk makes a brief appearance on his naturally surly face. It should look wrong there, but instead it looks at home. "Come on, I'm helping you out. I'm being a team player. Go team Grennedy."

I lean close, thoroughly irritated. "It did *not* help me out. In fact, I think it did the opposite of that. Graham says it's too late, that he waited too long, and now he's giving up."

"Then he's stupid. And you don't need stupid people in your life."

My look tells him I'm not amused.

Sighing, Blake steps forward, making me step back. "I know Graham. He's processing. When he decides to use his brain again, he'll figure out what he needs to do."

"Right. Which will probably not be what I want him to do."

"Have faith in your womanly wiles."

"Who talks like that? Also, how do you know how he thinks? It isn't like you two are close."

"We might not be close, but that doesn't mean I don't know my brother. I remember what he was like as a kid. He's a thinker." He pauses. "Actually, he overthinks things. He used to have anxiety even about dressing himself. I hate it say it, but, I even understand why he said that to you. Graham's a perfectionist. He wants everything to be exactly where and when it should, so in his mind, even though he wanted to tell you how he felt, he probably didn't think it was the right time."

He sighs. "Damn it, I am completely ruining my chances with you—not that they were ever too great. Might as well go for the gold," he mutters. Looking at me, he says, "He was thinking of *you*. He doesn't know how to be selfish, and even now, I see him struggling with what he wants and with what he thinks is best for you."

"What's best for me is him."

"Maybe. But does Graham think that way?"

"You know nothing," I tell him, but I'm really hoping he does.

"I know some things." He winks. "Like, you smell like bubble gum."

"Clearly you don't know enough. I don't do bubble gum."

He leans forward, tickling my neck with his breath and filling my nostrils with the scent of smoke and cloves. His soft hair brushes my jaw and I freeze, a deer stunned by the headlights of a car. "You're right," he says as he straightens, flashing me a quick grin. "It's more of an apple and vanilla smell. I like it."

"I can die in peace now, knowing you approve."

"Come now, be honest. You'd probably die in peace just from knowing *me*."

Something slams behind me and I jump, whipping my head around. A tight-lipped Graham takes another hardcover book and whacks it against the coffee table. There is a stack of books beside him, so I'm thinking this is going to be a drawn out event. I should have made popcorn.

"Hello, brother," Blake greets as he wrestles to get around me, giving me a chastising look when he wins—like I should have known better than to try to thwart him. He enters the living room and stops beside Graham. "What are you doing?"

"Just getting set up for a night of light reading. It's the way I love to spend all of my Friday nights," he says mockingly, keeping his head down as he abuses another book.

I wince, remaining close to the door and escape. He asked me to go to a movie with him tonight. I'm not sure if it was supposed to be a date or a just as friends thing, but either way, I had to decline due to my previous acceptance of Blake's fair proposal. He didn't even say anything when I told him. He just looked at me for a long moment and then walked away.

My whole being felt the loss of him as another crevice formed in the Graham-Kennedy pact of bosom buddies forever. I keep telling myself this is how it has to be. If we're ever to be anything more than roommates, our current friendship status has to be annihilated. I just hope we are not destroyed during the process of it. I am walking a paper thin line and I do not enjoy it, most likely because I fail at the balancing part of yoga every time. Which is why I never do it. Yoga and me do *not* get along.

"I have some books if you need something to read," I tell him, hesitation I have never before felt obvious in my tone. It's uncomfortable and I loathe it. "And if you get super bored, you can even alphabetize them. I know you like doing that."

He glances up at me and away. "I have plenty to do."

Blake's eyes narrow on me before he turns to his brother. "We'll be sure to bring you back some cotton candy."

"Don't bother."

"Graham doesn't like cotton candy," I say.

Blake's eyes twinkle as they meet mine. "More for me then. Ready?"

Graham straightens as his brother walks toward me. "The cotton candy isn't yours to have. Just remember that."

What the heck is going on? They're arguing over cotton candy now? I mean, really? Do their competitive natures know no end? They're dragging spun sugar into their war now?

Briefly pausing, Blake replies, "It is if no one else wants it."

With gritted teeth, Graham replies, "Maybe it isn't that no one wants it. Maybe they just don't want to pressure anyone into thinking they just want cotton candy and nothing else. Maybe they want to make sure everyone knows how much they really enjoy cotton candy, not just for now, but for always."

"But you don't like cotton candy," I point out to Graham, since I guess he forgot.

Rolling his eyes, Blake puts a hand on my arm and gently pushes. "Let's go, Einstein."

"Maybe I really actually *love* cotton candy!" he hollers as the door closes.

I look at Blake as we loiter inside the apartment building. "What just happened? He so doesn't like cotton candy."

He sweeps a hand over the top of my head without touching it. "Never mind. Some things are beyond you."

"That sounded like an insult."

"Did it?" His facial expression is all innocent.

"Apparently *that* wasn't beyond me," I mutter as we head out into the scorching heat of a summer evening, Wisconsin style. A mosquito immediately attacks my arm, making the ambience complete.

"How far away is the fair?" he asks, lighting up a cigarette.

"A mile—not too far. We can walk."

He pauses. "No. I don't do walking."

I stare at him in miscomprehension. "What are you talking about? You have legs, don't you? How can you not do walking?"

"I don't like walking. You don't do bubble gum, I don't do walking. We're all allowed to not do things."

"You went for a walk your first night here," I point out.

"It was a short one, and slow. And it was either that or find real beer."

I can tell by the look on his face that I shouldn't comment on that, so I return the conversation to me, where I like it.

"Look at my skirt." I fluff it up for his admiration. It's cream-colored eyelet that rests at my knees in a positively demure way. "I am not riding your bike in this skirt. And it's nice out. We should walk."

"No." He inhales nicotine, not looking the least bit disturbed by his refusal to give in to my whims.

"I'm walking," I say with finality. Are we really arguing over this? *Graham would walk with you. Graham* likes *walking.*

He shrugs. "Okay. I guess we'll meet there." And he starts toward his motorcycle—which entails walking, I might add.

I stare at him, sure he is joking. When he gets on his bike and looks at me, I see he isn't. Is he for real? As he continues to watch me, I have to believe he is. I ignore the rumble of the motorcycle's engine as he peals out of the parking lot, and when he toots the horn, I flip him off.

I am so walking like I don't have somewhere to be. With a long sigh and lots of mumbling, I begin my trek, kicking at a rock with my magenta sandal as I go.

Deciding to have a conversation with myself seems like a good idea, so I do that. "If this is his idea of wooing, then someone should let him know he totally sucks at it. Won't even walk a mile. A mile! How does he stay so fit-looking? Maybe he just smokes cigarettes all day and hardly eats. Maybe he doesn't need exercise to stay skinny 'cause he eats toilet paper like those models I read about. Graham likes to exercise. Graham likes to eat—and not toilet paper."

I begin to state the pros of Graham Malone, versus the cons of Blake Malone.

"Graham likes to walk. Graham likes to eat. Graham doesn't smoke cigarettes. Graham doesn't have a problem with addiction, which, crap, that bit endears Blake to me. Okay, moving on. Graham likes to exercise, which is sort of like walking, but I'm going to count it separately."

I wave at two young boys as they give me strange looks while coasting down the street on their bikes. "Graham has great taste in music. Graham is nice. Graham cooks good food. Graham is orderly and sort of anal about keeping the apartment clean, but that is still a plus. Graham would never do this to me," I say pitifully as longing shoots through me and makes my chest hurt. I could turn around, go back to Graham, ditch Blake, profess my love, and hope he professes his back.

And for my awesome conclusion, I end with, "Graham is not an asshat."

I generally walk a mile, depending on my amount of ambition at the time, within fifteen to twenty minutes. A look at my cell phone tells me I milked this baby out to forty-five minutes, which I think could be a record. I should contact Guinness and see. But I am not one for self-seeking glory, and so, I shall have to decline. Plus, like I have any idea who to get in touch with.

Multi-colored lights, the scent of buttered popcorn, a cacophony of boisterous voices, and foreign metal contraptions of fun and horror sticking up in the air tell me I have reached the fair—that and the sign that says 'Grant County Fairgrounds'.

I glance around the parking lot, looking for a familiar surly-faced guy or motorcycle and instead find something else. My heart squeezes as he strides toward me, although I am not sure if it is in pleasure or fear because, well, he doesn't seem very happy.

He looks up and sees me, his pace slowing as a frown mars his face.

Going for casual, I place a hand on my hip as I ask, "Did you do some heavy speed reading or what?"

"Aren't you on a date? What are you doing?" Graham demands.

"Apparently not. What are *you* doing?" A light breeze plays with his hair, somehow making it look even better, and I find myself distracted by the way the golden locks move up and back and down.

"Nothing." His eyes won't meet mine.

I nod. "I always wander aimlessly for miles as a form of doing nothing as well. It's a great way to waste time. And you know what they say about wasting time—actually, I don't know what they say about wasting time. Anyway, have fun doing nothing." I turn toward the fair, inwardly shouting at him to stop me.

"Kennedy—*Ken*," he calls.

I slowly face him. "Which is it? Kennedy or Ken?"

He takes a step toward me, his eyes never leaving mine. His expression alters from one emotion to the next until he finally, carefully, asks, "Which do you want it to be?"

This is a monumental question. Am I Ken to him or am I Kennedy? Basically—am I his buddy or something more? I open my mouth to answer him when something red, yellow, blue, and hideous, appears to the left of him. All good thoughts and feelings leave me in a whoosh of terror. If I was a screamer, I would so scream, but I am not, so instead only a strange, shrill sound escapes me.

I suck in a sharp breath and backpedal, wishing I could close my eyes so that I could pretend it isn't there. Graham is asking me something, but my heart is pounding in my ears, muffling his voice and all other sounds except for my terrified heartbeat. The thing approaches me, waving its oversized hand with a grotesque smile on its face, and I want to run.

"Get back," I tell it, only my vocal chords are tragically nonexistent at the moment, so it comes out a soundless rasp.

It starts to giggle, and I kid you not, my stomach cramps up in rebellion. Everything about it, constructed to be friendly and appealing, has a menacing quality to it. Its eyes are circled in black, its smile stretches to an abnormal width, showing yellow teeth, and even its bald spot seems garish. This—this right here—is why I hate clowns. There is *nothing* happy about them. And maybe my revulsion to them started out with the whole throwing up bit, but their appearance certainly didn't help.

And then it squirts me in the face with water and I shriek. What began as a tremble turns to an uncontrollable jerking of my limbs. It's still coming for me! What do I do? Where can I go? Where do I hide? I guess I'll stand in frozen terror—I seem to excel at it. My voice is especially loud when I tell it, "Get away from me! Shoo!" I even make a shooing gesture with my hand in case it doesn't speak English.

Its mouth tries to frown, but there is that perpetual smile painted on, and the whole thing just looks wrong, unnatural—like my mom's hair color.

Graham is suddenly between me and the obnoxious thing, cupping my face within his hands. "Hey. Look at me." He slowly smiles. "Hey there. Are you going to let a silly clown scare you? You're tougher than that. Come on, let's go. I'll buy you cotton candy."

"Fairs…are not…supposed to have…clowns," I say around chattering teeth.

Crinkles form around the striking green of his eyes. "I know. Who does things like that without consulting you first? There should have been a memo."

"At least."

A spray of cold water hits the back of Graham's head, and of course, once again my face, and I watch as he stiffens, the humor falling away like a superhero's cape when it's time to get real. He straightens, shielding me as he turns around. "That's enough. We get it. You're a clown. You do dumb things. Find someone else to pick on, okay?"

The clown giggles again and pulls an inflatable red bat out of its back pocket. It then commences to hit Graham over the head with it, which has my mouth dropping open. His profile shows me the tightening in his jaw. "Okay. Ha ha. You're funny. Now go away."

"Graham, let's go. If we walk away, I doubt it will follow." I'm really hoping anyway. I feel like such a wimp right now, but not enough to stop being one. Effort and all that.

"Yeah. Okay." He takes a deep breath, releases it, and starts to move—but not in enough time, because the final blow to cause Graham to snap is when the clown reaches around to poke him in the forehead with its fingers.

"What the hell?" he shouts, whirling around to shove the clown back.

The clown lifts its hands up innocently even as it is stumbling back.

"I'm okay," he tells me when I raise an eyebrow at him.

"Clearly."

"I'm okay," he repeats. As he turns toward the antagonistic clown, he says, "I apologize. I just—"

I really think the clown has a death wish and its next move supports this theory. It spins on its heel and takes a jab at him, putting a hand to its mouth when its fist connects with Graham's arm. I have alternating bouts of fear, laughter, and incredulity shooting through me as I watch the confrontation. I glance around, noticing we have a crowd forming around us. This is not good, not good at all.

Grabbing his arm, I yank him toward me when he starts for the clown. Placing my mouth close to his ear, I hurriedly tell him, "We need to leave. It's just a stupid clown. People are watching." I go still when I feel air fluttering the backs of my legs. I carefully turn around and glare at the cad. "You did not just lift up my skirt."

It shrugs.

I dive for the offensive being and grunt when an arm loops around my waist and pulls me back. "Easy, Cujo. We're both going to turn around and walk away, okay?"

I take what is meant to be a relaxing breath and nod. "Right. We're above this." I look at the annoying carnie as I say, "I'm going to write your employer a very stern letter about your conduct."

It spins in a circle, swinging the bat around its head as it does so, and thumps me over the head with it.

"That's it!" I shriek, running at it like a linebacker. I plow into its stomach with my shoulder and we both go to the pavement, its frumpy costume acting as a cushion for me. I grab the bat from it and begin to pummel it over the head with it. "How's that feel? Doesn't feel good, does it?"

Multiple hands pull at me and I snarl back, so wanting to annihilate all clowns, but finding comfort in being able to at least take this one down. I suppose maybe I am having a 'Happy Gilmore' golfing, or even a 'Billy Madison' penguin attacking, moment, but right now, I am okay with that. And at least I am not drunk—although, I sort of wish I was. Arms hook around me, lifting me up and away from the laughing clown. Who laughs while being attacked, even if the weapon is an inflatable bat? This clown is freaking nuts.

"Crazy clown!" I fight the bands locking me to a hard wall—I soon enough find out the bands are Blake's arms and the wall is his chest. "This is your fault!" I rant at him, twisting my face up to better glower at him. "If you had just walked with me, this never would have happened!"

"Yes, my lack of supervision is completely to blame for your 'roid rage. You should probably lower your dosage." He tips his face close to mine and says quietly, "Knock it off. Graham is trying to make you look sane for the nice cop over there. We all know it's going to take an impressive amount of acting on his part."

That slumps my shoulders. I look around, note the dispersing crowd, and focus on my roommate. He's gesturing wildly with his hands to a man in uniform, and I am sort of thinking he is not helping my case—especially with the way the police officer is staring at him like he is babbling nonsense. But then, maybe he is. I shake off Blake's hold and slowly make my way to the two men.

"—attacked her—"

I put a hand on Graham's mouth and press down. "Shh, there, there." Looking at the unimpressed cop, I say, "The clown is sadistic and should be put down." I ignore my roommate's groan. "Like, bullet to the head put down. I'm not lying. It—" A hand goes over my mouth and my eyes look up and to the left.

This has to look strange; my hand over Graham's mouth, Blake's hand over mine...

"These two are my responsibility. I thought it would be fun to take them to the fair, but they really can't handle social interaction at all. I should have known better. They're a little..." He moves the finger of his free hand in a circle by his ear, rolling his eyes.

I want to bite his hand, but instead settle with growling, which may or may not help my case. I guess it depends on how you look at it. I mean, if we're looking at a potential crazy person, then yes, I feel my growling is a plus.

I am an asset.

The cop eyes me and Graham, finally shrugging. "Take them home and we'll forget about it. The clown doesn't want to press charges."

"That clown—" I begin to sputter, but am unceremoniously shoved forward, my words cutting off as I fight to balance my position so that I do not land on my face. I glare at Blake, silently applauding his fabulous acting abilities that make it appear as though he is completely unconcerned over my unhappiness with his conduct.

"I feel bad for that clown," he mutters as we make our way from the fair.

"He's an asshole," Graham heatedly declares.

"Clowns are nuisances; they like to irritate people. That's what they do. People usually don't go all Incredible Hulk on them for it."

"I *hate* clowns," I say, sounding sort of spoiled brat-ish. "Especially that one."

Graham makes a funny noise and I glance at him. His eyes twinkle as they meet mine and he starts to laugh. I lift my eyebrows and he supplies, "You beat up a clown with an inflatable bat."

My mouth stretches into a wide grin as I laugh too. "I so did."

"Do you realize what else you did?"

"Somehow managed to look fabulous in a completely unflattering situation?"

"You got over your fear. I mean, you were livid. You can't lambaste a clown like that when you're scared of them. That was awesome." He high fives me.

"I am amazing, like Spiderman," I say with gusto, nodding in agreement.

Blake looks between the two of us, shaking his head. "You two are incredible."

"That too," I say. "Incredible *Hulks*," I add.

He lights a cigarette. "Incredible something. I take it the date is off?"

I see Graham stiffen out of the corner of my eye, refusing to look at him. I can visualize the tight-lipped expression he is sure to be wearing without actually having to see it.

"Was it a date?" I innocently blink at him. "I mean, don't dates usually entail the two people going somewhere *together*? That really didn't seem like a date to me. Me, walking. You, not walking. You didn't even wait for me. Where were you anyway?"

Eyes narrowing, he says, "Whatever makes you feel better in front of Graham." He hooks a leg over his bike. "If I'd realized it was going to take you an hour to get here, I would have better utilized my time. I was getting you this." He digs something small, fluffy, and white out of his jacket. It looks like a dead kitten.

I catch it when he tosses it my way, seeing that it is not a dead kitten, but a stuffed one. With furrowed brows, I stare down at it, wondering why he would get me such a thing. And then I sort of melt, because, well, it's so cute. And super soft. I rub it against my cheek as I lift my eyes to his, forgiving him for any annoying thing he's said or done since his arrival in Lancaster.

"Thank you."

"Unbelievable," is muttered to the right of me, which is where Graham is located. The voice sort of sounds like his too.

He winks at me as he starts the motorcycle, calling, "We'll do this again soon," before roaring out of the parking lot.

I turn to Graham, wondering what I will find. His eyes are locked on me, studying me, probably fantasizing about me as well. I'm pretty desirable, especially in this skirt.

I purse my lips and make my kitten dance in the air. "Hello, Graham, my name is Purr-Fecto." I drop my hand when he gives me a look that is not at all amused. "You know, like Magneto, only in the cat form." His features go blank and I sigh. "Come on, you grump, let's go home."

He flinches, his expression darkening, and suddenly I am being pulled roughly against him. He grabs the kitten from my hand and chucks it to the ground, interlacing his fingers with mine—all the while ignoring my perturbed demands that he tell me what is wrong with him, mind you—and slams his lips to mine. My words halt, my brain turns to mush, and I am a spark of fire turning into a blaze with his mouth teasing and loving mine.

Fuuuudge.

He tears his lips from mine, but doesn't release me. "My home. Your home. *Our* home." I open my mouth to ask him if the clown did mental damage with his deathly bat, but he's kissing me again.

"I'm competing, Kennedy," he breathes against my neck. "And I'm going to win."

I want to tell him that it isn't necessary, that I love him, which is so much more than the minor attraction I feel for his brother, but I don't want him to stop kissing me, so I focus on kissing him back, which isn't exactly a terrible thing to endure, and decide I'll let him compete.

chapter ten

the kitten is now gray with dirt, but I am floating on the beauty of Graham's words, so even that can't pull me down. But you know what can? Blake appearing beside me in the cereal aisle of the grocery store.

Without looking directly at him, I demand, "What are you doing?"

"Why are you carrying around that stuffed animal?"

"Fashion prop?" I actually forgot I was holding it when I decided we needed cereal for the morning and began the four block walk to the store, so I shoved it in my purse upon entering the building, and there it sits with its dingy head sticking out of the top of it.

"More like you couldn't bear to part with it."

I turn my head so that I can better squint my eyes at him. "Did you follow me here?"

"Yeah, I drove my motorcycle behind you in such a stealth-like way you didn't even know I was stalking you. You're not the only one who needs staples, you know."

"Go to the office supply store then. They don't sell them here."

He slowly closes his eyes and then reopens them. "Staples are food items too, like bread and milk. What school did you go to?"

"You know, I usually like sarcasm. Yours—not so much."

"I used to do drugs," he blurts out, immediately clenching his jaw, but meeting my gaze with defiance darkening his. "You probably already knew that."

The box of cereal drops from my limp hand, hitting the floor with a thump. "I'm sorry, what did you just blurt out, *in public?*"

He leans close to me, the proximity of him heating the air around me. "You want to know about me. I'm letting you know about me."

"In a grocery store?" My voice is high with disbelief. But, I mean, really? Talk about worst place ever to have a serious conversation. I shudder at the word 'serious'.

"I have a feeling I won't be getting much alone time with you from now on." His words tell me he suspects Graham has staked his claim on me. He doesn't seem surprised about it. "Seems like our interaction is working in your favor, if you're still hung up on Graham?"

I nod once at his inquiring look.

Rubbing his forehead, he mutters, "My dad is the definition of an asshole. He is a control freak, yells too much, and has been known to do things that wouldn't exactly endear him to others. My mom...my mom feels sorry for herself and the way her life turned out. Her whole world is focused on her and how better everything could have been."

I take a shaky breath, seeing a flash of pain in his eyes before it fades. My chest is tight as I say, "Do I need to pull up a chair? Maybe brew some coffee? I mean, how long is this heart to heart going to take?"

A grin lifts his lips almost as immediately as it falls away. "I like that about you."

I swallow hard, but don't say anything. I'm not going to guess what he is referring to, because, well, there are so many traits that could qualify.

"You avoid all things meaningful. You deflect from important conversations with your sardonic comments. Only, I do the same thing. It doesn't work on me."

"Can't blame a girl for trying," I grumble.

He reaches down, offering a now smashed-in box of cereal to me.

I take it and put it back where I got it from, glancing at him. "All those dead animals on the walls of my parents' living room? I put them there." When his eyebrows lower, I specify, "I mean, I didn't literally put them there, but I hunted them. I killed them. I am responsible for them being forever entombed on a gaudy yellow and white-striped wall. I used to hunt with my dad. A lot."

He takes a step back, visually sizing me up. "Wait. You don't eat a lot of meat. Graham told me when I got the pizzas."

My face instantly burns and I cross my arms, waiting.

Blake taps a finger against his unshaven jaw. "And yet you kill animals. Why don't you eat meat?"

I stare straight ahead, my jaw stiff as I mumble, "I eat some meat. But when I don't, it's because I think about the animals as a living creature and not the slab of meat before me and I can't eat it."

"But you can kill them."

"I don't kill them anymore!" People are beginning to look at us, and I lower my voice when I say, "I am not proud of my prowess as a hunter, okay? And every time I took a life, I felt horrible, but the sorrow I felt at taking an animal's life couldn't compare to the joy I felt knowing I had my dad's approval for something. It was like a blade of love and pain slicing me up each time.

"I was good at it, but I didn't enjoy it. So I stopped. And I don't eat a lot of meat. And, just for the record, anything we hunted was used as food, not trophies. I mean, I guess now the heads are trophies, but...whatever." I blink stinging eyes and want to race from the store.

"Hey."

I look up, finding his head dipped low so that his eyes are level with mine.

"I get it."

I faintly nod, grabbing the already mutilated box of cereal and smashing it against my chest some more. My grip is tight on the box, almost as though I am hugging it to me. "I love this cereal," I say lamely when he gives me a funny look.

"I can see that."

"It's my favorite kind."

"Okay."

"I'm going now."

He nods, a distant look in his eyes. "See you tomorrow."

I frown. "What?"

"You know, fishing with your dad. See you tomorrow." Blake looks at me, a smile on his lips.

"I'm not going."

"Sure." He sounds like he doesn't believe me, but I am overwhelmingly worn out from my small dip into the 'feelings' realm, so I walk away without further comment.

I am working on my second bowl of cereal in the near dark when there is a faint knock at the door. I heave my sleep-lodged body from the chair and stumble into the living room. Six in the morning is way too early for me to be awake. This is all Graham's fault. Even if I wasn't annoyed with the world over being awake at this insanely early hour, I'd still be annoyed with Graham, because, well, when I got home last night, we were back in the 'roomie' zone. At least, I think we were. I'm really not sure, which is the most maddening of all.

We watched a movie together, and yes, we sat extra close and we even kissed, but I don't know, I expected things to be more out of the friend zone than that. I didn't expect him to profess his eternal obsession for me or anything (because it's just a matter of time before he will), and I didn't really think we'd immediately be in bed or whatever (although, ya know, it would have been okay), but…what *did* I expect? Heck if I know. Something. Something more than what happened.

I open the door and glare my vexation at the one person who has the capability of annoying me more than, or at least an equal amount to, my imperceptive roommate. "This is all your fault."

He blinks. "What's my fault?"

I don't answer; I just continue to moodily scowl at him. If he hadn't shown up in Wisconsin and (maybe unknowingly, but probably not) messed with people's emotions, none of this would be happening. He got me all confused and Graham all confused and now everyone is confused. *You're not being fair.* Okay, so I'm not, but who cares? It's six in the morning and I'm going fishing with my dad, not to mention all the other stuff I am irate over.

"I take it you aren't a morning person?" are Blake's next chipper words. He's even smiling, which is bright enough to take over for the sun should it ever feel the need to go into retirement, but still not enough to make me happy. Plus, I know why he's smiling. "Funny thing, seeing you, here, awake. It's almost like you *meant* to be up. Like you have plans even," he continues.

I cross my arms, not finding him the least bit funny.

"All set for fishing?"

I turn around without saying a word, going back to the kitchen to finish my cereal, only to find that it is now soggy mush. With a sigh, I dump it out and wash the bowl and spoon.

"Where's Graham?"

I jump, somehow, in my semi-sleeping state, forgetting Blake was here.

He chuckles, moving within my view as he leans against the counter and crosses his arms. "How'd he get you to cave?"

My face burns and I tighten the lopsided rubber band holding my hair up, firmly pressing my lips together so that I do not acknowledge that question.

"Okay." He straightens. "I'll just go ask Graham."

"He didn't ask me," I mutter. "I volunteered."

His laughter is loud and rich and supremely aggravating. "You don't say?"

Graham enters the kitchen, looking positively perky. Guys shouldn't look perky, FYI. He's wearing old clothes—threadbare jeans that fit his thighs like I want my legs to and a worn deep purple shirt. His hair is messy, but that just makes him more appealing.

He nods at his brother and then turns to me, his eyes softening as he takes a good look at me. "You don't have to go."

I'm swaying on my feet, so when I try to put a hand up, it sort of flops around before going back to my side. "Sure I do. It'll be fun. You know me, love hanging out with the dad and doing macho stuff so that my gender role can be perpetually confused. It's the best."

He puts an arm around me and I slam into his side, liking the warmth and smell of him. I could probably fall asleep right here. "Such a trooper," he says, smacking a loud kiss to my temple.

Blake is watching us in that too in depth way of his, but he quickly looks away when I pointedly stare at him. "I got worms."

"You should probably go to the doctor for that."

He rolls his eyes, stealing a bottle of water from the refrigerator and uncapping it. "Doctors are overrated."

"Yeah, funeral directors too."

He pauses with the bottle halfway to his mouth, bewilderment filtering through his eyes. "I don't understand half of what you say."

"Well, at least you understand the other half of it. There's hope for you yet. I mean, at least a fifty-fifty chance, right?"

His eyes brighten. "There she is. 'Bout time you woke up. Good morning, Kennedy."

I mutter something that may or may not come out sounding like, "Fuck off," and stomp into the living room to await what is guaranteed to be an outstanding day. I can feel the awesomeness ahead.

Graham follows me, flipping a light switch and burning my eyes. "Did you just tell Blake to fuck off?"

"I can't remember. It was so long ago." I close my eyes and flop onto my back on the couch, hoping when I open my eyes it will be tomorrow.

He frowns. "You never say fuck."

"Fuck. Fuck fuck fuck fuck fuck. Fuckity fuck fuck."

"Maybe you should go back to bed."

"Maybe you should fu—"

A hand claps over my mouth, and I look up, finding twinkling eyes on me. "You're cute when you're upset."

I lick his hand and he yelps as he yanks it back. "Really, Kennedy?"

I smirk, finally feeling halfway decent. "Really. Carry me to the truck, servant."

The quiet grows, which makes me think he ignored me and left the room, but then I am being tossed over a shoulder. I begin to protest—loudly. "Graham! Put me down. This is no way to treat your roommate."

A hand smacks my rear and I jerk at the sting that comes. "Licking hands is no way to treat your roommate either. You wanted to be carried to the truck. I'm carrying you. Blake," he calls. "Let's go."

I watch black boots follow us as I am jostled around on a broad shoulder with pavement as my scenery. Cool air and gray skies sweep over us as Graham crosses the parking lot. I focus on his steady breathing, wondering how he can carry me without getting winded.

It isn't until we reach the truck that I realize his palm hasn't left my right cheek—butt cheek, that is. Blake gets into the truck, leaving Graham and me outside. His hand squeezes my cheek in a completely un-roomie-like way and he lowers me so that I slide down the front of him, catching me between his arms and the side of the truck.

Trapped by his arms, trapped by his eyes, trapped by my feelings for him, we stare at each other.

A smile flirts with his mouth and my stomach flutters. "I'll make you a chocolate cake tonight."

My mouth waters from those words. "Homemade cake?"

"Mmm. With homemade chocolate frosting."

I swallow thickly. "Why you gotta play with my emotions?"

"Why you gotta be so easily manipulated? Mention a cake and you're like putty in my hands."

"I can be," I breathe.

His eyes darken and he dips his head toward mine, his lips grazing the corner of my mouth as he whispers, "Not yet."

I think I'm going to fall to the ground when the horn blares and I jump straight up. "Fuck!"

Graham winks at me and moves away. "You're getting some bad habits, Ken."

"Can you be one of them, Barbie?" Oh yeah. I am *back*. Take that, Graham Malone.

He pauses by his door, looking at me over the hood of the truck. He shakes his head. "Nah. All I'm gonna be is good. You'll see."

I love competing Graham. He's fricking lickable.

I also take back every negative thing I thought about him last night when he refused to fondle me (he should just know to do these things)…and this morning …and…any other time I found him less than appealing.

Grandpa Jack is passed out on the porch when we arrive at my parents' home, which is one hundred percent awesome. What's even better is that he is wearing his pink scarf that looks like a bra, snoring away with a look of bliss on his wrinkly face. The lawnmower is parked with one wheel on the face of a garden gnome, but hey, at least it's turned off. Either that, or the battery went dead. I wonder if I get my super duper skills on the road from him?

This is not a funny matter. I get that. Alcoholism is a serious issue, and when I glance at Blake's white face, I see it hits him hard. He walks back to the truck without saying a word. Graham and I exchange a look, mine coupled with a loud sigh.

My grandfather is harmless, has never been involved in any criminal activities—well, other than drunk driving (which could have been bad if he'd ever decided to go out of town, but he didn't, and now he can't drive at all, so it's a moot point)—and he's happy this way. So we leave him alone. None of us enable him, but we also don't badger him. This is Grandpa. This is the way he's always been. He's close to eighty and isn't going to change. We just love him anyway.

I touch his cool brow. "Grandpa. Wake up."

He mutters in his sleep, clutching the scarf to his chest, and rolls toward the door.

I glance at Graham. "Do you think we can get him inside?"

He fingers a lock of hair that has fallen from my ponytail, his eyes a tender caress against my features. "Yes. We can do that. Blake and I," he adds.

"I don't think..." I look up, noting the cloud of smoke around Blake's head as he speed smokes like someone is after his stash of nicotine.

"It'll be fine. Go on inside. Tell your dad what's up."

I mentally groan at the upcoming confrontation—every event that involves my father and me turns into one, guaranteed. I could be like, *The sky is such a pretty blue today* (not that I would ever speak in such a nauseating way), and he'd be all, *Only girls notice the sky is blue*, or something equally lame. Because, duh, *everyone* knows the sky is blue, not just girls. Anyway.

I knock on the door once and check to see if it's locked. It swings open and the scent of burning toast hits me. I have dealt with my mother's non-cooking abilities for so long that I can distinguish which foods are, in fact, being decimated by her hand. Today, it is toast.

Rest in peace, crispy bread, I think as I enter the house.

"Mom? Dad?" I call as I avoid the dead eyes of deer staring at me from various positions on the walls, and head into the rose-themed kitchen, which is equally creepy.

My mom is staring at a plate of black, crumbly toast and my father is sitting at the table, watching her. "I don't understand," she mutters. "I had it on the highest setting."

"Hey, did you know Grandpa's sleeping outside?" I grab an apple from a bowl on the table and bite into it, thinking maybe the fruit will take the edge off the doughnut craving I am presently having. Three bites tell me it isn't going to work. I am not a quitter, but sometimes, even I must realize my limits. I chuck the apple and decide we'll be making a doughnut stop on the way to fishing. It's the least they can do.

"He must have thought this was home again. He's getting confused more and more," my mom says with a sigh.

"You don't have the toaster set all the way up unless you want burnt toast."

She glances at my father. "Why would I want that?"

He shakes his head and pushes himself up from the table, displaying his paunchy stomach. "Graham and his brother here?"

"Yeah. They're trying to wake up Grandpa."

"And what are you doing here?" His brown eyes I inherited zap me with their intensity.

I shift my feet, but don't look away. "I'm going fishing."

"Why? Thought that was a boy thing."

I set my jaw. "Did it ever stop you from taking me?"

"No, because you liked going."

"Maybe I like going now."

He snorts. "Maybe you got a thing for Graham."

My face heats up and I open my mouth to deny his words. Then I think, *The hell with it.* "Yeah? Maybe I do."

I see I surprised him when he narrows his eyes at me. He studies me for a minute and then nods. "'Bout time you liked a boy."

I toss my hands in the air. "You don't make any sense."

Scratching his head, he says, "I make all kinds of sense." He leaves the room.

I turn to my mom. "He doesn't make any sense."

"Your father…isn't good with emotions."

"Yeah. Figured that out a while ago." Like, when I was four and cried because our family cat died and he offered to have it stuffed as a means to make me feel better. It didn't.

She throws away the inedible toast and looks at me, her blue eyes sad. "I'm a bad cook."

My first inclination is to say, "You're just realizing this now?", but I don't. Instead I shrug. "You're good at a lot of other things."

"I can't crochet either."

I purse my lips to keep from agreeing. "Well…you—"

"And I can't sing. I don't even remember the shade of my natural hair color and I've had this outfit since the eighties."

I glance at her red top and tan pants. Yeah. Those should really go—along with a lot of other things in the house. "You're sort of making it hard for me to make you feel better when you keep tossing all the things you aren't good at, at me." I brighten. "You can dance! You're a great dancer."

"I'm having a mid-life crisis."

"You're forty-six," I scoff. "You're too young for that. I mean, maybe in four years…"

"I want to get fit, learn new things. Grow my hair out, maybe join a gym. Get a job. There's no reason I can't work. You're out of the house and I just burn food and have no reason to be at home as much as I am. I need some purpose, hobbies. I need a life."

My mouth drops open. She is so having a mid-life crisis. "But...you and Dad..." I trail off, not even knowing where I was trying to go with that. Somewhere awesome, that's for sure.

Mom starts singing 'Living Next Door To Alice', which in itself is strange, since her name is Alice, but I also think it is a diversion tactic, and also, maybe, a hint. Of what, I have no clue. A frown creases my brow as I watch my unusual mother I may or may not take after more than my father—either is a high compliment, of course.

"So—" I begin, and she just sings louder.

I shake my head and leave the room, but the living room isn't much better. Grandpa is propped up on the couch, still sleeping, with Graham and Blake on either side of him. His head bobs from one of their shoulders to the other, and it doesn't take long to find out why. Every time his head lands on one of them, the other one lifts their shoulder and he goes the other way. They also appear to be tangled up in his frayed scarf; one fabric tentacle around Graham's neck and another wrapped around Blake's arm. Both of their faces have resigned looks on them, and they appear to be having so much fun I would hate to disturb that. I don't find my dad in the room, and without saying anything to them, I walk outside.

I take what is meant to be a cleansing lungful of air, but instead I get a mouthful of the foul scent of cow manure, which is puzzling. How can I smell something through my mouth? Anyway. All the blissful smells of country life manage to seep into the town at the most inopportune times—like when I'm outside and breathing.

My dad hops down from the bed of his beat up Ford truck, wiping his hands on his jeans as he straightens. He barely looks at me when he says, "Wasting daylight. Get your boys."

"They're not my boys."

"Sure about that?"

Huffing, I round up 'my boys', both of which look beyond relieved to get away from the clutches of Grandpa's deadly pink scarf. We reach a small body of water in under ten minutes. Equipped with fishing poles, tackle boxes, and a cooler, the four of us amble down an uneven hill to a little known hot spot perfect for catching fish.

I strategically place myself away from the Malone men, which, unfortunately, puts me beside my father. Graham gives me a frown I ignore. I also pretend I don't see the smirk on Blake's face. I may have agreed to this fishing expedition, but they need to be together without the awesomeness of me getting in the way. I tend to do that. You can't hold back my light; it blazes far and wide.

So I pretend it's just me and my dad. We don't speak, me spearing the worms with the hooks and handing one pole to him. Minutes meld into an hour, the quiet actually relaxing, and when he finally does talk, a small shriek bursts from my lips as I jump.

He ignores that completely melodious sound. "Mom and me...we aren't doing the greatest."

I remove a hand from my pounding heart and glance sideways at him. We don't have heartfelt conversations. It is an unwritten rule. "Okay."

He scratches the side of his face and casts the line. "Think I should take her out on a date."

"What's your definition of a date?" I ask carefully.

He shrugs, looking at the brown water of the creek. A breeze catches the thin strands of his black hair to play with them, revealing his bald spot. "Haven't been on one before, really."

"Sure you have."

"Don't know much about them, but I am thinking tractor pulls and cans of beer don't qualify."

I almost smile at his dry tone. "Probably not, no. How about dancing? Mom likes to dance."

"You've seen me dance. Can't."

My father won't meet my eyes, his jaw set stubbornly even as his skin turns a startling shade of pink. I study him, something warm and fluffy going through me. Tenderness? An epiphany of what is happening sweeps over me, stunning in its clarity. My father is coming to me for advice. My father is talking to me like he actually wants me to act like a girl and think like a girl. It's weird.

I look over at Graham and Blake, find them quietly talking, which makes this moment all the more unusual, and turn to my dad. "I can teach you."

He looks startled. "No."

Situating myself directly in front of him, I set the fishing pole aside and stare him down. "I'll make you a deal."

Wariness creeps into his eyes.

"I'll go fishing with you one day a week until summer is over, and you'll have one dance lesson a week with me. You miss a day, I don't fish a day. Deal?"

"Why would I want to do that? Don't need you to go fishing with me that bad."

My face softens as I note the blustering tone to his voice and the way he will not look at me. "I think I've figured something out about you, but I'm not sure."

His jaw juts forward, like I am going to shout to the world that he lost his masculinity or something equally absurd. I mean, maybe if I had a megaphone...

"You love your wife."

"Of course I do."

"You want to spend time with me."

With a scowl in place, he replies, "Never said I didn't. You're the one that stopped wanting to hang out with me."

"Dad."

Rubbing his jaw, he mutters, "I know I haven't always been the way you want me to be, but I'm trying, all right? Don't know anything about girls. Never have. Hell, I don't even know how to take care of your mother."

I swallow at his admission, feeling my chest constrict at his inelegant honesty. "Okay. So. I have the perfect solution for this. I'll swap a dance lesson a week for a fishing day a week, and the end result will be mega-snappy dance moves cool enough to let your wife know you love and appreciate her, because, honestly, you really suck at showing it."

My dad glares at me.

I cross my arms and lift an eyebrow.

Finally, with a dramatic sigh, he nods. "Fine. I'll do it."

"Don't sound so happy about it."

"Trying not to."

"I noticed."

We go back to our silent fishing, but I'm smiling the whole time. The tension has dimmed. Well, until Blake shoves Graham into the river. A gasp leaves me, my mouth hanging open as I watch my roommate sputter to the surface of the dirty water. I drop my fishing pole, frozen in place.

My dad mutters, "What the hell?"

Blake throws his head back and laughs like I have never seen nor heard him laugh before. The loud and hearty sound is cut off short when Graham comes barreling out of the water, his body aimed straight for him, his eyes daggers of retribution. He lunges for his brother, wrapping his arms around his stomach and heaving him toward the water. Blake stumbles back, landing on his rear just inside the water. The sound of jeans smacking into water is sharp. He swipes water out of his eyes as Graham smirks at him.

"What is wrong with you two?" I demand, more annoyed than worried. They seem to be getting along, even if they are being brutish about it.

Suddenly I have the attention of two wet men, twin calculating gleams in their eyes. Graham is closest, his steps slow and purposeful as he approaches me.

"Don't even think about it." I put my hands out in front of me to ward him off.

His grin deepens as he reaches me. Water drips from his hair down his face to become one with his soggy clothes. "Don't think about what?"

A glance over my shoulder tells me a tree, the first form of cover I think of, is too far away. Not one to give up, I move for it anyway, but a wet, strong hand grabs the back of my shirt and pulls me away from where I want to go until I am flush with a cold chest. Cold clothes; warm body, I should say. His skin is burning through the dampness of his shirt.

"Graham, I swear, if you throw me in that water, I will never speak to you again."

His voice is low and close as he says, "You make it sound like that wouldn't be a good thing."

I haven't even finished my sound of incredulity before I am gathered into his arms, my arms unconsciously going around his neck to anchor me to him. His touch is gentle, his eyes are smiling.

"I mean it. This won't be good for you."

"Oh, I don't know about that." His arms swing out, and I tighten my hold on him, threatening him even as he is laughing at me. He does it again as we move closer to the water and I glare all my irk at him.

"If I go, you go."

He tilts his head as he studies me. His voice is unnaturally sober as he tells me, "That's fine with me."

I don't have time to process that before he lets go of me. I hit the water, refusing to let go of his neck, and we both go under. Lucky for me, the water is only a couple feet deep. Unlucky for Graham, I twist around until I am straddling him, keeping him down with my weight so the only thing above water is his head.

I give him a sweet smile. He doesn't return it.

"Hi," I purr.

He grunts in response.

"Fancy meeting you here."

"What can I say? Where you go, I follow."

I pat his cheek. "That's so sweet."

"I'm a sweet guy."

"*So* sweet," I agree.

"Hey! You're scaring the fish away." This from Blake, who is now standing near my father.

"The fish love me!" I declare, sweeping my arms out wide and losing my balance. I splash into the water, first laughing, and then choking as water goes down my throat.

Graham lifts me out of the water by my shirt. "The weight of your arrogance obviously tipped you over."

"It was more like the air couldn't handle all my splendor."

Half of his mouth lifts. "Something like that."

"Fishing with the three of you is impossible," Dad grumbles and stomps to the cooler, opening a can of soda and gulping it down.

For the remainder of the day, the four of us pretend to fish while we really enjoy tossing insults back and forth. My father is surprisingly good at it. I watch him joke around with the Malone men and feel pride feather its way through my chest. He's not so bad, I realize. I guess I'll keep him.

Graham produces a pan of brownies from the oven just as I walk into the kitchen. I knew he was making them, because the aroma of baking chocolate was tantalizing me the whole time I tried to relax in the bath. It's that blend of warm cocoa and sugar that makes you envision melting chocolate surrounding you, invading your senses. I got out early, way before I decompressed from work and finished my glass, okay, *bottle*, of wine, and now I am standing before him in a towel, dripping water on the floor, and salivating for a brownie—and my roommate. My head is fuzzy, which may or may not be from the wine. I can't be sure.

I take a deep breath and blurt out, "Can we move past the friend zone and into the next zone already?"

He freezes, looking comical bent over with a pan of brownies gripped in his red oven mitts. He's so domestic. "What are you wearing?"

"It's called a towel. Answer the question."

He frowns at me. "I—do you want to?"

I cock my head. It already feels like we're a couple, but focusing on it also makes me feel slightly ill. Because, commitment? *Scary.* Even so, this intimacy, this comfortableness, between us, comes naturally. It always has, even when he was stupid and thought he should date. I was the one he confided in, the one he snuggled against, the one to make him laugh. None of his ex-girlfriends ever had with him what we have.

"Yes," I say hurriedly and just as hurriedly add, "Give me the pan and no one gets hurt."

"You—what? You need to put clothes on." He swallows, slowly straightening. His eyes never leave me and I resist the urge to drop the towel. Why do I keep resisting the urge? Aren't you supposed to follow your instincts? He inhales deeply. "You can't walk around in towels anymore. It's forbidden."

"Since when?"

He closes his eyes and slowly inhales, popping them open as he says, "Since now. Right now. It's no longer allowed. It's a roommate rule."

"Roommate rule?"

He nods.

"We don't have roommate rules." Okay, so we do, just...I never follow them. Also, we made them up one night after some heavy drinking, so they really don't count, not to me. I search my head to see if this is, in actuality, one of the silly laws we made up while under the influence of alcohol.

Roomie Rule #1: Never put a gallon of milk back in the fridge when there is only an inch of milk left in it. (Graham's)

Roomie Rule #2: Do not put a knife in the peanut butter and then use the same knife in the jelly. (Graham's)

Roomie Rule #3: The television must be on football if football is on the television. (Graham's)

Roomie Rule #4: Use your own razor. (Graham's)

Roomie Rule #5: Any chocolate in the apartment belongs to Kennedy, regardless of who bought it. (Mine)

There's more, but I can't see the point in remembering them. Brain strain and stuff.

"You know," I begin, getting beyond irritated as I think of all the stupid rules he's made up since we began living together. "Your rules suck."

"Maybe you suck at following rules."

"Maybe you should suck—"

"Don't," he growls. "Don't even say it. Get dressed. Please."

"Why?"

"Because I'm trying to be decent right now and it's getting extremely difficult."

I stare at him, scrunching my face up as I consider his words. His expression is pained, tightness around his eyes and mouth. My inward debate lasts all of five seconds. I mean, look at him. I don't want him to continue to suffer. I lift my arms out to my sides and let the fabric fall, hearing his breath hiss through his teeth. No one has ever seen me naked before—at least, no one other than my family when I was a small child.

But if I want anyone to be the first—and only—to gaze upon my unclothed form, it is Graham. I can't be embarrassed about my boldness or lack of clothing, not with him. I trust Graham in all ways—with any secrets I feel the need to tell him, with me, even with my virtue. Also, I am impatient and we totally need to move this forward, or stop it altogether. Which, ouch to my heart.

The pan of brownies falls from his limp hands, clattering to the floor with the sound of sorrow, and he doesn't even notice. I do, of course. I shriek in horror and race for them, forgetting about how hot the pan is and burning my hands. Cursing, I tear the oven mitts from his frozen fingers and rescue about a third of the brownies. It doesn't register in my head that I am still naked until I glance at Graham and notice that I sort of put my breasts directly in front of his face, since he's still bent over. You'd think his back would hurt after a while. Also—he's turned on. Even if I didn't want to notice, it is just too obvious not to.

I slowly stand, but all that does is give him a better view. And then I decide I might as well work it, since, ya know, I'm naked and everything. I bend a knee and jut a hip out, placing my hands on my waist. I do this thing with my head that has my loose hair swinging around my arms and chest. He doesn't say anything—he just watches me with hunger in his eyes. It is so potent I feel a responding tug inside me.

He slowly straightens, and even that motions seems to bring him pain. His hand trembles as it raises and my breath catches, thinking he is going to touch my girls, but all he does is gently, with the barest brush of his fingertips along my sensitive skin, remove a lock of hair from my shoulder.

Graham's eyes meet mine and a charge goes through me at the heat within them. When he finally speaks, his voice sounds like gravel. "You're naked."

"Yes. Way to be observant. You said not to wear towels around the apartment anymore. I'm just following the *rules*."

His eyes flicker down and I feel his gaze on my skin like the hot brownie pan on my hands. It scalds me. They slowly raise to mine. "This isn't how the first time should be," he says bluntly, all of him burning into me, his soul an imprint upon mine.

"With you? Yes. It should."

"Your first time should be slow and careful, not crazy, frantic sex, and right now, that's what it would be. I don't want to hurt you. You deserve better," he says in an unsteady voice. "I want to do this right and this isn't the right time."

"What did you say about waiting for the right time?" I ask around a thick throat, feeling rejected. I reach down and grab the towel, quickly wrapping it around me once more. "That what you think is the right time is usually too late." He doesn't say anything, but his lips press into a thin line. My anger flares like flames of red heat. "You know what? You're a self-righteous ass. Have fun not having sex with me."

I start to leave the room, and glance over my shoulder to say the worst thing possible. "Maybe I'll call your brother. I know he won't say no."

I haven't even ended the lie before he is to me, his jaw clenched as he looms over me. "Don't even joke about that," he says slowly, thickness to his voice.

"Who said I was joking?" My body is shaking, part in fury and part in longing.

"Damn it, Kennedy!"

"Don't *swear* at me!" I yell, not really sure why everything he does and says is presently so irritating, but it is. Then again, I do know. My insides are all jumbled up, my mouth has a perpetual taste of something to it, and I feel...ugh, which is the most horrible of ways to feel. So horrible I can't even put a better name to it. I'm frustrated—mentally, sexually, emotionally.

My heart feels like it is cracked and I don't know how to make it whole again. I almost wish we were back to buddies, back before we kissed and said things and then became stupid. I also should have been honest long, long ago. That's what's between us; all the things we should have said before now and didn't. It isn't just me, and it isn't just him. We both messed up. Blake isn't really the problem—it's our own lack of bravery that's held us back.

"Can you just—can you just be honest, okay? Stop pretending to be someone you're not." His voice is pleading and his eyes are hurting.

"I don't pretend," I snap, although, yes, I do. I pretend I don't love him in the way I do, I pretend I am okay with just being his friend, I even pretend I am narcissistic, when really, I'm trying to hide all of my insecurities beneath sarcasm and a facade of insensitivity. I missed my calling as an actress. I missed my calling as a lot of things, I guess. The world will never be the same with all of my talent wasted working as a foot doctor's assistant.

"So you meant what you just said about Blake?"

I bow my head. "No," comes out in a meek voice.

"It's time to get real, okay? No more jokes, no more acerbic comments. Just you, me, and truth."

I freeze, thinking I should look up 'acerbic', and meet his gaze. "Fine," I say in a voice limp with resignation. It's past time to get real. "I'll get so real you'll wish I was fake."

He frowns at me.

"How's this for real?" I lean toward him. "I'm sick of being your buddy."

"I'm sick of you *being* my buddy."

Our faces are close, his red and tight—mine probably really unattractive at the moment. "We never should have been roommates."

He flinches. "You're right. We were not meant to be roommates. I know that now."

My breath hitches. "Why did you have to wait until your brother showed up to say anything? That makes me feel like this—whatever this is—isn't legitimate. Maybe you're just competing with your brother for the sake of competing. How am I supposed to know?"

He runs his hands through his hair. "How can you not know? Everything I say, everything I do, how I look at you. How can you not know?"

"Assuming things doesn't get anyone anywhere, Graham, you know that. People need to be told things, even me." Especially me.

He grabs my hands, his expression earnest. "I wanted you, Kennedy, from within minutes of knowing you. At first that's all I thought it was—an attraction. I realized it was more than that months ago, but I still felt like I shouldn't make a move, that it wasn't the right time. I didn't want to feel like I was pushing you into anything, ya know?

"And you're so much younger than me, you have so much living to do. How could I take that away from you? I tried dating others, but...I couldn't keep dating women when all I wanted was already living with me. I was going to tell you. I just...I wanted to make sure you felt the same. You joke a lot, but I never know what you really feel. Then Blake showed up and I panicked when I saw how you responded to him. I messed up. Big time. I don't even feel like I deserve a chance anymore."

I want to hold him, but I can't. Not yet. "I hate all your girlfriends."

"I haven't dated anyone in months."

"I don't care! I still hate them."

He shifts his jaw back and forth. "Fine. Okay. I hate all your boyfriends."

"I haven't had a boyfriend since I moved in with you." Like I wanted to admit that.

"Fine," he says through gritted teeth. "I hate all of your potential boyfriends."

"What potential boyfriends?"

His hands fly into the air. "I don't know! Potential ones. Any guy you look at, how's that?"

"Even Dr. Olman?"

"Yeah. Probably. If you smiled at him."

I grab Graham and squeeze him to me, feeling him slowly relax against me. This—him—this is all I want. Just him. The feel of his thundering heart against my chest makes me squeeze harder. He lifts his arms and holds me back, placing his chin on the crown of my head, and then rubs his cheek against my hair. He's upset. I'm upset. But even so, here we stand, together.

He sighs. "Now what do we do?"

"Make out?" I suggest hopefully.

He pulls back, his eyes flickering to my lips just before he brands them with his. It is a hard kiss, his teeth scraping my lips, his mouth punishing mine, telling me I will never, ever, *ever* be with anyone other than him. I already know it. The sweetness has been burned from Graham, and I also know I did that as well.

But I am not sorry.

I grab the ends of his shirt and tug. He obeys my silent command, removing his shirt and immediately locking lips with me. His hands find mine and thread our fingers together as he raises them over our heads, moving forward so I have no choice but to move back. Through the kitchen, into the living room, down the hall, never once do our lips part. He surrounds me, finally taking me, marking me as his with every touch of him.

He pushes me back, into his room, and I fall onto the bed, his body immediately covering mine. A low moan leaves me at the feel of him against me. "I'm done being the nice guy, Kennedy," he growls, his eyes flashing down at me.

'I'm Too Sexy' by Right Said Fred starts playing from my bedroom. I stare up at Graham. "Good. Because I like it when you decide to get crazy and not shave. You're so badass when that happens."

He places his lips to my collarbone, and I feel them smile against my skin as he kisses it. Graham moves over me and nips my lower lip, pausing as my phone stops and starts back up immediately. "Do you need to get that?"

"No."

"Are you sure?"

"Yes." I grab his face and smash my lips to his. Soon we're all tangled up limbs and hands and searing mouths, but then my stupid phone rings, again, and I want to scream.

Graham tears his lips from mine. "Answer your phone. It might be important," he adds when I reach for him again.

Grumbling the whole time, I race to my room and grab the cell phone off my bed, not looking at the number until I am back in his room. My brain produces a swear word and I press my lips together to keep it inside.

"Hello." My greeting is not exactly friendly.

"Hey."

My eyes latch onto Graham's. "What's up?"

Blake's voice is less than smooth as he says, "I need a drink."

I close my eyes against my roommate/almost lover's narrow-eyed look. "So get a glass of water."

"Kennedy." My name is a rough plea I cannot pretend doesn't cause a sting in my chest.

An apologetic look is on my face as I look at Graham. I say to Blake, "I'll be right over."

Graham stands, his mouth is a thin line of displeasure. "Let me guess: Blake?"

For some reason, my nakedness now decides to cause me to blush. I guess it's because the lust fever abated as soon as I saw the name and number on my cell phone. I get up and move for the door. Why did I listen to Graham and answer the phone?

Shame flushes my skin more. If Blake hadn't gotten a hold of me and instead took that first drink of alcohol, I have this idea that it would have been really disastrous for him. I'm glad he called. I just wish it had been in, I don't know, thirty minutes or so. I don't know why he called me, specifically, but I can't not go to him. That would be cruel and I am not a purposely mean person.

"Yeah. He isn't doing so hot."

"It's like he has some super powers that let him know the worst possible time to be around, even if only in spirit," he mutters, swiping a hand through his hair and causing a chaotic mess of golden strands to form around his head.

"Come on, have a little empathy."

He glares at me, gesturing downward. "Empathy isn't really what I'm feeling right now."

I grab the first article of clothing I find—a sock—and hold it over my breasts. "I'm sorry. You have no idea how sorry I am. For real."

His eyes scour the surface of my skin, up and down, making me hot and shaky. "I'm sorry too."

I want to be flippant and suggest a rain check, but his whole being is telling me that wouldn't be a good idea. I edge toward the door. "Really sorry."

He nods, not looking at me.

Tossing clothes on, I feel excruciating tightness in my throat, to the point where it hurts to inhale. There was something so resigned about Graham, like he was flirting with the idea of giving up on me. He won't. My positive self is hopeful, and maybe delusional. But then, so am I, and I tell my negative self everything will be okay. It has to be.

Determination and annoyance stiffen my jaw as I drive to Blake's. He's sitting on the steps outside his apartment with his hands dangling between his knees and his head lowered. His broken form swipes the irritation from my brow as I sit beside him. "'Sup."

"Today is the anniversary of my girlfriend's death."

"Bummer." The word sounds callous, but it's not. I just don't know what to say.

Blake seems to understand. "Yeah. I thought I would be okay this time, but I wasn't—I'm not. I never am. Every day I fight my past, and sometimes, I wonder why I keep fighting it." He takes a deep breath before dropping the bombshell he isn't aware I already know. "I was driving the car. It's my fault she's dead."

My lungs exhale in a deep sigh of sorrow and apprehension. I do not want the burdens Blake keeps unloading on me, but I also know someone needs to take them. "Did you love her?"

He shrugs. "I guess. As much as I knew about love to be able to feel it."

"It wasn't intentional."

"Tell that to the judge and her family."

I watch as stars make their presence known, flipping on like tiny lights under the canopy of night. "Part of living is accepting you do not control everything."

His laugh is cutting, blades of displeasure against my spine. "I haven't been able to control any part of my life."

"So take control."

"You don't know what it's like—"

My head turns lightning fast, his words falling away as our eyes connect. "Save it, Malone. Every day is a new day to be awesome, and you, my friend, choose to not be awesome more times than should be available. It should be like a Pez dispenser of unawesomeness, and eventually, it should run out. I think yours should have been bone dry long ago—without the option of refilling it. Right? Right."

"You're crazy," he murmurs, but there is the hint of a smile in his voice.

"Crazy like a fox."

He snorts, shaking his head. "I think about her a lot—not really her, I guess, but the fact that I took away any chance of her life getting better. Neither one of us was all that level-headed then. Young and dumb. Reckless. But there was always the chance it could get better, and because of me, it was never able to, not for her. Her parents hate me. She has a younger brother...I ruined all of their lives by my stupid actions."

"You can only ruin someone's life if they allow it."

"I don't think they would have allowed me to kill their daughter and sister, if they had had the choice."

"Nobody likes a whiner."

He looks down at his clasped hands. "Her name was Billie."

"Was the middle name Jean?"

He gives me a blank look. "No. Jo."

"So you're saying the kid is not your son?"

"Wow."

"I know." I bump my shoulder against his. "Talk."

I realize my comments could be seen as insensitive and macabre, and yet, as he shares pieces of his past with me, and I make my twisted quips, he relaxes, starts to smile, looks brighter than his usual gloom and doom self. I'm telling you, I got skills. Unorthodox skills, but skills nonetheless.

Blake steps away from the edge of self-destruction one more time, and I hope he can find it in himself to continue to do so. He has to realize he's strong on his own. Otherwise, he'll never believe it's true.

The apartment is dark and quiet when I get home, which is odd because it's not even ten yet. I stumble around in the dark, not wanting to turn on any lights—why, I am not sure. Because Graham turned them all off, I suppose, and turning even one on, would be letting him win, in some stupid, childish way. But, hey, have I ever once said I was mature? If I did, I was totally lying. Just so you know.

"Why is it that you say you don't have a thing for my brother, and yet every time I turn around, you're with him?" The voice is low, too even to be natural, and creepy since there is no body to accompany it.

"Why are you turning around all the time? Maybe you turned around a few times and got super dizzy so you just think you're still spinning around, only you really aren't," I spew forth in a rushed manner only a truly gifted person is capable of.

A light turns on and I feel all 'naughty girl caught in the act'. Of what, I don't know. I blink in the sudden light and focus on Graham's form. He's standing against the wall opposite me with his arms crossed. I pay a little too much detail to his bare chest, but I am merely reacquainting myself with a sight I have missed, so it's totally acceptable. His golden hair is standing up in a few spots, he's sporting a scowl, and he looks so good my mouth goes dry.

"You know he needed someone to talk to."

"They have shrinks for that. Since when is he your responsibility? Last time I checked, even with how orally gifted you are, you do not have a license to be dragged into the mess that is Blake's mind."

Orally gifted. Why did my face just burst into flames? And I feel like giggling. I school my features into a mask of calmness. "What happened to being real? What's really bothering you?"

He gives me a look, shaking his head. "You know what I find funny? Women say they want a nice guy, but who do they usually go for? Not the nice guys. Any woman ever given the choice between someone sweet and someone rude, takes the rude guy. And you know why? Because women like to think they want the nice guys, but they really don't. Nice guys look good on paper, but in real life, not so much. Women don't even know what they want, so how do they think men are ever going to figure it out?"

"That should be on a shirt. And are you trying to imply something?"

"No."

"Graham."

"*I'm* the nice guy here." He rubs his face, giving me a bleary-eyed look as his hands drop to his sides. "I feel like a complete ass, but I have this—this *insecurity* inside of me, telling me you want Blake. It's this monster of doubt and I keep telling it to shut up, but it just isn't going away."

"Well, I want you to seduce me, but that isn't happening either, so I have my cross to bear as well."

"What?" His voice is faint.

"Nothing."

Graham's expression tells me he didn't appreciate that jab. "What happened to being real?" he mocks.

I scowl. "Can you make brownies again? I have too many clothes on."

His jaw tightens. "There are brownies in the kitchen."

"It's just not the same as when they come fresh out of the oven."

"Did you sleep with him?" His voice is blunt, razor-edged. He doesn't even sound like Graham anymore. I thought I would like that, but I don't. I want old Graham back. He was so much sweeter.

My good humor dissipates likes droplets of water under the sun as his words sink in. "You did not just ask me that."

He shrugs, his shoulders stiff under the guise of nonchalance he is trying to portray. "You said if you didn't get it from me, you could get it from him. So? Did you?"

"You know, I change my view on you. You...are an asshat."

"Whatever."

Whatever. I'll give him whatever. My mouth puckers up in distaste and I storm past him to get to my room. He grabs my arm as I pass by, but I jerk it away. I slam the door behind me and slide down its length, my butt firmly planted in the carpet beneath me. I stare into the darkness, seeing nothing but blobs of black over more blobs of black. What has happened to us? Our relationship used to be so effortless. We've turned into these two insane people that snap at each other and make little sense. I mean, I'm pretty much the same, but Graham? What the hell happened to Graham?

You happened to Graham.

Shut it.

I figure he's gone to bed, but then his voice talks from the other side of the door, startling me so that I kick my leg out and my foot connects with my bed. I inwardly curse, rubbing at the throbbing toe as I listen.

"You want to know why I chose to be a golf instructor?"

So you can flirt with women all day? I bite my lip to keep the words unspoken. He's not really a flirt. He's just a super nice guy and women like to think he's flirting with them because he's attractive, and attention from an attractive guy is hard to come by sometimes. I have it all figured out. Don't ask how many hours I spent analyzing it all.

"I hate confinement. I acted like I didn't know what Blake was talking about when he said the same, but...I know exactly what he meant. I just—I didn't want you to know how truly messed up my childhood was. Blake has no problem playing the victim in his own twisted, sarcastic way, but I can't do it. I won't."

There are other jobs that require being outside, my hateful side sneers.

"I mean, yeah, there are other jobs I could have picked and still been outside."

I whip my head around to frown at the door.

"But I actually do like golf. And I like teaching people something they want to learn, not something they have to or need to learn."

"Why are you telling me this?" I whisper, not sure if he can hear me or not.

Silence is my answer for a long time, and then, quietly, he says, "I just want you to know me. All of me. Even the asshat parts, but especially the non-asshat parts."

I twist around so that my head is resting against the door, and somehow, I feel that Graham's is as well. I do know him. And I love him—every part of him, even the ones that would be considered flawed by many. I have to, 'cause I have been given no less of the same from him. Friends or roommates, lovers or nothing, he's always cared about me, even when I was probably unlikable.

I hear him sigh. "Good night, Kennedy."

"Good night, Graham."

chapter eleven

It's sort of awkward showing up to an event with your "date" not really speaking to you, but that's how we apparently roll today. I dislike mute Graham a lot. He's no fun at all. I think of telling him how much fun he isn't right now, just to further irritate him, but his clenched jaw tells me I probably shouldn't. I don't know what his problem is this time. All I said was that Blake was coming alone today and maybe we could have him ride with us.

Needless to say, he didn't ride with us.

I'm wearing a lemon yellow top and white shorts I know will not be white by the end of the day. Part of me wants to toss the whole 'I love you and want to have your babies' fantasies from my mind and just go back to being roommates, but I can't do it. And anyway, no matter how good of friends we have ever been, I always wanted more. Craved it. Needed it. I can't go back to feeling a way I never really felt.

"Want a drink?" He doesn't look at me as he says this, his body turned partially away.

I roll my eyes at his behavior. "Make it scotch."

That gets his attention. "You don't drink scotch."

"How do you know? Maybe I'm a closet liker of scotch. I have my secrets too."

"Really?" He becomes much too engrossed in me. "Like what? Tell me one."

"Okay." I pretend to think about it. "Sometimes you put too many marshmallows in the hot chocolate and it turns out less than delicious."

He puts his beautiful face right next to mine. "Maybe you should make it from now on."

"Maybe I will."

He opens his mouth as though he wants to say more, snaps his lips together, and heads in the direction of a drink cart. I really hope he isn't bringing me back scotch.

The sunshine has its game on today and is making my skin a pretty pink that might turn into an unflattering shade of lobster red if it continues on its present course. There are people everywhere, milling about the rolling fields of green. The country club is closed to the public for this wondrous event, so everyone I am looking at either works here or is here with someone that does. But then I notice something that makes my head throb.

Graham is standing by the drink cart, his hair sexily disheveled and the neon green of his shirt a direct line for anyone hoping to get blinded. He is such an attention seeker. My lips compress in displeasure at the sight of the woman beside him. It's the ex I puked on. I really don't regret that right now. She tilts her head back as she laughs, placing a hand on his forearm. I want to dismember that arm from the rest of her for ever thinking she has the right to touch Graham, regardless of the fact that she once had every right. Even then she didn't have the right. I should tell her that. My feet start to move.

At either the worst possible time, or the best, reality seeps through the crazy in my brain in the form of Blake. A hand touches my arm. "I wouldn't."

Without taking my eyes from the pair, I grind out, "Wouldn't what?"

A cold cup is placed within my hand. "Whatever form of torture you're thinking of performing on her—I wouldn't."

I take a big gulp from the cup, my eyes widening as straight vodka slides down my throat. "What the hell?" I gasp, my esophagus on fire.

"You looked like you needed a drink."

"I generally drink vodka with something else in it—other than just ice cubes." I finally glance at him, noting the gray shirt and jeans and face twisted into an expression of innocence. "What are you doing carrying around booze anyway?"

"Helping a friend in need."

I slam the rest of the drink, its descent much smoother than the first time around. "Didn't you say I shouldn't drink to feel better, only to feel even better? Or something ridiculous like that?"

"Don't you feel even better than you did a moment ago?" His smile is much too sweet. He pats me on the back so hard I stumble forward. That could also be the effect of the booze, I suppose. Vodka tends to work quickly and effectively.

"It's nice to know you actually listen to me when I'm talking."

Kate Minson—Graham's ex-girlfriend—leans in close to my roommate and whispers into his ear. He looks momentarily surprised, but quickly covers it up with a flash of a smile. Forget the fact that it looks slightly strained. *I'll show him slightly strained.*

I smash the cup with my fist. "What did you say?"

He sighs. "Never mind. Going all Hulk, are you? Would you look at that; you're even turning green."

Graham looks up, his gaze shooting right to me. Even with the distance between us, I see his jaw stiffen as he takes in who I am standing next to. I offer a dramatic hand wave and he narrows his eyes, turning back to the brunette beside him.

"I puked on her once."

"Who?"

"Kate Minson. His ex-girlfriend that's all over him right now."

"If you keep drinking at the rate of your first cup, you'll be able to have a repeat. Guaranteed."

"I need a refill."

"On one condition."

I finally look at him. "You know I can go get my own, right?"

"You could, but you're lazy, and you'd rather not."

"How do you know me so well?"

"I pay attention."

"To my laziness? The highest of compliments right there, let me tell you."

Blake grins. "Let's golf."

"I don't know how to golf."

"Hey, with alcohol, anything is possible."

He starts to walk up the hill, but I hang back. "I get the feeling you have some nefarious agenda you don't want me to know about, and alcohol plays a key role in it." Nefarious? I didn't even know I knew that word. I guess what they say is true; alcohol does make you smarter. Or is it dumber? Nah.

"You should have been a detective," he says over his shoulder.

"I should have been a lot of things," I mutter, following him.

"Where are you going?" Graham demands as I sweep by, my nose toward the sky.

"To golf," I sniff. "Isn't that why we're here?"

"You don't know how to golf."

"Thanks for the drink," I say pointedly.

"Is that Kennedy?" Kate questions, her pretty face scrunching up like she just bit into a big, juicy bug. "She's still your roommate?" she continues, her voice going faint as I hurry my pace.

I used to get drunk and act stupid. Then I realized I don't need alcohol to be stupid. Then again—it doesn't hurt. Two drinks later—this time with orange juice mixed in with the vodka—I decide I am the best golfer ever. Blake agrees. Silently—but he agrees.

"Isn't there something wrong with this picture? The alcoholic supplying the booze?"

"Just go with it, and anyway, I don't need to drink when I'm around you. I can just get drunk off the fumes seeping out of your pores." He's standing behind me, his upper body close to my back as he resituates my hands on the club.

"So romantic."

"Tell me about it. Ready?" When I nod, he steps back. "Okay. Swing."

I do. Only I also let go of the club. I whirl around in time to see Blake staggering back with a hand to his head. "Are you okay?" I shriek, rushing for him.

He puts a hand out, halting me as it connects with my face. "I'm fine. Really."

I shove his fingers from my nose and mouth. "Let me see it."

"It just clipped my temple. I'll live."

"Deadly with a golf club. Never knew you had it in you."

I turn to face Graham. He is trying to smirk, but his mouth is too tight to fully allow it, so it looks more like he is grimacing. "You don't know everything about me."

"I think we established that already," he replies coolly.

I look past him, my hands flexing into fists when I see Kate is close by, chatting with a couple. I'm not sure if I'm making the fists because I want to hit her, or so I don't wrap them around her neck. I'm so conflicted. Punch her...strangle her...either possibility is much too tempting. She continually glances our way, her eyes locked on Graham in a creepy, stalker-ish way. *I* would never look at him like that.

"Why is she here? She doesn't work here."

"Apparently as of this coming Monday, she does," he says slowly, all expressionless about that fact.

"Hello. Injured party over here." Blake's voice is mocking, so I totally know he is fine. He just wants attention. It must be a family thing.

"She works here," I state, pinpricks of light bursting behind my eyelids. I think it's my sanity, finally leaving me.

"Yep." His tone is way too cheerful as he says this. "Why? Does that bother you?" He's watching me closely as he waits for my response.

I smile tightly. "Not at all. Excuse me. I have balls to hit." I put just the right amount of airiness to my voice as I flounce away, making a beeline for the nearest drink cart.

"Balls to hit?" Blake murmurs, appearing beside me.

I sip my drink, impulsively grabbing a bottle of water as well. I don't need to be sick, not just yet. I chug the water and toss the empty bottle into the nearest garbage can. "I'm hungry. Let's eat." I leave without waiting for an answer or to see if Blake is coming with me. He is a lurker by nature, though, so I'm pretty sure he'll show up sooner or later.

But he doesn't. Graham does. His face is like stone as he wordlessly stands beside me. I get a hamburger and so does he. I grab a bag of chips and he does the same. I refuse to look at him, but I can feel him. He's sucking me in by mere proximity alone. What sorcery is this? I spin on my heel and find a picnic table to sit at. He sits across from me.

"What are you doing?" I finally demand when I've had enough of this silent...whatever this is.

"We came here together."

"You are so perceptive."

A tick forms near his eye. "Why are you hanging out with Blake?"

"Why are you hanging out with pukey Kate?"

He leans toward me. "She was only pukey because of you."

"She was still nauseating, either way." I take a large bite of the manufactured hamburger patty and swallow the dryness down. It should make me feel better to know that I am most likely not really eating meat, only...there's the question of what I *am* eating.

"Are you jealous?" He pops a chip in his mouth and crunches away.

"Are you?"

"Yep."

I slowly set my hamburger down, not expecting that admission. Although, can you really blame him? I open my mouth to ask him why we both are such morons, but then Kate ruins it with her face, and the arm she puts around Graham's shoulders, and the lopsided hug she gives him. My bag of chips become dead chips as I watch. I relax my hand around the bag once its unfounded destruction becomes known to me. Those chips didn't deserve that kind of an end.

Her face is flushed, making me think she is drinking booze—the bottle of flavored beer in her hand is a good sign of this as well. She tugs on his arm. "Graham, come on. I want some golf lessons from a pro."

My eyes narrow. "Then you're talking to the wrong person." Graham is a good golfer, I'll give him that, but he is certainly not a professional. Never mind the fact that she knows this and was most likely trying to give him an ego boost. Ego boosts are lame, unless they're for me.

"Come on, Graham. Please?" Her voice is all whiny, her eyelashes fluttering at him.

"Do you have a bug in your eye?" The glare she aims my way is lethal, but I can do better.

A voice behind me says, "Ready for round two, Kennedy?"

And just like that, Graham shoots to his feet, throwing his food away. "Let's go, Kate."

The scowl on my face doesn't fade even when they are no longer within sight. I turn it on Blake and he shrugs. The way his lips twitch tells me he is enjoying the current debacle that is Graham and me more than he should. I elbow him as I stalk past, a smirk replacing the glower on my face when he grunts.

Somehow we manage to be set up right beside Kate and Graham. And by "somehow," I mean that I purposely stand next to Kate and Graham. All the better to be nosy. Blake just rolls his eyes at my obvious antics and demonstrates the proper way to stand and hold a golf club. I drink my drink and pretend to pay attention, but all the while my mind is on the couple beside us. How did this happen? How did Kate steal my roommate/date away? How did I get stuck with Blake?

"Kennedy? You want to try?" he asks when I finally drag my eyes to him.

"I hate golf," I mutter, grabbing the golf club from him and whacking at the ball. I miss.

I shouldn't say "stuck". Blake is a good time, don't get me wrong. He's just—he's not my good time. Graham is. And Kate totally snatched him away. I'm not sure how many drinks I've had, but I at least have had four by now. Every time Graham looks at me, I look away. My face is hot and I feel dizzy, but I am blaming that on the sun. The sun can do that.

"Are you sure it's golf you hate?" Blake's eyes go to Kate and back to me.

"Shut up."

"Pretend the ball is her face. It might help."

I stand as directed. "This is the most uncomfortable position. How do golfers do this?" I visualize Kate's smiling face and swing. And miss again. A curse word slips out. "You're a terrible instructor."

"I never realized how much you complain."

Taking a deep breath, I look at Blake. "You like golf too."

"I do."

"You seem pretty good at it."

"I am."

I nod, swiping sweaty hair back from my cheek. I hear Graham's low voice off to the side and want to annihilate the girl standing next to him. I glance over, noting how close Kate is standing to him. He isn't looking at her, but she is devouring him with her eyes.

"I can't take this anymore," I mutter.

"Why does your voice have an ominous cast to it?" Blake reaches for me when I start to walk away, ushering me back to our proper spot. "What are you doing?"

"I'm going to kill her," I say with calmness that should be admired, not followed by the incredulous look on Blake's face.

"Focus, okay? It's seriously messing with Graham that you're hanging out with me, so this is working in your favor, right? Just act like you're having fun, which shouldn't be hard to do. You *are* with me."

I, completely by accident, toss an empty water bottle in the direction of my roommate and his ex. It hits his shin just as I turn away.

"Subtle."

A ball flies by my face and I whirl around, my gaze touching on Graham's wide eyes before focusing on Kate. "Whoops," she says with a shrug. "I guess I need more one on one coaching, Graham."

"It would help if you were standing in the right direction," is his wry comeback.

Kate laughs shrilly and my insides go chaotic even as I am frozen. "I know. I'm so bad."

Blake gives me a look. "Breathe in, breathe out."

"I'm not having a baby."

"No. Just a meltdown. Isn't this fun? I couldn't imagine having a more fun time."

"Because you get off on sick, sick things. He broke up with her months ago." I shred the lawn with my club. "Why is he even talking to her?" The lawn gets in the club's way again. "She is so *fake*." A sound of frustration leaves me and I fling the club down.

"Somebody ate their grumpy pills today." Her voice is sweetly snarky and I am *done*.

"Do you *eat* pills?" I demand as I face her, closing the distance between us. She blinks and backs up a step, a furrow forming between her perfectly arched eyebrows. "I mean, if you're going to try to go for cute, at least make sense."

"You're so demented."

"You're right. I am." The next instant has me doing something crazy—demented, even. I'm going to say it's heatstroke messing with my head, but in any event, I snatch Blake's glass of water from him and toss it in her face. "I'm super demented."

A shriek leaves her as she hops up and down, but it isn't long before her eyes are blazing and she recovers enough to shove me. Blake rights me when I haphazardly stumble into him and Graham tells Kate not to touch me again, which further irritates her, as does, I'm sure, the smirk on my face as I toss my Screwdriver at her. I'm all about the drink throwing today, apparently.

"Kennedy, knock it off," Graham warns.

I stick my tongue out at him, totally not scared.

"The only reason we broke up was because of you always butting into our relationship! You were just there, all the time." She stabs a finger at me and I slap it away.

"You wish that was why. And I live there. What did you expect?"

When we both advance a step, Graham shoots between us, raising his hands to keep us from attacking. "That wasn't it, Kate, and you know it," he says, looking tired and sounding like he's had this conversation many, many times before. I know he has—I was sitting next to him during many of the aforementioned conversations. Granted, I was pretending to read, but still.

"It could have been the vomit. That was pretty unflattering. You have to admit," I say to my roommate with a shrug.

She makes a hissing sound as she inhales, her hands clenching at her sides. "That was the most disgusting thing ever."

"Tell me about it."

I hear a snicker and look over my shoulder. Blake is watching us with a thoroughly amused look on his face, arms crossed over his chest. He offers another glass of water with raised eyebrows. I wonder who his supplier is.

Graham's lips are turned down, telling me he doesn't appreciate my commentary. Looking at Kate, he says, "You look like you might want to go home. Do you have a way there?"

Wet with booze, looking like a wilted flower, she beams and somehow manages to come off angelic. I scrunch my nose up. I hate people that look cute even when they shouldn't.

"My dad dropped me off and he isn't coming back for a few hours. Can you take me home?"

"He is not taking you home. Ever," I say in a super controlled voice.

"Oh, he already did. Plenty of times," she purrs.

Blake guffaws and I want to smack him.

"Past tense," I hiss like a snake. I feel like one—all venomous and whatnot. "Meaning, never again," I clarify.

"You don't know that."

"I so know that."

"Okay. That's enough, both of you." This from Graham.

"You're right. It is. Let's go home." I put emphasis on "home" with a pointed look at Kate, in case she forgot we live together. He shall be going home with me and no one else. He will take me home and no one else.

A spray of red, sticky flavored beer hits me in the face, neck, and chest area. A gasp falls from my mouth as I freeze in disbelief. She did not just do that. Okay, so I guess I may have deserved it.

"Sorry," she trills, a satisfied smirk on her berry-colored lips.

With a battle cry, I sprint at her with my hands out and aimed for her neck. Amazingly, no one stops me. She screams and tries to run away, but I am faster. I grab her around the waist and we both go down, right into the soggy grass left in the wake of our alcohol and water abuse. Mud and other things become imbedded into my skin and clothes. I knew these shorts were going to get dirty.

"I don't like you!" is all I can think to say. Hey, sometimes keeping it simple is the way to go.

"I don't like you either!" she yells with her eyes closed.

Shoving me off of her, she staggers to her feet. Her hair is a matted mess around her face, her dress is stained with unknown substances, and she looks ready to cry. And yet she somehow holds it in.

Leaning close to my ear, she whispers, "Just remember, starting Monday, I'll be working with him." Straightening, she gives me an evil grin before strutting away like she isn't receiving puzzled stares from people.

And now I want to cry. A hand appears in front of my nose. I look up, see a grim-faced Graham, and ignore his offer. A curse word fills the air as I stand and he wraps his arms around me, holding me to him.

"I know, very sentimental moment. One I'll be sure to tell the grandkids. What are you doing?" I try to push him away, but he doesn't budge.

"Blake," he barks.

"Yeah?" He looks from my face to Graham, supremely pleased.

"Do you have a jacket on your bike?"

"I do."

"Get it."

He angles his head. "I don't know. She looks fine without it to me."

A growl leaves my roommate.

With a wink, he heads for his bike.

"What's your problem?"

"Your shirt is wet."

"So?"

"It's revealing more than it should."

"Says who?" I try again to dislodge him, but he won't allow it. "Come on, Graham. It's too hot for this. Get off me."

His arms tighten. "No."

With a resigned sigh, I stand still as we wait for Blake to get back. "I really don't like Kate."

"Got that."

"And I'm annoyed with you."

"Completely mutual right now."

I sigh again. Looking up, I tell him, "Blake doesn't have a jacket."

"What?" He spins around so that I am facing an elderly couple and he can see his brother. "Damn it. Where is it?"

With a grin, Blake pulls a thin, lightweight jacket from his back pocket with a flourish. "Compact."

Graham manages to get the coat over me without letting my front be visible to anyone other than him. I watch him as he zips the jacket, the lines around his mouth obvious signs of his displeasure, the way his eyebrows are furrowed proof that he is not happy, and I just want to kiss him. But he is unapproachable, everything about him telling me to stay back.

"Make sure Kate gets home," he says to his brother, one hand around mine as he pulls me toward his truck.

I know he isn't concerned about her personally, simply her welfare, a fact that makes my heart swell with even more love for him. That decent part of him doesn't know how to go away, and I admire that, even as it irritates the snot out of me.

The ride home is silent. I stare out the passenger side window and Graham watches the road. We are at an impasse once again. Maybe I should give up. I realize how immature my behavior was, but it is to be expected, so I do not fully understand his anger with me. Maybe it's at the situation, maybe it's because he thought I was what he wanted and now realizes I am not. I can't believe that, though, and so I choose not to. Maybe I just need to grow up. I cross my arms and watch as cornfields turn blurry under the guise of my tears.

I'm pretty sure I'm as grown up as I'll ever be.

Dr. Olman and Sally show up at work Friday morning—together. The beams on their faces make me nauseous. This week has been horrible, and not just because Graham and I have barely spoken or hung out, but also because my dad and I started his dance lessons. I have swollen, throbbing toes.

It's true; he really can't dance.

And that isn't the worst of it. My mom made me take her shopping Tuesday night. Trying to conform her from the eighties to the two thousands took work—and wine. Lots of wine. She does look smoking hot now, so there's that. The look on my dad's face when she got home was priceless. I should have taken a picture. His gaping look was definitely frame-worthy.

"Why are you two so happy?" I ask, going for casual and coming off sounding sour. I guess I can mark acting off my list. I'm not *that* good at it.

Sally gives me a look and then grins. "We're engaged!" A diamond flashes my way, momentarily blinding me, and then Phoebe and Sally are squealing and hugging.

I look at Dr. Olman. "I don't understand. You weren't even dating." The mocking tone is one hundred percent real, as is the smirk I give him.

He flushes red, matching his shirt. "Oh...well..."

I give him a quick hug. "It's okay. I won't tell anyone about the closet. Congratulations."

He pats my back. "Thank you."

"Just so I'm prepared...are you going to get married in a closet? Because, if you are, we might want to clean it out first. Limited seating in there too. Bummer."

His back goes stiff and he pulls away. "Remind me why I hired you?"

"For my slap-stick humor?"

"No. That's not it. Keep going."

The urge to laugh takes over me. "Um...awesome dating advice?"

He is not amused.

"I know! No one else wanted the job."

"Close. Get to work."

He's lucky I like working here. Never thought I would, but then, even though I know an astronomical amount, I can't know everything. The rest of the day is spent listening to Phoebe gush over Nathan, who she apparently is in love with already. I fight not to roll my eyes, but the glow on her face and the softness of her smile work me over as the day goes on, and I find myself truly hoping they can make a go of it. I just hope their babies don't come out with feet for faces or cigarettes in their mouths. Shudder.

Post-work Friday afternoon, I knock on Blake's door, not surprised when he opens it with a smug smile on his face. He enjoyed last weekend a little too much. Not wanting to talk about anything, really, I've been ducking and weaving him like a cat against the promise of a bath. Apparently this past week has been the week of avoidance.

I toss the jacket on the back of the couch. "Thanks for letting me borrow it Saturday."

"No problem. You looked better without it though."

With narrowed eyes, I say, "I bet I did."

"Graham didn't agree."

"No. He didn't," I agree, crossing my arms. He about had a heart attack and the evil part of me enjoyed it. Jealous Graham is almost as much fun to see in motion as all the other dysfunctional parts of him—except for mute Graham. I've had enough of him lately.

"What's going on with you and Graham anyway? Little trouble in paradise?"

"Nothing's going on with Graham and me." Which is the problem. Everything has been put on pause.

"You barely talked last weekend. Until you were shouting. Is it because of me?"

"Well, you don't help. Did you take Kate home?" A bitter taste enters my mouth as I say her name.

"Oh yeah."

"Did you...?"

"Did I...what?" He lifts his eyebrows.

"You know, have sex with her."

He smirks, just a flash of teeth and lips and it's gone. "You're blunt. I like it. No. I didn't. I'm not that kind of guy."

I snort, pretty sure he *is* that kind of guy.

"You'll be happy to know she's been following me around at work all week instead of Graham. She must have acquired exceptional taste since last weekend."

My body freezes up. I have been going insane imagining all the possible workday scenarios at the country club, most of them involving Graham and Kate sneaking off to do the dirty deed. "So she isn't pursuing Graham?"

"Nah. He shot her down cold on Monday. Told her there was no way they were ever going to get back together. Ever. There's stodgy Graham for you, no fun at all." He pauses. "Before Kate scoops me up, why don't you lay claim to me? We both know you're infatuated with my body."

I blink, turning my confused face his way.

"You're fun. I like your mouth—both the things that come out of it and the way it looks. I like you. I mean, yeah, I'm leaving soon, but nothing is set in stone. I could finish my degree up somewhere other than Illinois. And I don't have to leave the country when I'm done with college. Or you could go with me. We could even date for a while and realize at the end of summer we aren't for each other. But I think we should at least give it a chance, and I know part of you wants to do the same."

His eyes are locked on me. "I mean, didn't Graham have his chance? He had over a year to tell you how he felt, and he waited until I showed up. Why? And you're with me right now, and not him, so what does that tell you? Because it tells me you care about me."

He is partially serious, or maybe more than partially. I can tell by the intensity of his gaze and how it does not waver from me. What is ironic is that I think if I had met Blake first, and there was no Graham in the picture, I would have dated him and I could have fallen in love with him. But with Graham I can see forever and I don't know if that would have been the case for Blake and me. I'm thinking it wouldn't have been. He's too needy. Not for me, in other words.

"I do care about you," I answer truthfully. "But you don't know me well enough to think what you're saying. You like the idea of me more than me personally."

"Don't tell me what I do or don't feel or think. I know enough about you."

"I think we get along so well because we both have the same defense tactics. Can you imagine us in an actual argument? We'd be endlessly flinging sarcasm back and forth."

"It would be pretty awesome." His lips twitch.

"Awesome, yes, but productive? No. Anyway, I think part of the appeal is that I have feelings for your brother and your issues with him compel you to try to steal me away from him."

"It's not really stealing if you aren't even his, now is it?"

A slap to the face couldn't have hurt more. "That was cruel. And Graham cares about me. We both know he does."

He curls his upper lip. "I'm a cruel guy. And, yeah, sure, he cares about you, just like I do—but does he love you? Has he ever specifically said those words?"

I shove his words away, along with the sting that comes with them. "None of this is really about Graham and me, or even you and me. It's about *you*—you and your brother. You want people to think all of these bad things about you, only none of them really fit. You hurt and you feel things and you maybe feel things more than others because you know what it is to screw up, to lose someone, to be at fault, to want to go back and change the things you cannot. You know what it is to feel like you aren't good enough. You know what it is to let something control you and you know what it is to have to be stronger than the need."

I begin to pace before him, wanting to blast the truth of my thoughts at him so completely that there is no way for him to refute the validity of them. He has to know this. He has to believe what I am telling him. "None of that makes you bad. Hiding the real you doesn't make you weak. Wanting to replace pain, to numb it, with alcohol and drugs doesn't make you irredeemable. It makes you human. It makes you...it makes you..." I struggle to find the right words. "It makes you a complex individual worthy of second chances and trust and hope. It makes you strong. You're strong, Blake. You just need to believe it yourself. And you and your brother need to start acting like brothers. You need him more than you need me. Trust me."

I've barely finished my words before he is moving for me. The fire in his eyes makes them shine silver as he reaches for me. His hold on my neck is hard as he slams his lips to mine. The longing and need in the kiss makes me want to cry for him. He needs so much. He needs more than I can give. He breaks away when he realizes I am stiff within his arms and not kissing him back, quickly moving to put distance between us.

"I'm sorry," he says roughly, his taut back to me. "You should go."

"Blake—"

"Go!" he roars, whirling around. He glares at me, anger hiding the hurt.

I fight tears as I slowly move for the door. Once there, though, I cannot go, not without saying what I have to. I stare at a small crack in the wood. "One day you'll find someone you don't have to feel the need to hide from. She won't be something you think you want or need. She won't be your redemption. You'll know when you find her, because you'll want to change for you, not for her. I was just another addiction, just something else you thought would make you whole. Nothing can do that for you but you."

I open the door and walk through it, quietly closing it behind me. Something shatters inside the apartment and I flinch, methodically putting one foot in front of the other as I slowly make my way down the stairs and away from Blake. I can't fix him. Only he can do that.

Graham doesn't fill a hole inside me. He doesn't fix what is broken. He just makes everything brighter. He makes me smile and he makes me laugh; I am better because of him, but I also realize I would be okay without him, and that is the difference between Blake and me. He is looking for a savior. One day he'll realize that he's the only one who can save him.

Wow, I totally just impressed myself with how mature I can be when I feel the need to be. High five to me—but not really because anyone looking would think I am clapping at nothing.

I show up at the apartment, all ready to finally tell Graham I love him like more than a brother from another mother—because I can't not tell him any longer—and halt in the doorway. Something doesn't belong in the room. Oh, right, it's the burly, black-haired man with Graham's eyes that is watching me from where he stands in the center of the room. He looks rich and asshole-ish.

"Who are you?" I demand. Maybe I should work on my greeting skills.

"Who are you?" he retaliates, flicking a piece of imaginary flint from his black polo shirt, and I know it's imaginary because, hello, black shirt? Everything shows up on black, except, well, black things. Moving on.

"Kennedy. Where's Graham?"

"Ah, the roommate." Something about his tone makes me like him less than I did a second ago, and that was already nil.

I know who he is.

"You're his dad." My voice is not welcoming.

"Benson Malone, yes." He pauses. "I'm looking for my son."

I lift an eyebrow. "Is he hiding?"

Amusement flickers through the eyes that should not be in his face. "Not Graham—the other one."

I cross my arms and lean against the door, forgetting I never shut it. I stumble back into the hallway and take a deep breath, carefully walk inside the apartment, and close the door. "Let's try that again." And I resume my earlier position.

Something that could pass for laughter sounds from Benson.

"Why are you looking for Blake?"

His brows furrow and he opens his mouth, but Graham happens to make an appearance before he can respond, which is either good for me or Benson. I can't be sure. "Kennedy," he quickly interjects. "I see you've met my father."

"Sure." If that's what you want to call it. "He's—"

"He stopped in to see if I've seen Blake recently, but I had to tell him that unfortunately, no, I haven't." He widens his eyes at me, telling me to shut up without telling me.

Stopped in? He makes it seem like he lives on the other side of town and not in another state. Something is up. I mean, *obviously*. Graham just saw his brother today at work. I frown, but amazingly manage to keep my mouth shut as I look at the man who fathered two exceptional beings and probably doesn't even realize it.

"Okay." That's all I got.

"You know Blake," his dad states.

"Noooo." I glance at Graham to see if this was the correct response. He does nothing, so I figure it must be.

"You said his name."

"Well, yeah, I mean, Graham's talked about him a lot, so, yeah, of course I know his name." I try to laugh, but it sounds like I am instead being strangled, so I stop.

"There was familiarity in your tone." His mouth is pulled down with suspicion.

I lift my hands. "I don't even know what that means, sorry."

"Which word?"

Dude. So uncalled for. I ignore him and look at my roommate. His hands are fisted at his sides and a tick has formed in his jaw. "Why is he looking for your brother? What's going on?"

"I'm right here. You can ask me."

I look in his direction as I say, "Don't you live in South Dakota or something? You just come to Wisconsin on some strange search and rescue attempt for your son who probably doesn't even want you to find him?"

"North Dakota," he tightly supplies.

"Blake's mom is sick. He wants him to come home to see her," Graham tells me.

"Like, a cold sick? And you couldn't call him to let him know?"

Benson stiffens up like a board. "She has cancer. He switched his phone number without giving me his new one. I've been trying to get a hold of him for weeks. Showing up here was my last resort."

That blows most of the wind from my sails, although, there's probably a reason Blake changed his number and didn't give the new one to his father. Like, he doesn't want to talk to him. I take a closer look at Graham's father. His skin is sort of pasty beneath the tan and there are black lines under his eyes. I can't hate a man who looks like that.

Shoulders slumping, I say, "I'm sorry to hear that."

"Not as sorry as I am," is his grim response. He turns to his eldest son. "If you're in contact with him, please let him know it's urgent that he gets in touch with me. I'm staying at The Cozy Inn for the night." He hesitates. "Maybe we can meet for breakfast in the morning before I head back, catch up."

"I'll let you know," is Graham's noncommittal response.

He nods at his son, pauses near me, and then quietly leaves.

Some of the tension, but not all of it, leaves with him.

Graham eyes me. "You were with Blake?"

Guilt stabs through me—for being with him when I know Graham hates it, and for how I left Blake, especially after what I just found out. "Yeah. I gave him back his jacket." I rub my forehead, dropping my hand to face him. "You should call him, or…maybe go over there and talk to him." I wince, wondering what state Blake will be in when and if his brother shows up.

Not your problem, I remind myself.

"I will, but only because of the circumstances." His jaw clenches. "You've apparently made your choice. I was going to tell you to move out, but…I don't think I can stand living here."

My lungs deflate. "No. You have it—"

He shakes his head. "We'll talk later. I have to let Blake know Dad's here."

I collapse on the couch, staring at the closed door Graham just walked through. I want to say I am devastated, but actually, I just feel numb. I am not one to sit and mope, so instead I go on a cleaning, chocolate-eating binge. The apartment becomes spotless as I consume large quantities of peanut butter cups. My thoughts race around what Graham said to me before he left and if he really meant it; wondering what's going on with Blake, how the news of his mother is affecting him, how both of them are dealing with their father being so close.

Is Blake is okay? Is Graham is okay? It's past midnight by the time I call it a night on the cleaning bit, plopping onto the couch and closing my eyes. I realize I am holding a peanut butter cup in my hand and, with eyes still closed, make it disappear.

I am magical.

Five minutes later I decide I can't take it anymore, and so, clad in purple pajama pants with black stripes and a neon yellow t-shirt, I head out into the night. Lucky for me, the streets are deserted, so I don't have to worry about all the inattentive drivers that are usually out during the day forcing me to drive badly. So that's a plus. Graham's truck is parked along the curb outside of Blake's temporary residence, and a shiny silver SUV is in the driveway. Frowning as some inner sense tells me that the SUV shouldn't be there, I climb out of my car and head up the stairs.

Loud male voices stream out to me through the closed door and I swing it open without knocking. I'm taken aback by what greets me, and it isn't just Blake clad only in his boxer briefs. Although—*hello*. His body is cut with that of the fine strokes of an artist's brush, all muscled and enticing. I shift my gaze away from his body, redirecting it to the scene before me. There are three male forms standing in the middle of the room, all angry-faced as they eye one another.

Benson reaches for his son, saying, "You're coming home with me, now."

Graham cuts him off, standing protectively before his younger brother. "You can't make him leave. He isn't some kid; he's twenty-six years old. He isn't yours to shove around anymore."

"He's a drug addict who can't take care of himself. I can, and I will. How long do you think it is before he's back to his pills and booze? He always goes back to them. Nothing has ever mattered enough to him to keep him sober for long. At least at home, there's less of a chance of it. His mother needs him," he adds.

"My mother needs many things, but none of them are me," Blake says in a low voice.

"Your mother is sick!"

"My mother was sick before I left! My mother's always been sick!" he shouts back. "And maybe it wasn't cancer then, but does it really matter?" He takes a deep breath, struggling to calm down. When he speaks again, his voice is softer. "There was always something keeping her apart from me. This isn't any different. She doesn't need me and I'm not going—not yet, not until I want to."

"If you do not come with me now, I will make you, and you won't like it. I got you out of that rehabilitation center once and I can put you back in it." Their dad's voice has turned to ice, and any empathy I felt for him at the apartment has dissolved like sugar in water. I hate this guy. Seriously. Totally. And it irks me like I can't explain that Graham and Blake were ever subjected to him, let alone stuck with him for years. At least Graham got away—Blake wasn't as lucky.

"You're going to have to get through me," Graham grimly tells his father.

Okay, so I'm sort of surprised they haven't noticed me yet, but this time, for once, I am all right with that. This is epic. And sad. I want to run in front of the Malone boys and save them from their big, bad dad, but this one I need to sit out. I see Blake's face when his brother says this, and my heart squeezes. Such vulnerability on a face usually constructed from stone is strange to see. His dark eyes lift and meet mine before he quickly looks down. Doesn't matter—I saw the glistening in them. He finally got his big brother back. Maybe I should have called Benson Malone when Blake first got here to speed up the brothers' reunion. I so would have. Well, maybe.

"You don't think I will?" Benson saunters toward them and both sons stiffen. "You might be older and bigger now, but you're still my son, and you will obey me."

When he gets close to him, Graham spits out, "Hit me and it will be your last time."

Benson laughs, and it is a cruel sound.

I freeze at Graham's words, and at his father's reaction. I lift my eyes to Benson and then they flicker over to where his son stands. He hit Graham? That man hit the sweet, loving boy I cannot imagine life without; the one that makes everything brighter and better? I thought I had it bad. My father has tried to turn me into a guy for as long as I can remember, but never once has he threatened or abused me. I know he loves me, even if I'm a disappointing girl instead of a rock star son, because it's just a given I'd be a rock star if I were a boy. Whatever misguided issues I've had with him are small potatoes to this. Never have I looked at him with a mixture of fear and defiance, not like Graham and Blake are currently looking at their dad.

They have been abused by this man.

If it hadn't already been apparent from Graham's words, I would have been able to tell by the way their shoulders hunch as if to protect them from an oncoming blow. It is evident in the way they won't meet his eyes for too long and flinch as he advances.

When he takes another step toward Graham and Graham straightens as though preparing for physical contact, I state, "Touch either one of them and I'm calling the cops." I even have my phone in hand and posed for emergency assistance because I am well-organized.

Three pairs of eyes swing my way. I see the color drain from Graham's face and I don't know if it's because I'm here, because I'm witnessing this, or if it's a combination of both. "You shouldn't be here," he says harshly. Ouch.

"He's right. Run along. This is family business and doesn't concern you."

I straighten and turn my dagger eyes on Benson. "It does concern me, and do you know why it does? Because Graham *is* my family. And anyone that hurts my family, deals with me." Blake groans and I ignore that. I may not be fluent in defensive skills, but I am totally adept at kicking a set of nuts. He really doesn't want to push me.

I don't look at Graham, because I don't want to take the chance of being hurt by whatever I see in his face. I'm sticking up for him, whether he wants me to or not. I love him, and that's what you do for people you love. You have their back, always.

Now that I have Benson's full attention, I'm sort of wishing I didn't, especially when he starts to walk toward me. "Do you know what I do for a living?"

"Stripper?" I guess hopefully.

His brows lower, almost completely obliterating his eyes from my view. "No. I'm a businessman. Do you know what businessmen get?"

"Free ice cream cones on Sunday?"

"Whatever they want," he answers darkly. "Your mouth—"

"Is amazingly gifted." I almost want to stop with the one-liners, but I am nervous, and so, they just keep spouting forth.

"Is annoying," he corrects.

"Well, that too." If you want to get technical.

"I'll go with you," Blake announces, stepping between his father and me. "I just—let's get this over with. Kennedy doesn't need to be pulled into our mess, and Graham deserves to be left out of it too." Can my heart get any tighter?

"You're not going with him," Graham angrily tells his brother. "This shit should have ended a long time ago. You are allowed to live your life without his influence on it. In fact, you'd probably be a lot happier without it. And...you can stay here, you can stay with me, for as long as you need. You don't have to go back. You don't—" He pauses, swallowing thickly. "You don't have to go anywhere, okay?"

The brothers stare at each other, understanding and acceptance falling over their faces like drops of rain. I know men are bullheaded, but, *come on*, they should have figured this crap out long ago. They need each other. I guess sometimes you can't see who your allies are unless there is a common enemy. As I watch them, I realize something as well—I love them both. Not in the same way, never that, but one as I should love a man and the other as I should love a friend. That's okay, I decide. My heart is big enough for two Malone men.

I look at their dad. But three? *Hell no.*

"This is ludicrous. How do you think your mother is going to feel knowing you refused to come back?"

"You don't have to tell her any of this, and really, you'd look better if you didn't," Graham informs him.

"Your mother was a whore, and I'm sure your roommate is too," is his awesomely inaccurate comeback.

I gasp, not so much by what he said—because I know his mother loved his dad and that's probably the only reason why she put up with his bullshit, and I'm a virgin, so his words are one hundred percent false—but by how I know Graham is going to react, and he does. He swings a fist at his dad and impact with his nose is made.

Benson Malone staggers back into the wall and slowly slides to the floor, his eyes unfocused and a stream of red coursing from his nostrils.

"You loved my mother once. Did you think she was a whore then?" he bites out, staring down at his father, his hands fisting at his sides.

Benson makes an unintelligible response, which is just as well, because, like anyone wants to hear any more from him anyway.

I look at my roommate, wondering if he hit his father for me or his mom, then figuring it was probably both. I ache that he did that, even though it was completely deserved. I ache that I can see the regret mixed in with the fury on his face. He wishes he hadn't done it—he wishes he'd had no reason to. He is breathing heavy as he glares his father down. Already his knuckles are pink and swollen. I want to take him into my arms and hold him until the pain goes away.

Also, he's been punching people a lot lately.

"I was supposed to do that," I tell him.

He shakes his hand out. "Actually, I think I was supposed to."

"Well, if you really feel it was necessary for it to be you."

"I really do."

I hit a button on my phone and widen my eyes. "Oh. Wow. I can't believe it, but I somehow, accidentally, totally without meaning to, pushed the button to call the cops." I look up into a pair of knowing green eyes. "Since they're probably almost here already..." I shrug and look at his dad. "I guess we should just tell them that he refused to leave and then attacked you. I mean, that's what I saw."

"Sounds good to me," Blake says, eyeing his partially conscious dad.

The cops arrive, the situation is explained, and Benson Malone is hauled off, hopefully never to harm—verbally or otherwise—his sons again. The air becomes strained with just the three of us standing around, avoiding eyes. I mean, not that it wasn't strained before, but this is a different kind of tension. This is the kind people with *feelings* for one another get when too many things have been said, not enough has been said, and no one knows what to say now.

But foremost, Blake and Graham need to be alone to talk. I may be in both of their lives, but they have a life, a connection, that has nothing to do with me. I need to make sure Blake is okay and I need to make sure Graham and I are okay, but for now, *they* need to be okay.

I blow out a noisy breath. "You two should talk. I'm going to go home." My eyes shift to Graham's. Is it still my home? I know my face gives this thought away.

His jaw tightens, but he doesn't say anything. He doesn't tell me to pack up and get the heck out, so I am going to go with it is still my home, at least for now. Which means I'm totally going to lounge about in his bed and eat doughnuts as I read a smut book—or just sleep. It is pretty late. Sleep equals fantasies about my roommate, so I'm really not too upset over the way the rest of my night may go.

I give a half-hearted wave and depart.

chapter twelve

W hen pacing around the apartment for an hour doesn't produce Graham like I feel it should, I go where I want to be, where I can feel closest to my roommate when he isn't around—his bedroom. Is that creepy? Maybe. I don't care. I can be a creeper. I'm cool with that.

And so, with the lights out, I crawl into his bed, feel his scent wrap around me, and hug his pillow to my chest. I guess if he kicks me out, at least I can have this until I get the boot. Something cold and suffocating punches me in the throat like the sharp edge of a sword, and I realize, it is fear. The thought of being without him is impossible to imagine, and I squeeze my eyes against the hated foreboding that slithers along my spine in the dark. Instead, I search for my happy place, finding it in the image of bright green eyes, and fall asleep to their truths, and to their secrets.

At some point during the night, I wake up, knowing I am not alone. I slowly sit up. In the black of the room I see a form sitting on the edge of the bed, unmoving. Other than a hazy outline, I can't see much of Graham. But I don't need to see him to know he is hurting. Gloominess rolls from him like a whip curling back up after it has lashed all the joy from a being. I crawl over to him, flip onto my back, and lower myself so that my head is resting beside his leg. I stare up at him, seeing the faint glow of his eyes, barely able to make out the line of his hard mouth.

"I didn't want you to see that." His voice is low, rough with emotion.

"See what?"

"The asshole that is my father."

I take a deep breath. "Asking you if you're okay would be lame."

"Ask me anyway."

"Are you okay?"

A finger brushes hair from my forehead and I shiver. "No. But I'm better than I was before I walked into this room."

"Such a charmer," I murmur, really meaning it and somehow managing to sound sarcastic. Sometimes gifts can be curses too, I suppose. "Is it the bed?"

"That. And the person in it."

I want to crawl into his lap and cling to him. I don't. Instead I say, "We need to talk."

"Yes." Resignation hangs from that one word.

With a sigh, I sit up, turning to face him, and cross my legs. "We need to talk about us, but we also need to talk about you. Why are you afraid of the dark and don't like walls around you?"

His head tips forward, golden hair presently painted ebony with night. "It isn't hard to guess."

"Right. I know that. But I want you to tell me. I mean, if you want to tell me." I blow out a noisy breath. "Do you want to tell me?"

He lets himself fall back so that his legs are hanging over the edge of the bed and places his hands behind his head. "You want to know something really macho?"

I remain quiet, knowing he doesn't really want me to answer that. Sometimes paying attention really does have its pluses. Like knowing what's going on. That's always a plus.

"I used to pee the bed." He cringes, but I just look at him, not judging. It's whatever. It happens. Apparently even adults do it—not me, but other adults. Usually there is alcohol involved.

"My dad used to lock me in a closet when I misbehaved. Even if it wasn't anything that bad, like if I forgot to wash my hands after sneezing or something. He wasn't just strict—he was controlling to the point of being cruel. And it wouldn't be for minutes; it would be for *hours*. I'd sit in a closet barely bigger than I was, scared and hungry, and I had to stay like that until he let me out. Sometimes—sometimes it got so bad, and I was in there so long, that I literally pissed myself." Shame coats his words.

His hands move from his head to his face. "And then I'd have to stay in there longer for doing that. My mom—my mom didn't know. He never did that shit when she was around and I never told her. My dad told me only babies ran and told their moms on their dads. I believed him.

"It got to the point where I couldn't sleep at night if the lights were out. I was terrified. And my dad wouldn't let me have them on, and...*fuck*. I would pee the bed at night. My mom didn't understand what was going on; she just thought I had a weak bladder. Ironically, it only happened when my dad stayed over, or when I had to stay at his place. I guess I was scared of him even as I slept." He pauses. "This is embarrassing."

I touch his arm, squeezing gently. "Hey. This is me. I wear embarrassing like a velvet coat of awesomeness. Continue."

He continues. "The bed-wetting went on for a few years, to my complete humiliation. I couldn't even stay at any of my friends' houses because I was worried I would pee the bed and end any friendships I had." The bleakness of his tone repeatedly punches my heart until I fear it will be bruised indefinitely.

"It was just this horrible cycle. I'd do something wrong, he'd punish me until I did another thing wrong, and then he got to punish me some more. It never ended, not until I quit going there. The abuse changed in form over the years—more verbal than anything, but he was always an asshole. And then I abandoned Blake to it."

"You were just a kid," I whisper, my chest and throat and everything inside me aching for him.

His hands drop from his face and he slowly turns his head toward me. "Yeah. I was. But so was Blake. And he needed me more than I needed to be away from our dad. I should have been there for him. I should have done more, taken more, and been what my brother needed so he didn't feel like he had no one. That's what big brothers do, right? They protect their younger siblings. But I didn't. I left."

"He's here now and you're helping him."

"Too little. Too late."

I touch his sharp jaw and he turns into my hand, brushing his lips against my palm. I lean toward him, our faces so close I can see his eyes looking at me. "Stop it. Right now."

"I'm trying, I am. Am I really helping him? I don't think so. I think he would have been better off not coming here at all, and I'm not saying that just because of you. We just—we don't have that brotherly bond or whatever the hell it is."

"I'm glad he came."

He freezes, and then sits up, moving away from me.

"Because," I prod on, closing the distance between us. "If he hadn't come here, where would we be? We'd still be stuck as Ken and Barbie, platonic BFFs for life. And even if things haven't exactly gone smoothly, at least they've *gone*, ya know? I see a different you and you see a different me, and it needed to happen, even if it sucks. And you're wrong," I add.

"About?"

"You and Blake do have a brotherly bond. You stuck up for him in front of your dad. That took a lot of guts. High five." I raise my hand. He ignores it. I drop my hand with a sigh.

"You care about him."

"Yes. Am I not allowed to care about another guy?"

Graham gets up from the bed, his movements jerky and ungraceful.

"Where are you going?" I demand when he starts across the room.

"I can't sleep here."

"But...it's your bed."

He pauses. "You're right. It's my bed. You get out."

I cross my arms. "No."

"Fine." He opens the door, slamming it behind him.

I blink in the empty, dark room, and then dive for the door, frustration pushing me forward with the wings of an angry bird. Which—totally love that game.

I grab the glass of orange juice he just poured, glaring at his scowling face, and chug it just to irritate him. His face darkens and he grabs another glass from the cupboard, pouring more juice. I take that one and slam it down as well. We're going to go through a lot of glasses at this rate.

"Knock it off, Kennedy!"

"You keep pouring them, I'll keep drinking them," I declare, even though I doubt it, 'cause my stomach is already rebelling.

He goes for water next and I drink that down too.

"You're such an infantile," he says with disgust.

"You love that I'm such an infantile!" I shout at him.

"You're right! I do."

I frown at his words and facial expression. It looks like he surprised even himself by admitting that. He stares at me for a minute and then shakes his head, looking away.

I muster up my irk to say, "Then don't say it like you don't love it when you so love it."

His lips press together and he charges toward the patio door, but I beat him to it. I know I am being *completely* infantile, but I don't care. I need his attention, however I can get it.

"What are you doing?"

I place my palms against the glass and block the immediate exit. "I'm putting myself in front of you."

"I see that. Why?"

I shrug. "It seemed like a good idea."

"It wasn't." He puts his hands on my shoulders and firmly moves me to the side.

"Neither was that," I mutter and hop on his back as he walks through the patio door.

"What the hell? Are you out of your mind?" he thunders, reflexively grabbing the backs of my legs so I don't fall. I knew he cared.

"Yes!" I scream. "I'm out of my mind and you already know this so why are you acting like you don't?"

He somehow twists his upper body as he reaches for me and pulls me off of him and in front of him. Hands on my shoulders, he shakes me. "Quit doing these crazy things!"

Words spew forth in a chaotic rush. "You don't get it. I need to be like this. I don't want to be some over-emotional chick that cares what everyone thinks about her. That can't be me. I hide myself behind layers of me and it works, for the most part, but right now, with us, it really hasn't worked. It was safe. I thought safe was good. I hate safe. I don't want safe. I can't pretend this is okay anymore. I can't keep hiding."

"Meaning what?"

I fall into the patio chair and feel it sway beneath my weight. As if I needed *that* to make me feel better. "You're so blind, Graham," I whisper.

"Twenty-twenty vision," he replies wryly.

I lift my face and scowl at him. "Not where it matters, not when it counts."

His body descends into the chair beside me and he rubs his face. "Maybe you should explain it to me then."

"Okay. Fine. Blake is only hitting on me to aggravate you. Did you see that?"

"No. He is hitting on you because he wants to die," he says darkly.

"He's probably attracted to me, a little, but he's just lost, ya know? And he thinks he needs someone to make him whole. But more than that, more than me, he wants his brother, and he can't just come out and say that, so he thinks he has to be the annoying kid brother, because no matter how old you two get, he'll always be the little brother. Why can't you see that?"

He doesn't speak for a long time, staring into the night. "I do," he finally says. "I do see it. When I can think straight. But then I see the two of you together and I think of the two of you together and I go mad. You liked kissing him." His jaw is tight, his hard body coiled like a wire.

"Well, it wasn't terrible."

He jumps to his feet and goes inside, leaving me outside. That just isn't going to fly. I need confrontation and he's going to give it to me. I've had enough of this tension. It sucks ass. Big time.

He's standing in his room, staring at the only framed photograph in it. My chest clenches at the sight of it sitting on top of his dresser.

"Tell me the truth, what's going on with you two?" he asks, not looking at me.

"What's going on with you and pukey Kate?" I demand, holding my breath as I wait for his reply. I could take Blake's word for it that there is nothing between them, but I need confirmation from Graham. He needs to tell me.

She was never good for him. When they were dating, everything was about her, not him. It was like she cared more about how he looked with her than him. There was always this vague look in her eyes—she wasn't really seeing him, not like she should have been. She didn't realize how amazing he was when she had him, so she can't have him back. I decree it.

It takes him a while to answer. "I guess I'm not as nice of a guy as I thought I was."

"Why do you say that?"

He looks at me. "Because I can't stand pukey Kate. I was only talking to her to make you jealous. A nice guy wouldn't do that."

"She's pretty," I grumble, just to be fair.

"I guess. That doesn't mean anything. Pretty girls are nice to look at, but that's about it."

I look down, knowing I don't fall into the customary "pretty girl" category. I guess that's okay. I'm awesome enough without being beautiful as well.

"Why do you like me so much?" I blurt out. And then I keep going, because sometimes, I don't know when or how to shut up. "I've never really had a serious boyfriend. Or female friends. I annoy people, exasperate them. I say the wrong things. And you...you're pretty close to perfect. You could have just about anyone."

Rough fingers graze my jawline and I look up. "I prefer girls with sharp tongues, questionable morals, and quirky personalities, all of which, in my estimation, are sure signs of beauty. And your face doesn't hurt either." His hand drops from my chin. "I am far from perfect. You live with me. You know this."

"Right. You have all kinds of flaws." I roll my eyes.

"I do," he says earnestly. "I have a little bit of OCD. Everything has to be orderly and clean. I imagine it gets irritating at times having to deal with my neurotic habits."

I want to roll my eyes again. "Yeah. You're a horrible, horrible person."

He doesn't seem to hear me. "Yes, you're a pain in the butt, but in your own way, you have sweetness to you. I look at you, and I want to smile, all the time. I never know what you're going to say or do next, and I like that. No one could ever say you're dull. But you're wrong." His mouth compresses. "If I could have anyone, I'd already have her."

My breath hitches. "Aunt Jemima?"

Graham's brows furrow.

"I know about your syrup obsession."

He picks up the photograph and brings it to me. Two people with goofy expressions on their faces look back. Tapping a finger on the face of the female in the picture, he says, "Her."

I swallow thickly, staring at our happy faces. The picture was taken on New Year's Eve last year. We went to a party together, danced, made fun of the drunk people around us, got drunk ourselves, and ended the night by falling asleep on the couch with our feet in each other's faces. It was the best time ever.

"I mean, it's obvious, right? Look around my room. See any other framed pictures?"

I nod toward the painting of a run-down barn with endless blue skies and rolling hills of green. That is the lone piece of artwork in the room. Graham likes simplistic decorating, because to him, that means clean. I know, I don't get it either. Messes are chaotic, yes, but they're also interesting.

We're sort of a mess, I decide, fighting a smile.

"Of people." When I don't say anything, he continues. "When is the last time I dated anyone? Haven't you wondered about that?"

"Figured you were finally getting some decent taste," I mumble.

Graham rubs his face. "I'm...tired. In general, but about this too. Any girlfriend I've had since you've been my roommate I've compared to you and always found them lacking. I gave up trying to delude myself into thinking I could fall for someone else and just decided to enjoy what I could get of you. But it isn't enough now, and it hasn't been for some time."

He takes a deep breath, that paused inhalation of air telling me he is about to say something big. "Answer me truthfully, okay? Do you want Blake or do you want me? Or do you want neither of us? Because, I want you. And not just for a little bit, and not just in my bed, but all of you, and I hope, for always. Whatever you tell me, I'll try to be okay with it. I just want to know."

I wheeze, trying to breathe. He did not just say that. Only he did. My heart is pounding a scary beat in my chest and I suddenly feel dizzy. I open my mouth, but only a squeak comes out.

He stares down at me, his features harder, and at the same time, more open than I've previously witnessed. I see yearning in his eyes—this look of wanting something always just out of reach. He slowly begins to talk. "I hate that you're attracted to my brother. It makes me want to punch him in the face, but more than anything, it makes me want to rip my own heart out, just so I don't have to feel pain every time I think about you looking at him like you used to look at me.

"I thought you were mine. I mean, even though we'd never actually said it, I just...it was...it was *there*. Ya know? I could see it, I could feel it. It was this certainty, this one thing I knew to be true, out of the many things I didn't. It didn't have to be said."

He swallows thickly, turning his eyes away so that his sharp jaw is within my view. "And now I realize it should have been said. There was no doubt in my mind it would happen when the time was right. I wanted you so bad I just knew you had to want me too—I'm such a clueless asshole."

"You're not an asshole. I mean, not all the time. Sometimes, though, you are clueless. But so am I," I hurry to add.

He gives me a look. "Why is everything so difficult with you? I literally feel like I'm going out of my mind every time I'm around you."

"It's because you love me," I tell him just to annoy him.

"I do," he responds raggedly.

I go still, unable to look at him. "What?"

"Look at me."

I shake my head. I can't breathe, and if I look at him, I'll probably die.

"Kennedy."

I briefly close my eyes at the ache I catch in his voice. It wraps around me like a vise and I have no choice but to do as he bids. I look up.

"I do love you."

"I know. As a friend with possible benefits."

"*No.* Not just as a friend. And that friends with benefits crap? *Hell no.* You're right. I shouldn't have been keeping how I feel a secret for so long. And I do regret that. I wish I could have been braver than I was. I just…I didn't want to lose you. But I do love you."

I stare him down. "As what? What exactly do you love about me? In what way do you love me? Tell me. Tell me now or don't ever tell me." I so just gave him an ultimatum. I hate ultimatums. I also hate fresh tomatoes. Random.

"Fine. All right? Fine. I love everything about you."

"How could you not?" I'm going to die. For real.

He makes a sound of frustration and shows me his back. In the next instant he is whirling around with sparks in his eyes. "I even love how annoying you are. And you're lucky, because right now, tonight, you're being *extremely* annoying."

"Wait." I cover his eyes. No idea why. I guess to further confuse him. "Did you just say I'm annoying? I've never been so insulted in my life." My heart is going to pound right out of my chest. Why can't I stop deflecting? Because I'm a wimp way more than I want anyone to know, I answer myself.

He pulls my hands from his face. "You are so incredibly annoying. More annoying than anyone I have ever known before."

"Dude." I guess he is allowed to say that, especially with me throwing that ultimatum bit in his face. That was uncool of me.

"You make me laugh, every day. You exasperate me. You charm me. And even when you're being your crazy self, I can see past that. I know you think Blake understands you on some level I cannot, because of his schooling or whatever, or maybe just because you think you're a lot like him, but just because I don't analyze you and your personality doesn't mean I don't understand. Just because I haven't responded to situations in the manner you would have does not mean I don't know why you do the things you do."

"Really? Prove it." I cross my arms, awaiting the wonderfulness about to be bestowed upon me.

"Prove it? Okay. Fine. I know you're messed up because of your father acting like he wanted you to be his son, but I also know he did that because it was the only way he knew how to connect with you. He was scared of you, intimidated. He didn't know how to be a father to a girl, so he did the best he could, the only way he could. You need to give him some credit. I'm not saying he isn't an ass or that he couldn't have been more sensitive to you, but I also know he loves you, and he is proud of you.

"And...I think you need to know that, even if you'd never admit it. You don't always have to joke around, or hide what you love to do. You can like fishing and still like dresses. You can even go fishing in a dress, and you know what? I recommend that the next time you and your dad do your weekly fishing adventure."

He grins and I grin back, feeling all warm and fluffy. Like a cat. "You don't have to choose. I know you think you do, but you don't. You don't have to hide you, or be in constant rebellion against what you think your father wants you to be. I think no matter what you are, he'll love you, and he always has. Some of us don't get that. I never had that, not with my dad. You're lucky even if it doesn't seem like it to you. I know you, even if I can't say it in a pretty way. I know you, I know how you think and feel, and I think you're exceptionally original. And I like—*love*—that about you."

He looks at me. "I want you. And I am not a needy man, but even I will admit that I need you. My life is so much better with you in it. It took a while for me to see why and I'm sorry about that. Sometimes it's hard to see what you have when, in your mind, the possibility of losing it is never a thought." He pauses, smiling. "Your crazy makes my crazy make sense."

"That makes absolutely no sense at all."

"Exactly."

"So...you love me? Like, love me like you want me to have your babies." I grin, knowing that'll spook him.

He is exceptionally mature about it, only going a little white. "Yeah. Like that. What about you?"

"I don't want you to have my babies. Men aren't cut out for that. Wimps."

"Do you love me?"

"I love you." No joking, no sarcasm. Just simple and even. I look up, meeting his shining eyes. The look on his face is so purely earnest that I bite my lip to keep from ravishing him immediately.

"Why do you sound like you're making fun of me?"

"What?" I sputter. "I just said I love you!"

"I know, but your tone..."

"Ugh." Why do I even bother?

Grinning, Graham takes me into his arms. "Kidding."

Just before his lips touch mine, I tell him, "You suck at kidding."

A cool wind plays with my hair, making me think it might have a thing for me. I hug myself against its advances, watching tree leaves get moved around by it as well. Apparently it likes to play the field. I squint at the rising sun, feeling its arms wrap around me to warm me up. This summer, I have to say, has been more interesting than any other I've previously experienced. I suppose that's good. I've grown up a little, which is a shame, but also a necessity.

You can become an adult at the oddest age, ya know? Eighteen is not the magic number. You don't have your birthday and morph into someone that knows everything. Being an adult doesn't mean you're suddenly stuffy and boring—it just means you're more responsible, more considerate. Well, that's my definition of what being an adult means. And I'm always right, so, ya know, that's what it is.

I'm close to twenty-three and am only now figuring stuff out. I guess I'm a late bloomer. I glance down at my chest, wondering when they're going to decide to bloom. Sighing, I pull hair from my mouth, knowing that ain't gonna happen, not without cosmetic surgery. And surgery for me? No way. Knives really don't do it for me.

The low rumble of an approaching contraption of metal and power alerts me that I may have a visitor. I sort of think he's probably here for his brother, but I totally have words to say to him, so he'll have to listen to them—at least until he walks around me and goes inside. I sip my hot chocolate, watching a lean frame dismount from a bike and stride for me. I admire him as he approaches, but it's sort of a clinical assessment, like how I would admire a really good pedicure. I appreciate what I am looking at, but the toenail polish isn't for me. I don't feel regret about that. All I have room inside of me for is a feeling of contentment.

Apparently phenomenal sex does that. Who knew? No crying ensued, FYI. Well, Graham was probably crying on the inside from sheer joy. Of course, the first time hurt, and was over quickly—that was totally Graham's fault. The second time was better; much better. I smile, thinking I should do a shout out to the world about my non-virginity. Or not.

His dark hair is windswept, and I think it likes him more than me. *Fickle wind*, I muse. Blake's face is hard, but then he glances down to where I am sitting on the steps of the apartment building, and they soften microscopically. Which, is a huge change for the features that are usually blank. His thin jacket is the color of slate and dark jeans are wrapped around his legs like the arms of a lover. He stops a few feet from me, squinting down at me.

I return the squint, though there is no reason for it as the sun is behind me. "I like squinting," I say when he continues to silently regard me.

Shaking his head, he drops down beside me, stretching his long legs out. "You know, I've been watching you and my brother. I mean, I was watching you a good deal too, but I was really paying attention to you two. You really do go well together. It's like he accepts your weirdness and you take the edge off him."

He takes a deep breath, staring straight ahead. "You were right. I don't think it was really that I wanted to steal you away, or anything like that, I just—I just wanted what the two of you have, I guess. I went about it the wrong way. But, hey, at least you were strong enough to stay smart and not mess things up with Graham, right?"

"I am a genius." I don't point out that I let him kiss me. I don't mention I wondered what sex with him would be like. And I especially don't bring up the fact that for a nanosecond I was tempted to go forth with the whole 'let's have a casual thing and see what happens'. He doesn't have to know all of that. It would just make it impossible for him to move on from the magnificence of me, and we don't need that kind of drama.

"I wish I was more like Graham. I mean, I used to wish it. I even hated him a little bit because I wanted to be like him so much, only no matter what I did, or said, or how I acted, I could never reach the status he had. He was always stronger, ya know? Stood up to our dad, didn't get sucked into booze and drugs, never reckless. He was able to realize things I never could."

"Like what?" I ask, an ache in my chest.

He shrugs. "He was better than all of that. He knew he was worth something and it didn't matter what anyone else told him." He shakes his head, pausing to rub his face, then resumes his distant stare. "My dad is a prick and my mom is self-absorbed, but neither of them put drugs in my hand. Life can suck, but it was my fault that I chose to deal with it the way I did. No one made me do any of the things I did."

He swallows, becoming quiet as I wordlessly thread my fingers through his. At first he resists, but then I feel his body sighing as he relents, letting my hand hold his. "You're right," he says after a while. "I need to depend on me, and no one else." He unhooks our fingers and slowly stands. "Which is why I decided to go ahead and go to Australia."

I tilt my head. I thought the plan was always to go to Australia.

As though knowing my thoughts, he faintly grins. "There was a moment when I seriously considered not going, but then I woke up and realized I would be staying here for nothing—nothing for me anyway. You're Graham's; always have been, and even if you weren't, you still wouldn't be mine. Know why?"

I shake my head, stunned by how mute I can be when I think it's a good idea. I have lots of good ideas. I should patent them.

His smile grows. "Because you, Kennedy Somers, belong to no one but you. No one can own you. You should be glad of that." He turns, saying, "I'm going to say 'bye to Graham and then I'm taking off for home."

"Home?"

"Yeah. I need to say some things to my parents before I go. Make amends, if possible. Not so much with them, but with me."

"Be careful, okay?"

His mouth lifts in an uneven smile. "I will. No one gets to control me anymore, not even my parents."

"What about your mom? And her cancer?"

His expression twists and then clears. "It sucks. But my father left out a detail when he was trying so hard to get me to come home."

"Oh?"

"She's in remission. Has been for a while. My dad was lying about the seriousness of it." He pauses. "Even though I didn't keep in contact with my dad, I did with my mom."

"Which is why you seemed so heartless when you refused to go home to your dying mother," I muse.

"Well, I am that."

"You are not that," I tell him sternly.

"Kennedy: the girl with the big heart who doesn't want anyone to see it."

"Blake: the guy with the goodness in him he doesn't want anyone to know about."

"Touché."

We share a grin.

He's almost to the door when I say, "Blake?"

He faces me, one eyebrow lifted.

I feel a smile stretch my lips. "I'm glad you don't have a thing with the word red."

He briefly closes his eyes. "This is why you two are perfect for each other. No one else would get that."

"And I know you're going to be fine," I continue, standing as well.

"Thanks."

"Send me a postcard."

"You got it."

He enters the apartment building and I turn away, reaching down for my mug. I finish the lukewarm cocoa, deciding to go for a walk while I have some ambition. It doesn't matter that I am clothed in red and blue polka-dotted shorts and a yellow shirt with red hearts on it. I walk around the square that embraces the courthouse, pretty sure the only reason it's one way all around is to confuse people like me.

By the time I get back to the apartment, the air has transformed from cool to warm and a fine sheen of perspiration covers my skin, making it appear dew-kissed. Too bad I don't smell dew-kissed. I grab the empty mug from the steps and head inside.

Graham is sitting on the deck, nursing a mug of coffee. He's facing away from me and I kiss his bare shoulder as I sit beside him. I wait until he looks at me to ask, "Did he go?"

Sadness flitters through his eyes before passing on. "Yeah. It finally feels like I have a brother and now he's gone."

"Not forever," I say, brushing hair from his forehead. He catches my hand and kisses the palm of it, his lips hot against my skin.

"Not forever." His face lights up as he grins. "He wants us to fly out to visit this winter."

"Really?"

"Yeah. You game?"

"I am so game." I ignore the pounding of my heart, trying to tell myself it is not terror I feel thrumming through my veins, even though, yeah, it is. I sit up. "Wait. It'll be warm there when it's cold here."

He laughs. "It's pretty much warm there year-round."

"Right. So it will be warm there when it's cold here."

"Good deductive skills."

I so got this. Warm weather totally trumps flying for the first time. "When are you going to tell my dad you're my boyfriend?"

His coffee cup lurches in his hand and brown liquid falls over the lip of the mug. "What?"

"Yep. My dad. When are you going to tell him you're my boyfriend? I mean, first you'll have to convince him I'm not a guy." I frown. "Well, either that, or you're gay."

Graham chokes as he tries to swallow.

I thump him on the back. "I know. I never would have guessed." I perk up. "You seriously could do gay. I mean, you bake and clean and are prettier than me. Glad that's settled." I sit back, trying not to laugh as he stares at me.

Without taking his eyes from mine, he begins to sing 'Walk Like A Man'. No idea why. I guess probably because he's almost as quirky as me. Almost. I study him, admiring the curve of his yummy lips, the sparkle of his eyes, the way the sun hits him just right and makes him all sigh-worthy. I mean, his singing is terrible, but at least he looks good.

"What are you doing?" I finally ask.

"I'm serenading you."

I slowly nod, fiddling with the strap of my tank top as I say, "You know those people that naturally sing really well and you could listen to them for hours and hours?"

"Yeah."

I look up. "You're not one of them."

His lips twitch. "Isn't it about effort?"

"Not with singing, no. It's about talent. You don't have it."

"I love you."

"That's not going to make you sound any better."

Laughing, he reaches for me and pulls me to his lap. "I love you so much I even love it when you stink. Like right now."

"I may stink, but at least I can sing," I huff.

"You cannot sing. I've heard you."

I kiss his nose. "I can't be good at *everything*." I lift my hand. "High five."

Shaking his head, he smiles and gives me a high five. "Stop being such a roomie."

"Never. That's how I got you, and I'm keeping you." I grab his head before he can say anymore and pull his mouth to mine.

He murmurs against my lips, "You better keep me."

"I'm so keeping you." I smile and kiss him.

about lindy:

Lindy Zart has been writing since she was a child. Luckily for readers, her writing has improved since then. She lives in Wisconsin with her husband, two sons, and one cat. Lindy loves hearing from people who enjoy her work. She also has a completely healthy obsession with the following: coffee, wine, Bloody Marys, and pizza.

You can connect with Lindy at:

Twitter.com/LindyZart
Facebook.com/LindyZart
Lindyzartauthor.blogspot.com
Amazon.com/author/lindyzart

Listen to the playlists for Lindy's books on Spotify.com
Get an ebook autograph from Lindy at Authorgraph.com

CPSIA information can be obtained
at www.ICGtesting.com
Printed in the USA
LVOW04s1835021116
511368LV00010B/1303/P